Wyatt leaned toward the bed and held Mia's good hand between both of his.

The contact satisfied nothing. He wanted a reaction. He wanted her to wake up, squeeze his fingers and reassure him that she really was alive. How pathetic had he become?

Mia Fiore needed someone to watch out for her and keep her from putting her life at risk again. She needed someone to show her that she was worth more alive than dead. She needed someone to love her beyond all reason.

That someone wasn't Wyatt. He only lived within reason. When he was with Mia, he lost every bit of common sense. That was an unacceptable flaw. He'd been trained to be a doctor, not a lovesick fool.

He held on to her hand, reluctant to let go. He'd forgotten how well her hand fitted inside his.

Dear Reader,

My mother is a retired RN. She worked full-time through her first three pregnancies. When I came along (the last of four and the only girl) she stopped working, as raising four children required full-time hours. When I was in seventh grade, my mom decided to go back to nursing. A few weeks into her return to work, she came home and told me that she was considering quitting. She'd been out of the medical field for a while and the learning curve had increased over those years.

My mom says that I told her that she wasn't allowed to quit. That she wouldn't let us quit something until we'd given it a year, or a full season if it was a sports team. I also added if she gave up, she'd be teaching me that it was okay to give up, too. I don't remember this conversation, but I love the memory my mom gave me. My mom never quit all those years ago and just like my mom, I knew I couldn't give up on my dream of writing because I didn't want my daughters to ever give up on their dreams. I have her to thank for that childhood lesson that has stuck with me.

I love to connect with readers. Check my website to learn more about my upcoming books, sign up for my mailing list, or chat with me on Facebook (carilynnwebb) or Twitter (@carilynnwebb). If you know someone in the medical field, give them a hug today and tell them thanks for all they do.

Cari Lynn Webb

HEARTWARMING

The Doctor's Recovery

Cari Lynn Webb

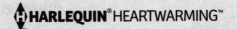

Recycling programs
for this product may
not exist in your area.

ISBN-13: 978-1-335-63364-4

The Doctor's Recovery

Copyright © 2018 by Cari Lynn Webb

Printed in U.S.A.

www.Harlequin.com

Cari Lynn Webb lives in South Carolina with her husband, daughters and assorted four-legged family members. She's been blessed to see the power of true love in her grandparents' seventy-year marriage and her parents' marriage of over fifty years. She knows love isn't always sweet and perfect—it can be challenging, complicated and risky. But she believes happily-ever-afters are worth fighting for.

Books by Cari Lynn Webb

Harlequin Heartwarming

"The Matchmaker Wore Skates" in
Make Me a Match
The Charm Offensive

Visit the Author Profile page
at Harlequin.com for more titles.

To my daughter, Hannah, who believes in dragons, too. I love you more than you can imagine. Don't ever stop believing in magic.

Special thanks to Diane S. for your guidance with all things hospital related and Michelle W. for sharing your physical therapy expertise. To Melinda Curtis and Anna J. Stewart for your support and friendship. And thanks to my husband and family for their patience and understanding during deadlines and for keeping me focused, even when I just wanted to watch TV with you guys.

CHAPTER ONE

MIA FIORE COLLAPSED on the deck of the *Poseidon*. Hands tugged, rolling her over. Faces blurred above her. The ringing in her ears dulled the shouts snapping into the wind. Her arm burned from wrist to elbow. Her toes and legs tingled as if pricked by a thousand sea urchins. Every breath hurt as if her skintight wet suit crushed her ribs together. An oxygen mask covered her mouth. And when she considered drifting into the beckoning oblivion, one of her crew yelled for her to keep awake.

Each smack of the dive boat against the choppy surf of San Francisco Bay pounded through her body, short-circuiting her thoughts as if rearranging time itself. Her brain skipped through images like a slide show on fast-forward: the predive equipment check, the pair of leopard sharks posed for a picture, her dive knife drifting to the ocean floor, fishing line—so much fishing line—wrapped around her, no air to ascend. Dinner with her film crew in the city. Her father's laughter. A different dinner with the crew. In a different time. Different place.

Another jolt of her body against the unrelenting bay waters. Another command from her dive partner, Eddy, for Mia to stay with them.

More hands lifted her from the boat onto something soft. The straps across her legs drove those tingles deep into her bones. A woman with calm blue eyes and a paramedic uniform replaced Eddy beside Mia. She rattled off numbers and ordered Mia to stay with her before the sirens drowned out every thought.

The effort to remain conscious exhausted Mia. If she could only rest. Close her eyes. Five minutes. Ten minutes. Recharging moments, her father would call it.

Nausea rolled like a powerful riptide through Mia, jarring her awake. Mia gasped at the loss of clean air.

"Easy." A hand pressed her back. Another mask covered her mouth.

Fluorescent lights had replaced the sky above her head, and a "code blue" announcement replaced the sound of sirens. Even more hands prodded, shifted and poked at her. Still the pain bored through her, the tingles pricked.

Mia rolled her head when she heard Eddy's voice beside her. Eddy, his wet suit gone, held her cold hand, but he never looked at her. "Dr. Reid? Wyatt?"

Another voice rumbled on Mia's other side. She'd once known a doctor named Wyatt Reid. But that was a lifetime ago. In Africa when Eddy had needed immediate medical attention and her father had still been alive. That was all in the past, wasn't it?

"Answered prayers, Mia." Eddy squeezed her hand. "Dr. Reid has you now."

But Wyatt Reid had never had her. She'd never had him. Not then. Not now. Mia strained, pulled by the warm touch on her forehead. She knew those ash-gray eyes. Knew that face. Knew that inflexible, gritty voice.

He repeated, "Mia, stay with me."

But Wyatt had to know that he asked the impossible. Her eyes refused to focus and she finally gave in, succumbing to her body's insistent need for a recharging moment. As she drifted away, she wondered if Wyatt Reid realized that her heart had never left him.

WYATT WOULD'VE SWORN Mia mumbled something about her heart always belonging to him. But the Mia Fiore he'd known would never put her heart up for the bargaining. He added delirium to her list of symptoms from severe decompression sickness.

Wyatt issued several more orders to the nurses and paused to look at Eddy Fuller, one of Mia's longtime film crew guys and most likely to be listed as Mia's emergency contact. "Stick around, Fuller. We'll need the details about the dive."

"It was only supposed to be an exploratory dive. To get the layout, make lighting adjustments before we filmed later this week." Eddy thrust his fingers into his hair, the mass of thick curls cushioning his scalp from his tense grip. "Fishing line snagged her and her equipment."

Mia was an experienced, well-trained diver, as was her entire crew. She'd never have attempted the dive without Eddy beside her. "Where were you?"

"She'd given me the all clear to ascend." Guilt saturated the man's voice, and his shoulders sagged.

"But she wasn't with you," Wyatt accused.

"She must have turned to photograph something." Eddy crammed his hands into the pockets of his cargo pants. "It'll be on the film."

Wyatt nodded. Of course, Mia's camera

would've been rolling the whole time, capturing every all-consuming second. He'd known she'd give her life for the right footage for one of her documentaries despite her protests back in Africa. Her heart could never have been with Wyatt when it belonged completely to her work.

Eddy's gaze twitched several times to the double doors that separated them from Mia. Wyatt added, "She's going to be admitted for more than a night. She needs hyperbaric treatments and wound care."

"We're on deadline." The fatigue settling into the dark bruises beneath Eddy's eyes softened his protest.

"Adjust your schedule." Wyatt stepped closer to Eddy. He didn't have to stretch to look the tall, lanky man in the eyes. "She almost died this afternoon. The only deadline she has now is to heal."

"So she isn't going to…you know…" Eddy lost his voice and only managed to swallow several times before his gaze fixed on the closed double doors and his skin paled.

A fall from a rappeling accident in Africa had broken Eddy's femur, snapped six ribs and readjusted several internal organs. The villagers had insisted only Wyatt could save such a damaged man. Mia had swooped into the medical camp and insisted death wasn't a viable option before making Wyatt vow to save her friend's life. She'd never flinched when Wyatt had requested her assistance. Only one thing had ever made Mia retreat.

Eddy would likely faint and make Wyatt catch him if Wyatt told the man he required his help now. Thankfully, they stood in Bay Water Medical Center, not an understaffed, undersupplied medical hut in Central Africa. Wyatt squeezed Eddy's shoulder. "Mia isn't going to die tonight."

Relief shifted through Eddy and spread into his grin.

"However, I make no guarantees about her life once she's discharged and on her own again." On her own, Mia embraced adventure and dared life to challenge her more. Stopping to smell the roses would only perplex her. She'd wonder why anyone would stop for the ordinary when they could traipse through the Everglades to glimpse some rare orchid.

Eddy lifted his hands. "As her doctor, it's appropriate that you give Mia her recovery orders."

"I'm only her doctor while she's in the ER, but I'll make sure she has the best care upstairs." Wyatt scanned Eddy's face, searching for twinges of discomfort or latent distress.

He'd been in the water with Mia. Decompression sickness wasn't always instantaneous. "No numbness or pain?"

"Only the same twinge in my thigh that keeps me from taking too many risks these days," Eddy said.

Too bad Mia didn't have a similar internal monitor to keep her safe.

Eddy tipped his chin toward Wyatt. "You sure you can't treat Mia upstairs, too? I owe my life to you."

"We got lucky that day." And he intended to continue being lucky. Despite what he'd told Eddy, Mia was far from in the clear. Yet living was the only viable option for Mia, as well. He walked toward the double doors and looked back at Eddy. "She'll have a skilled team taking over her care, but I'll check on her."

Eddy's mop of curls bounced. "Wait till I tell Frank and Shane that you have our girl."

"Once she's stable, I move her out of my care." *And out of my life.* Wyatt shrugged at the empty hall. Eddy had already escaped into the waiting area to find his friends.

Mia Fiore had arrived as a patient, and she'd leave as one. Their relationship was nothing more than doctor and patient. They'd set that status two years ago in Africa after one night of confessions and secrets revealed. A night that had ended with a kiss that had offered acceptance and hope and promised something more. But sunrise had clarified what the darkness had concealed. The truth: their kiss had been nothing more for Mia than an unspoken goodbye. Until tonight, he hadn't seen or talked to Mia Fiore in several years. If he'd thought about her more than once over the last twenty-four months, he'd never confess.

Wyatt squeezed the back of his neck and rolled his shoulders, rushing the past into place beneath his stethoscope and medical degree.

Mia needed the doctor now. The one who saved lives with methodical care and single-minded focus. Besides, once he transferred Mia out of the ER, she'd no longer be his concern.

MIA GLARED AT the TV bolted to the wall across from her hospital bed and the exuberant talk show host with her wide smile and unfiltered laugh filling the flat screen. That same laugh had woken Mia yesterday afternoon like an abrasive alarm clock. The first night, she'd slept through cinching blood pressure cuffs, needle pricks for IV lines and seven hours in the hyperbaric chamber. She hadn't been as fortunate last night.

Sleep had come in sporadic snippets. Mia preferred the nighttime cacophony of insect songs in the rain forest to the beeps of monitors and stat pages for doctors. The light of a full moon never startled her quite like the hall light streaming across her face when the nurses arrived to draw blood or redress her wounds.

She'd always pushed herself to the limit when she was awake to give her body no reason to avoid sleep. Now pain disrupted her dreams. But awake she forgot to breathe through the intense muscle spasms that locked her shoulder inside its socket. Awake she forgot and tried to massage her knotted thigh muscles and only drove those invisible pins and needles deeper into her bones. Her nerves misfired like arcs from live wires brushing against each other, and her body never deflected the shock.

Miscommunication surrounded her like that time Eddy and Mia flew into Grenada in the Caribbean Sea and the rest of the crew landed in Granada, Spain. They'd laughed about that mishap, sipped piña coladas on the beach and waited for the crew's arrival. The urge to laugh failed to overtake Mia now.

An absentminded rap on her door interrupted the TV show's relationship expert's monologue about confidence in the workplace and beyond. Dr. Hensen pumped exactly two drops of antibacterial gel into his hands from the container on the wall by her bathroom. Six steps brought him to her bedside. He moved with precision, as if he preserved his physical energy for the cell-sized version of the doctor who typed away wildly inside his brain. She suspected Dr. Hensen was a certifiable genius who had graduated medical school at the age of sixteen. Since she'd met him yesterday, she'd wanted to know if he could legally consume alcohol.

Mia muted the volume on the TV as the relationship expert exclaimed, "Fake it until you make it, ladies."

If only Mia had brushed and braided her hair. If she looked put together, Dr. Hensen might believe she was. She nodded, as that also improved confidence, according to her new TV advice expert. She was confident that her doctor would see his way to sign her discharge papers.

She'd risked two questions yesterday while Dr. Hensen examined her, and he'd looked as if she'd interrupted his latest theory on DNA regeneration. Today she waited for him to finish. He removed his glasses and pulled back as if adjusting the viewing lens on his microscope before inspecting the deepest part of her cut near her ankle. She had no explanation for slicing her right shin open in a ten-inch jagged arc.

He covered her leg wound and applied the same scrutiny to her arm. The memory of her dive knife flaying her wet suit and skin open from wrist to elbow came in quick spurts like ten-second sound bites scattered throughout a nighttime newscast.

Finally, Dr. Hensen peeled off his latex gloves and blinked three times as if slowing his brain.

Mia launched into the silence. "It's been almost forty-eight hours since the accident. Today seems like a good day for stitches." She smiled to cover her flinch and hoped the good doctor dismissed the wince in her voice. The throb from his deft prodding pulsed through her entire arm, goading her to press the pain medication pump on her IV.

He repositioned the bandage on her arm, tugging in increments until satisfied. "The paresthesia has subsided in all extremities?"

Mia paused to translate Dr. Hensen's medical textbook speech. "After the hyperbaric chamber this morning, I moved my entire right side." She skipped over the nerve pain and continued numbness that absorbed most of her skin, restricting a full range of movement. But she was better than yesterday. Certainly, that counted for something. "If you won't close my cuts, then can we add more sessions in the chamber?"

Dr. Hensen patted her shoulder, the motion awkward as if he'd closed the textbook, yet she found no comfort in the fit of his bedside manner. "The body heals at its own pace, Mia. We must respect that."

"But the chamber helped me move today." She swallowed, pushing the panic down her throat. Her cuts needed to be stitched because normal patients suffered through sutures, then got discharged. Routine patients received discharge papers. There was nothing routine about another night in the hospital. Unease skimmed over her, leaving a sticky chill across her skin.

"You'll continue daily sessions in the hyperbaric chamber and physical therapy. We'll need to keep monitoring you for infection."

"But you won't stitch it all up?"

"Lacerations sustained in a marine environment are susceptible to uncommon pathogens. There is a serious risk for infection in extremity trauma such as yours." Dr. Hensen added another stiff pat on her shoulder, once again stepping out of his textbook. Compassion softened his voice. "Sutures won't get you discharged."

Her skin absorbed that unease, kicking her pulse into overdrive. How would she convince her Bay Water Medical team she was ready to leave?

The information dry-erase board across from her bed listed today's wound care nurse: Kellie K. Her hyperbaric physician: Dr. West. Her physical therapist: Robyn. Her team's lead: Dr. Hensen along with a handful more support staff. The hospital employees overseeing her care outnumbered her documentary film crew by three to one. As if she was a critical patient.

If she was critical, she'd have to admit the severity of her injuries, and that meant admitting she'd made several crucial dive mistakes. Those phantom pins and needles pierced through her stomach, letting the dread and distress leak in. Her father had died from his mistakes.

But she'd promised her dad she'd honor each of his final wishes. She'd always coveted her father's love, and that meant she'd take over the Fiore Films business, continue his life's work and not fail him. *You always lacked discipline and focus, Mia. But now you can make me proud.* She didn't have time to debate her character with her father's ghost. She had one too many open wounds to contend with now.

"So I'm supposed to just lie here and do nothing? Then lie in the chamber and do nothing again?" She'd only ever been a visitor at the hospital. She'd never been the patient waiting on her own visitors. "And just keep on *doing* nothing."

"Your body needs rest to facilitate healing. It may seem like nothing, but restoration of injured tissue is a complex process." Dr. Hensen looked at her, his smile a small twitch. "Healing is quite an exhaustive process for the body."

"But I have an actual job." She clutched Dr. Hensen's arm, holding him in place. The startled look behind his round glasses hinted at his retreat back inside his mental textbook. Mia continued, "And an important deadline to meet."

A brisk knock and sure footsteps preceded the order from a familiar voice. "Right now, your only job is to heal."

Dr. Hensen tugged his arm free and darted toward Wyatt Reid. Relief coated Dr. Hensen's voice and slid into his extended handshake with Wyatt. "Nice to see that they let you out of the ER, Dr. Reid. We could certainly benefit from your skills up here." He pushed on his glasses and glanced at Mia. "I agree with my colleague, Mia. You need to concentrate on your recovery. Don't fight the process. I'll see you tomorrow."

Mia nodded. This was so not how she'd envisioned her first meeting with Wyatt. She excluded their ER encounter, as her hallucinations and her reality had collided and become indecipherable throughout the night.

But there was nothing imaginary about Wyatt now from his navy scrubs to slate eyes to his hair still long enough to run her fingers through and rearrange. That was all wrong. Confusion must be a side effect of her pain meds. The only running she intended to do was out of the hospital and away from Wyatt. The blood pressure cuff squeezed her arm as if on cue to censure any thoughts about leaving.

An IV line and monitors tethered her to a hospital bed. That she couldn't tether the giant moths that escaped her stomach and fluttered through her chest annoyed her. Why hadn't she prepared for this better? Of course, seeing Dr. Wyatt Reid again had never been on her schedule. Neither had an extended stay in the hospital.

She held on to her smile until Dr. Hensen

closed her door before glaring at Wyatt. "You didn't have to admit me. You could've treated my wounds and sent me home with Eddy."

"Should I have sent you home when you passed out in the ER? Or after the hyperbaric chamber when you passed out again?" He moved to the foot of her bed and stared at her. "And the blood loss? Was I supposed to give two CCs of blood to Eddy to pump into you that evening?"

The logic in his questions and composure in his tone grated on her. That something inside her sighed at his presence shoved her into the irrational. "I have a job."

"So do I." He gripped the bed frame and leaned forward, fully prepared to take her on. "I took a Hippocratic oath to save lives, including yours."

An oath that he lived and breathed. Always. Just like she lived for her job. She tipped her chin up and held his gaze. "I cannot miss my deadline."

"It can wait."

"Easy for you to say," she said. "You're walking around, doing your job just fine like always."

"You'll be back doing your job soon enough."

"Not if I miss this deadline."

"They'll understand."

He didn't understand. She wasn't supposed to be the patient. She didn't make mistakes that could cost her her life or those of her best friends. Those pinpricks turned her stomach inside out, stealing her breath. If they'd just let her leave, then perhaps it wasn't such a big mistake. And her life could return to normal like she wanted. Why did her old life make her hyperventilate now? She loved the life she'd built with her father.

Wyatt tilted his head and studied her. "Are you afraid to be here?"

"Of course I don't want to be here." Not with Wyatt close enough to touch, but so far out of her reach. But that was all wrong. She wanted discharge papers, her old life back more than she'd ever wanted Wyatt. She pressed her fist into the bed. "You do know what happens in places like this."

"Yes, I know what happens in hospitals." The softness in his voice slid into his gaze, tempering the cool sleet color. "We save lives."

"Or not." She scowled at the fragile crack in her voice and blamed Wyatt for making her weak.

Wyatt walked around to her side and lifted his arm toward her.

Everything in Mia stilled. The air in her lungs, her pulse, all of her waited and wished.

He made a midcourse correction to adjust her IV line, denying her his touch. "I'm really sorry about your dad."

Mia buried her arm under the covers. She didn't need his support. She'd never needed that. She'd handle her grief like she handled everything else: on her own terms. Besides, it was his fault she was there. Not entirely, she admitted, but she needed someone to blame to keep her sanity. Otherwise she might crumble beneath the ramifications of her accident. "Why are you here?"

"I work downstairs in the ER."

"I know that." She tugged on the blankets, refusing to look at him. "Why are you up here?"

"My mother is down the hall, recovering from a second hip replacement."

That brought her focus to him. "I'm not your mother."

"I've noticed." The laughter in his voice melted into his smile.

And ping-ponged something warm through her like the first sip of homemade hot chocolate. She remembered that comforting feeling from their time together. But she hadn't missed him. She'd chosen to leave and live her life. "Why are you in my room specifically? I'm not your patient." His name wasn't on her information board. She was thankful for that, wasn't she?

"I can't check up on a friend?" he asked.

"Is that what we are?"

"Unless you prefer another definition for our relationship."

They had no relationship. Wasn't that the point? "We haven't spoken in twenty-six months."

"That's rather exact," he said.

"Yet true," she said.

"I promised Eddy I'd check on you."

"Eddy was here?" Relief rushed through her. Nothing had happened to Eddy. Her friend hadn't suffered because of her error.

"Eddy, Frank and Shane have all been here." His eyebrows pulled together, highlighting his perplexed voice. "Your crew still follows wherever you lead."

"They work with me because they want to," she said. Unlike Wyatt, who'd never follow. He'd wanted to be with her, too, at one time. But only on his terms. And those were terms she would never accept. She crammed her pillow behind her head. "Well, you've checked up on me. Dr. Hensen told me to sleep and let my body heal. Could you dim the lights on your way out?"

"I'll be back." There was a hint of warning in his tone.

With any luck, she'd be asleep. Mia closed her eyes, shutting him out and severing her awareness of him as anything more than a doctor. Wyatt Reid was a doctor first and always, same as she was a filmmaker first and always.

"If you need me, the nurses know how to find me," he added before the lights dimmed and silence rushed through the room.

Mia wanted to stuff the pillow over her face and scream. That would no doubt get her another specialist for her care team and a psychological evaluation. There had to be at least ten hospitals in San Francisco, and she'd ended up at the one where Wyatt Reid worked. Not even fate could've conjured that twist.

CHAPTER TWO

THE DOOR TO Mia's room clicked shut, soft and quiet, despite Wyatt's tight grip on the steel handle. Slamming the door might've satisfied him, but he doubted that would be enough to disrupt Mia's determination to greet her father in the afterlife. Stubborn woman couldn't see past her current deadline. She'd almost died. *Died.*

Yet she railed at him for admitting her as if the entire incident was his fault. As if he prevented her from finishing her precious film. Had she learned nothing from her father's death? She'd brushed off his condolences about her dad like a decade-long chain-smoker given a pamphlet on how to quit.

Still he'd treat her like any other patient, the same as he'd declined to make an exception for his mother. He refused to lose his objectivity only to have them suffer for his misstep. Emotional lockdown was the only prudent course of action. Not that he had to worry with his mom. However, Mia triggered something inside him, something that rattled that lock and disturbed his composure. He simply had to regulate his neurological response to Mia with more precision and resist any urge to be more than a doctor who knew what she needed even if she didn't. It was past time Mia slowed down, reassessed and grieved.

Of course, knowing what was best for someone didn't guarantee the person's agreement or cooperation. That much he learned every day with his mother. He seemed to be surrounded by difficult women. Good thing he'd never walked away from a challenge.

Wyatt slowed at the nurses' station and met Nettie's gaze, waiting for the charge nurse's signal. Wyatt believed in gathering as much information as possible before any confrontation, and when it came to his mother, he'd gather information from any source willing to release it. Nettie smiled. Her thumbs-up allowed the breath he'd been holding to slip out.

His mother's references to her final days had quadrupled since her first hip surgery eight weeks ago. It'd gotten so bad, her parting line most evenings had been: *you'll need to look for me in the morgue tomorrow if you wish to visit me.* After her second hip surgery, she'd revised her morgue commentary and now suggested suitable places to scatter her ashes depending on the season she'd arbitrarily determined would be her last. Fortunately, his mother hadn't referenced pushing up daisies in the last three days, and every signal from the charge nurse had been positive.

Wyatt knocked on his mom's door and entered the room. His mother wore her receiving pajamas, the ones with roses and vines that she'd deemed appropriate attire for visitors. That made three days in a row. Wyatt frowned as his mother muttered. Her face was pressed close enough to her notepad screen that her nose would leave an imprint. Even with her glasses on, the strain could trigger another seizure. He'd need to talk to her primary care physician about her seizure medications after her discharge.

"Mom." He kissed her wilted cheek and imagined she leaned in for his greeting like she'd used to when he was a clumsy kid climbing onto her lap for a good-night hug. But mother and son had stopped leaning on each other years ago. He shoved his useless childhood memories aside and nudged her notepad lower before enlarging the image on her screen with his fingers. One quick glance confirmed the photographs that absorbed all of her attention. He'd forwarded that latest set of pictures he'd taken in her greenhouse to her email account last night.

"Well, that's much better." Her focus remained fixed on her screen, but appreciation tinged her voice.

While his mother continued to check the vitals on her precious plants, he took an inventory of her, searching for anything the medical team might've missed like last time: new bruises on her arms, involuntary winces of pain, signs of infection. Anything that might signal another unexpected decline.

"The begonia needs to be repotted before the weekend." She flipped through several more photographs. "The snapdragon seedlings need more light." She glanced at the window, her eyebrows pulling in behind her round glasses at the fog swirling against the pane. "Bring them into the house and put them under the lights for the next few days."

"We already put the primrose seeds under the house lights," he reminded her. Newborns with jaundice belonged under special lights. Preemies required such meticulous care and attention, not plants. But that wasn't an argument he intended to revisit with his mother. Her greenhouse was a sacred place; everything inside those glassed walls was her family now.

She flicked her hand back and forth as if sweeping away his words like spilled soil. "The pots aren't too big. They can share the space."

If only everything in life was so easy and simple. Wyatt and his mother struggled to share the same space.

"You could buy a new light." She lifted her gaze above her oversize glasses.

No way. He wasn't adding another UV light. Soon enough the DEA would be knocking down the door to bust him for growing illegal substances, as he had too many lights going now. Either that or the neighbors were convinced he had a deep-seated fear of the dark. The lights matched his night-shift schedule: on all night, off in the morning. With his work schedule changing to days, he'd have to change the plants' schedule, too. His mother preferred consistency, but it was the best he could do to keep everything alive. In another time, she'd concentrated on her family with the same meticulous consideration. Now her devotion belonged to her plants and the nursery she'd built in her backyard. Not that he wanted her fawning over him as if he was one of her struggling plants. "I'll make it work."

She smiled and pulled up another photograph. "The orchid has taken to the new food mixture. There's happiness in the blooms now."

But not in his mother. He hadn't seen real joy in his mother in over five years, long before his brother's unexpected death. He remembered the lightness in her laughter and happiness on her face when his father would come home and dance her to her seat at the dinner table every night. He'd even witnessed the same dance, the steps slower and more cautious, when he'd returned home from college, months before cancer stole his father and dimmed his mother's light. Still there'd been moments after the grief had settled and the memories no longer stung. Then came Trent, when love had proved to be a poor antidote to his brother's inner turmoil and anguish and nothing had slowed his downward spiral. Then not even Wyatt could reignite any sort of happiness in his mother.

He cracked his knuckles. The pop realigned his bones and his focus. He hadn't slammed the door to Mia's room, but he could slam the door on memory lane and lock it.

Besides, he needed his mother to concentrate on her recovery and talk about her living situation after room 326 on the transitional care floor at Bay Water Medical. After her discharge, all of his mother's love could return to her flowers. He only cared that she was safe when she left the hospital. That was his duty as her son. He had her love as a child, that was enough. Something scraped across his insides like a dull razor, leaving deep gouges in its wake. He rubbed his chest and discarded the phantom ache. "Your neighbor in the Craftsman brought over his cactus last night. It's dead."

"You didn't tell Samuel that, I hope."

"I suggested that he drop it in the recycle bin on his way back home," Wyatt said.

"I raised you with better manners than that."

He smiled. He did consider dropping the pathetic plant in the recycle bin himself on his way to work. Even a tempered truth had less cruelty than false hope.

His mother eyed him. "Where's the cactus?"

"Sitting beside the other neighborhood plants begging for resuscitation and prompt care." His mother had a plant-based ER in her nursery. The neighbors and her so-called friends were obviously taking advantage of his mom's green thumb skills. Her greenhouse wasn't the local garden center at the hardware store or inside one of the city's impressive parks with multiple staff to attend to it.

She was one person, living alone, among her plants. In his opinion, her garden and greenhouse had gotten more than a bit out of control. She needed to say no more often.

"What kind of cactus is it?"

"The cactus kind." Wyatt dropped his keys and cell phone on the window ledge and crossed his arms over his chest.

"Really, Wyatt. If you asked for details about a gunshot victim downstairs, you'd hardly accept bullet wound as an appropriate response."

Bullet wounds and his patients were not even in the same stratosphere as a dying cactus. Especially a cactus that could be replaced with a trip to the local home improvement store and a five-minute walk through the garden center. Wyatt sighed, picked up his mother's tablet and searched cactus images on the internet. "Maybe this one, if its shoots weren't all shriveled up."

"Ask Samuel if this is his great-grandmother's Christmas cactus that he told me about," she said.

"If you get on email, you could ask him yourself," Wyatt suggested.

His mother waved her hand. "This is quite personal. You don't talk to your patients' family members through email when they come into the ER."

He wasn't adverse to the suggestion, especially given some of the family members who'd confronted him in the past few months. But again, plants and patients hardly belonged in the same sentence. "It's a *cactus*." Wyatt stressed the word because it needed repeating. A replaceable cactus.

"Yes, but it's been in his family since his great-grandmother settled in the city. The plant has deep, meaningful roots."

He once had meaningful roots in the city, too. But that was the problem with roots—when they died, it hurt all the more. At least the neighbor needed to grieve only the loss of a plant, not his family. What was wrong with him? He blamed Mia Fiore for stirring up the unnecessary emotional pot inside him. "Tell me what to do with Granny's cactus."

"Bring me a stem." Helen powered off her notepad. "In the meantime, look for the cactus food. It's on the third shelf to the left of the door of the greenhouse."

In the meantime, he'd be working in the ER, looking for nitroglycerin to treat chest pain and injecting alteplase to dissolve blood clots in the brain or giving morphine to decrease crippling kidney stones. "That's the only neighborhood plant SOS from yesterday." Wyatt injected lightness into his tone. Still, his mother looked crestfallen at the news, as if rescuing neighborhood plants gave her a reason to live. "Mom, we need to discuss…"

"Discuss these applications for the foundation," she finished for him and pulled out a stack of papers from the drawer in her bedside table.

His level of frustration soared. Two months ago, before her fall, his mom had decided to give away the family money to local charities through her newly formed foundation. They'd already talked about that. Right now, they had to discuss assisted care and her living arrangements after her discharge. Once he knew she was safe, he could return to Africa and the medical aid program he'd started there. The one that depended on his return to expand into more remote locations. "You were going to cancel the ad and put the foundation on hold for now."

"You decided that, but I decided differently." The warning rapped through her voice like marbles striking a tile floor.

She'd approached helping Trent the very same way, agreeing to Wyatt's suggestions but then doing exactly what she'd wanted, and look how badly that had turned out. If his mom had only accepted his brother's addictions and risked revealing the truth of Trent's condition to friends and family by admitting his brother to an in-patient rehab center, Trent might be alive today. Wyatt straightened, met her gaze and smoothed the boyish plea, as if he was six again and wanted a puppy, out of his voice. "But we already talked about this."

"No, you told me that I'd be stopping the foundation funding like you instruct your patients on medicine and follow-up appointments. I doubt you use such an overbearing tone with them." She smoothed the clear tape over her IV line port. "But I've reasons, good ones, for continuing to disperse funds from the foundation."

Doing it because he didn't want her to was not a good reason. Nor was her insistence that her days were limited. Her days hadn't been limited since they'd cleared the infection from her femur bone and replaced her hip for the second time. "These applicants need to be vetted. You don't even know if they're real organizations or not." He swiped the first application from the pile and scanned the messy handwritten form from Project Save the Leprechauns. "It's nothing more than a mad money grab."

"There's nothing mad about it." She patted her hair into place as if her perfectly set updo would keep all the dissenters at bay. "I wish to see the family money put to good use while I'm still alive. It isn't as if you need it. You can go through the applicants and I can write the checks."

Wyatt dropped his chin to his chest and jammed both hands into his hair. That stack contained at least a hundred more pages. He had real work: patients to care for and conference calls to attend with his partners overseas. "You want me to go through all of these?"

"Yes. I need to concentrate on my therapy." She pulled her robe tighter across her chest. "I don't want to disappoint the charities that are relying on my money to keep up their good work."

"Yes, I'm sure Project Rescue the Dust Bunny is impacting the needy in the city with its wonderful deeds." He crumpled the second application from the pile in his fist. One vetted, only ninety-nine to go.

"I promised to help fund local charities in my ad, and I'll keep my word. I only need the best twenty from that pile."

She was going to be bankrupt before her discharge. "I'll do this, if we talk about the brochures I left with you."

"I threw those out." Satisfaction, not re-morse, steadied her gaze. She never flinched, as if she was a heart surgeon wielding a scal-pel.

He squeezed the crumpled paper tighter, trying to squeeze the irritation from his voice. "You cannot move home."

"I most certainly can." She raised her voice with the same dignity she'd raised two boys. "And will."

"I cannot ensure your safety at home." His cell phone rang.

"You won't have to ensure anything. You'll be back in Africa, where you'd clearly rather be right now." Disdain hardened her voice, and disapproval shifted into the scowl she aimed at his phone. "It must be eight o'clock. Africa calls at this time every night you visit me."

"I've already explained that my partners and I expanded our clinic before I left. My schedule and the time change make it diffi-cult to talk, and there are things that only I can handle."

"Yet you aren't the only doctor within your organization. But then you must prefer the in-terruption. After all, there are twenty-three other hours to choose to schedule your con-ference call."

Silence swelled inside the room.

She acted like he'd traded her for Africa. He'd have talked to her about his plans for his medical aid work if she'd gone to her own son's funeral five years ago. But neither her youngest son's funeral nor her oldest son's departure to a foreign country had been important enough for her to leave her precious gardens unattended. Resentment ricocheted through him, nothing new there.

But the sting that hitched his breath and tightened his chest was too fresh, as if his mother's absence still hurt. Yet he wasn't wading into that emotional quicksand. That was the past. Not forgotten, but past. Now wasn't the time or the place. There'd never be a time or place for that particular discussion.

He closed off his emotions. Sentiment only ever distorted the logic and rationale he'd come to depend on in the ER and every other part of his life. Was it too late to steer the conversation back to her nursery? If only there'd been another neighbor with a plant emergency. "My life is in Africa."

"Then you should return."

But not stay. Not ever stay. She'd never ask that of him. "When you're settled."

"You need to live your own life, not dictate mine."

As if he'd returned only to boss her around. Not because they were the only family left and needed each other. Wyatt squirmed at the thought. "I came home for you."

"I never asked you to," she said.

The last five years their conversations had been trivial: her plants, which friends had passed away and who had moved in on her street. She wouldn't ask when he was coming home, and he wouldn't volunteer to return. She hadn't even asked him to come home when she'd first fallen and injured her hip. He'd come back at the request of a distant cousin. He pushed out of the chair, wanting to push the past back in its place and get moving again. His agenda: move forward. To always keep moving forward. Perhaps then he just might outrun all the what-ifs. "A good son looks after his mother." And Wyatt was determined to be a good son, even if his mother didn't appreciate his interference.

"You've done that," she said.

"I'm not finished."

"I can take care of myself now." His mother tugged on the belt around her waist, but the flimsy fabric refused to stay tied, and the satiny bow unraveled in her fragile hands, discrediting her claim.

"Not in your house." Wyatt set his hands on his hips and eyed his mom. "Not alone."

She wouldn't meet his gaze, but her chin lifted. "Being alone is nothing new. Besides, I have wonderful neighbors."

Neighbors who Wyatt believed needed nothing more than his mom's green thumb. A distant cousin had been the one to find his mother after her fall, not one of her supposedly wonderfully attentive neighbors. He hadn't been there either. Not that she needed him. He turned his back to all those complicated emotions. "You're obviously tired."

"Not especially."

Well, he was. Exhausted. Wyatt pressed a kiss against his mom's pale cheek. "We can talk about this tomorrow. I'm on days this week, and I need to sleep."

She reached up as if to touch him, but her fingers stirred only the air between them. "My mind is made up."

He wasn't sure if it was the bed rail or something else that held her back. Not that it mattered. He'd long ago outgrown his need for motherly affection.

Besides, his mind was made up, too. He might be surrounded by stubborn women, but that wouldn't stop him from doing what was right.

CHAPTER THREE

MIA TUGGED ON the twin ties on her hospital gown and gritted her teeth. She'd needed only one day to learn to tie her shoes in grade school. No way was a flimsy gown going to beat her. Of course, in elementary school her fingers hadn't been numb or her arm stiff and sore from even the smallest movement. Still, she'd tie her gown closed as she had nothing else to do until her morning physical therapy in an hour.

This was the perfect catnap opportunity. Yet her mind refused to let her sleep. Every time she closed her eyes, images from her accident bombarded her. She wasn't certain what was real and what was manufactured by her nightmares. Real or imagined, fear rippled through her like the explosive screech of a frightened red fox and retreated only if she opened her eyes. She'd never considered herself stupid or irrational. Until now. Clearly three days without decent sleep had taken its toll.

At least she had a plan. Because another night of no sleep was unacceptable.

Her fingers trembled, and the thin strap slipped from her grip. Numbness absorbed her arm, and her leg throbbed from Dr. Hensen's routine exam. Tears pooled in her eyes. She refused to cry, especially over stupid things. Still her chin sagged toward her chest, and her arms drooped to her sides. Everything inside her went limp, and defeat rushed in.

"You better not be crying." Eddy Fuller's voice filled her room, the nervous tremor in his tone increasing his volume. His curly hair always reminded her of a cup of coffee sweetened with too many creamers and complemented his usual laid-back style.

"I'm not." Mia mumbled into her chest and avoided looking at her best friend and her father's longtime video editor.

"Good. Tears are annoying." Eddy stopped just inside the room and set the bags he carried on the floor near his feet. "Then what are you doing?"

"Trying to tie my gown." And squeeze her stupid tears back behind her eyes.

Eddy made quick work of the ties behind her neck before retreating against the wall near the bathroom. His skin looked faded. He pinched his lips together as if struggling not to breathe too deeply. Eddy and hospitals did not play well together.

Mia latched on to her friend's discomfort like a life preserver, pulling her out of her own self-pity pool. "You watch criminal and medical dramas in marathon sessions every week. How can my cuts bother you?"

"They look worse today." His gaze lowered from the abstract art hanging on the wall behind her to her face, where it stuck. "You're pushing too hard."

She ignored the last part. She wasn't pushing hard enough to get out. "You didn't even look at my leg."

"I don't need to look at the ooze and pus to know it's there." Eddy's gaze never wavered, unlike the ashen color that rolled over his skin.

"It's supposed to look like this. It's healing." She hoped. The throbbing in her leg had become steady and constant, even before Dr. Hensen took the culture of her wound that morning. "Give me the laptop and I'll release you from this torture. I really appreciate that you came all the way to my room."

Eddy pushed away from the wall and kept his focus on Mia. "Will you still appreciate me when I tell you that I called your mom?"

"You talked to my mom?" The back of her

head pounded like someone had smashed the abstract art frame against her head.

Eddy squeezed the wedding ring tattooed around his ring finger like he always did whenever doubt seized him. "She needed to know."

"That I'm fine," Mia added.

"That you're in the hospital and working toward being fine," Eddy clarified.

"You told her everything?" Everything would only make her mom worry. And her mom already made a worrywart sound like an optimist. The throb extended around to Mia's temples and stabbed.

"I explained that you had a diving accident during a filming session."

That was more than enough for her mom to book the first flight from New York to San Francisco. Almost seven hours in the plane for her mom to fret about how Mia should live her life with less risk. To strategize about how Mia could still express her passion for saving the wildlife by donating to charities rather than camping out in the wilderness as if she was a native. Seven hours for her mom to torment her already high-strung nerves into a full-blown anxiety attack over Mia's refusal to make a big difference in the world from behind a nice, secure cherry-stained desk.

Mia grabbed her phone and texted her mom, stalling any flight confirmations and keeping her mom at home, where she'd always been the calmest. Still, Mia had to finish her film and get back to her life before her mom arrived to turn Mia's world inside out. "I'll deal with my mom later. I just need the laptop now."

Eddy tilted his head and studied her, his curls shifting as if to emphasize his internal debate. "You can watch Shane's footage from Sunday on your phone."

"I don't want Shane's edited version." Mia motioned toward the laptop bag that sat on the floor. "I want to watch all of it."

"You need to concentrate on healing, not reliving the accident." Eddy made no move to pick up the computer bag. "It wasn't easy for us to review."

That was Eddy's sensitivity to blood and hospitals talking. Besides, she already relived the accident every time she closed her eyes. Every time she fell asleep. If she watched the footage, maybe her dreams would find new content, instead of replaying the same thing. "We're going to need new footage to finish the film."

Eddy's gaze skipped away from her, but it wasn't the pus and ooze chasing off his focus this time. It was doubt. Doubt that Mia could get new footage. She'd never seen Eddy second-guess any of her father's decisions. He'd never questioned her father's ability to get even the most difficult shot.

But Mia wasn't her father, and Eddy made that fact more than clear when he said, "We need to wrap it up with what we have and just be done."

She wouldn't *just* be done until she finished the film to her father's standards. Nothing else would ensure his legacy. Nothing else would ensure the recognition and accolades her father had always coveted in life. Nothing else would ensure her mother's lifestyle remained the same just like she'd promised her dad. "We'll be done when it's finished like my father expected and it's worthy of the Fiore name."

Eddy stiffened. "You sounded like your dad just now."

"Excellent," she said. Yet confusion creased into the edges of his eyes and uncertainty tipped his chin down. Her friend still doubted her. So be it. She'd become who her father had planned for her to be and prove Eddy and everyone else wrong. "I'd think the more like him I am, the better for all of us."

Eddy set the computer bag on the bedside

table. "Just be careful you don't lose yourself in your father's ghost."

Her father wouldn't be a ghost if she'd stepped further out of her comfort zone. *Only the lazy and uninspired curl up in their comfort zones, Mia. I raised you to be more than that.* Now she had to be more to keep from disappointing anyone else. "I'm upholding the Fiore family legacy."

Her duty as an only child was to continue the Fiore filmmaking tradition as her father had always envisioned. Her responsibility as the only Fiore child was to take care of her mother just as her father had always done. Just as she'd promised him she would.

Eddy pulled a smaller leather case from the paper shopping bag he'd brought in and dropped it on her lap. "The guys and I got you something."

Mia unzipped the top and gaped at the digital camera tucked inside. "What am I supposed to do with this?"

"Take pictures. Open your creative mind," Eddy said. "It'll be a good distraction while you're here."

Her creative mind was open and ready to finish the final documentary in her father's acclaimed series. Her creative mind was already at full capacity with her film work. *Art must always send a message that impacts many lives, Mia.*

Pictures of IV lines, needle containers and hand sanitizer hardly impacted lives. Portraits wouldn't pay the mortgage on her mother's house. Unless, of course, those same pictures were taken in the aftermath of a bombing in the Middle East. Yet she wasn't in Syria and Bay Water Medical wasn't inside a war zone. Photojournalist wasn't her job title. Neither was photographer.

Besides, only her body had been damaged in the accident, not her mind. Not her creative side. She ran her finger along the zipper, the uneven edge matching the uncertainty knotting through her. What if she'd lost something more precious like her passion? Not possible. More than just her livelihood relied on her finishing this film and securing new contracts. "You expect me to take pictures? Here?"

"It's a camera, Mia, not a bow and arrow." Eddy swatted at the air as if annoyed by a pesky mosquito, not his good friend. "We aren't suggesting you have target practice out in the hallways."

No, it was worse than that. Her friends suggested that she betray her father's memory by wasting her time with still photographs.

"What happened to crossword puzzles and books to fill the time?"

Eddy grinned and walked to the door. "Have to think outside the box to keep the creativity lines open."

He'd quoted her father. But her dad had meant with film work. With the important work that touched many lives. With the film work that supported her mother all these years. The soft knock on the door followed by the cheerful greeting from her physical therapist saved Mia from correcting Eddy's misconception. She set the camera bag on the rolling table and pushed it away, along with her doubts.

Time to concentrate on therapy and exercise. Walking without pain. Moving without pain. There was nothing wrong with her creative mind. Nothing that a camera could fix. The hospital walls compressed in on her. The bland, dull paint made everything stark, barren and exposed her uncertainties. Clearly, she'd been alone with her own thoughts too much. She needed breathing space. "I want to walk the entire floor today, not just this hall."

"How's your pain?" Robyn unclipped several of Mia's monitors.

"Tolerable," Mia said. Numbness and pain wouldn't interfere with her therapy. She had to prove she'd made progress, and that had to start now. With every hour she remained inside Bay Water Medical, her resolve leached into the pale walls like blood into white carpet.

"We'll take it slow and easy," Robyn said.

"We can stop at the nurses' station," Mia suggested. "Take stock. Turn back or keep going." She had no intention of returning to her room until she'd walked every linoleum-covered inch of the third floor.

Mia managed to cover only one hallway before she leaned against the nurses' station and tried to wrestle her pain back into submission. Another physical therapist accompanied a woman. Her pure-white hair and the unsteady grip of her hands, all knuckles and veins, on her walker betrayed her age even though gravity had failed to diminish her height and transform her into one of those pint-sized seniors. The pair paused beside Mia.

"Helen, let me see your hand." The charge nurse, Nettie, leaned over the counter toward the older woman. "I swear you must have a green arm because no normal green thumb could've saved my plant."

The silver woven through Nettie's black hair broadcast her experience with life, making her a cross between the neighborhood's favorite nana and the matriarch of a dignified political family. Nettie's straightforward nature and disdain for sugarcoating made her one of Mia's favorite nurses on the floor.

Nettie tapped her phone, spun the screen around and grinned proudly. "I was ready to toss that gardenia into the Dumpster, and now look at it."

Mia assumed she'd have a dead thumb if she tried to grow anything. Her mom believed in silk plants and Waterford crystal to decorate a home with life. Her father believed nature belonged in its native habitat. Mia wasn't sure if she agreed, but she'd need more than a home for a plant. She'd need to give it her time and attention, and that was in short supply.

"Isn't it just lovely." Helen pushed her glasses up. Her smile bloomed up into her eyes, filling her fragile skin with light. "The scent when it flowers will fill your entire house."

Roslyn, a nursing assistant with the ink still drying on her certification, glanced at the phone over Nettie's shoulder. "The city gardeners could learn something from you."

"I'm an amateur with no formal schooling," Helen said.

But the older woman had passion even without formal training, and that mattered.

A passion that glowed from within her like the sunrise streaking burnt gold across the plains in Zimbabwe, rousing the wild to life. Only Helen awakened someone's love for nature.

"You're a plant whisperer, Ms. Reid." Awe lowered Roslyn's voice into a church whisper.

"Nothing like that." Helen patted her hair as if she'd revealed too much and needed to tuck her secrets back in place. "I've grown my share of gardenias over the years. Once you understand their temperament, they thrive and blossom."

"If only you had a cure for a temperamental man, Helen." Nettie's grin lifted her eyebrows. "We could bottle it, make millions and retire in style."

"I have better luck with plants." Helen reached for her walker, her movements slow, as if someone lowered the dimmer switch inside her.

"Nonsense." Nettie looked at Mia. "She's got a son working more hours than sanity recommends down in the ER. You raised him right, Helen."

The plant whisperer is Helen Reid. As in Wyatt Reid's mom. The one Wyatt had told Mia was recovering from hip surgery down the hall from her. Helen had an inch or two on Mia even hunched over her walker. Wyatt's height hadn't come from only his father's side. But Wyatt's personality fit into every inch of his six-three frame. His willpower alone displaced any soft spots. Nothing on Wyatt appeared weak. Everything about Helen was fragile, from her thin frame to her shaky grip on her walker. She reminded Mia of one of those flamingos at the zoo, standing on one thin leg, regal and proud yet looking as if the slightest jostle would topple her. "Are you Wyatt Reid's mother?"

"He's my son, but he hasn't needed me as his mother in quite some time." Her voice wilted like her white curls that drooped against her head as if faint from dehydration.

"Wyatt mentioned he was on his way to see you when I spoke to him last night," Mia said.

A three-point walker turn and small shuffle brought Helen face-to-face with Mia. Her eyes, not slate like Wyatt's but hazel, blinked behind large round glasses, reflecting an all-too-familiar calculated focus. Mother and son were not that different.

Only one blink interrupted Helen's slow study of Mia, as if Mia squatted under a microscope. "He cannot be your doctor, dear, as he only treats patients in the emergency room."

"He saved my life the other night," Mia

confessed. Wyatt required no boost to his ego. Yet his mother should know the depth of her son's medical skills. "Although we'd already met several years ago in Africa."

Helen winced, as if in pain, but never reached to massage her tender hip or sore side. Only that flinch of discomfort pinched her skin, flexing the age lines across her face. "Do you volunteer with Wyatt's organization, too?"

"No," Mia said.

Helen's face cleared and her mouth softened, as if the phantom pain receded. Her wispy eyebrows lifted above her glasses, her only encouragement for Mia to continue.

"I'm a documentary filmmaker." Mia sank into the older woman's open gaze, recognizing the flicker of loneliness in the hazel depths. Mia knew all too well about feeling alone, even in a crowd. Helen's gaze hooked inside Mia and prodded her to keep talking. "One of my crew fell from a cliff, and the locals told us to take him to Wyatt in the neighboring village. They were convinced only Wyatt could help him."

"And did he live?" Robyn finished writing her notes and tucked the paperwork in the back pocket of her scrubs.

"Thanks to Wyatt." Mia maneuvered her walker next to Helen's.

"Like I said before, Helen, you raised him right. And a boy raised right always needs his mama." Nettie set her phone on the counter and turned away to answer a patient's call on the intercom system.

"That's kind, but it's utter nonsense." Helen's quiet laughter failed to mask the sadness that burned into the dark rims around her eyes.

Robyn stepped up beside Mia. "Okay, ladies, we've rested and it's time to walk."

Helen's PT joined them. "Ready to head back, Helen?"

"I suppose it's my only option, unless you're going to let me make my escape." Helen pointed her thumb over her shoulder at the main elevators. "You'd only need to look the other way for five minutes."

The women laughed. "You can rest in the chairs at the end of the hallway until Occupational Therapy arrives. There's a good view of the elevators from there. You can run on OT's watch."

Helen set her hand on Mia's walker. "They're not going to let you leave either, dear. You might as well tell me about this filmmaking while we walk. You'll save me from answering more questions about my pain level and bathroom successes."

"It's a family business," Mia said. "Or was until my father passed last fall." She always remained detached in the retelling. *Always.* Until now. With Wyatt's mom. Now the grief cinched around her lungs like some medieval corset, replacing air with tears. *Save the emotion for the film reel, Mia.*

"I'm sorry." Nothing false slipped through Helen's words. "Now you're left with the burden to carry on alone."

The sincerity in Helen's voice crested through Mia, and the understanding in her gaze loosened several tears. Helen knew loss. She also recognized loneliness. The similarities between mother and son clearly ran only skin deep. Mia brushed at her damp cheek. "My dad taught me everything I know, and I can't fail him."

"Of course you won't, my dear." Helen squeezed Mia's arm with the same confident strength that bolstered her voice. "Now tell me, what do you film?"

"My father started with human rights before transitioning into environmental issues. His last two series covered endangered wildlife around the world and the effects of urban sprawl on their habitats. I'm finishing the final film in the series about the human impact on the environment for the Nature Wildlife Network." Mia inhaled, searching for air to clog the wheeze in her throat. Walking and talking had never before left her winded.

"If you're traveling for your films, where do you call home?" Helen asked.

Lately wherever her tent stakes stuck in the ground. "I'm a bit of a nomad."

"Or perhaps you haven't discovered that one place you want to settle in," Helen suggested.

Nothing relaxed inside Mia at the idea of living in the same place. Her mother had established herself in New York. But Mia wasn't a stayer like her mom. She wasn't made for settling. Her father had taught her to live her passion. Documentary films weren't made behind a desk, scouring the internet for video footage. To be a success she must embrace her father's lifestyle and not *settle* for anything less. "I've settled into being a nomad."

"My husband never liked to travel." Helen paused and held out her hand, curving her arm like a graceful ballerina. "I always wanted to dance through a field of heather or touch a red ginger flower in the wild or collect seashells along a white-sand beach."

Mia had dug more than her toes in the white

sand in the Gulf of Mexico. She'd crawled across the beach on her stomach, filming the rare Kemp's ridley hatchlings emerging from their nests to crawl home to the ocean. Sand stuck to places it never should've been weeks after they'd wrapped filming. She hadn't exactly danced through the field of heather; more like trampled the purple flowers, tracking the sea eagles on the Isle of Skye. Yet the cloud of midges and her severe allergic reaction to the bites from the hundreds of tiny bugs downgraded the trip from cherished to agonizingly itchy. If only she hadn't followed her father up the mountainside for a shot that had never made the final film cut.

However, she could envision a younger version of Helen Reid sashaying through that same field, pausing to greet each flower like a garden fairy from the ancient myths. The images clicked through her mind, vivid stills of moments captured and preserved. But Mia wasn't creating a memory book for Helen. "You could celebrate your full recovery by traveling to Scotland with Wyatt."

"He has other important commitments and I have my gardens. At least for now." The steel in Helen's tone gave the sadness in her quiet gaze a backbone.

"Have your doctors restricted you from gardening when you get home?"

"My doctors like to tell me I've a bionic hip now." Helen patted her leg. "I may need to replace the other one so it can keep up with its new-and-improved partner."

"When will you be back to your gardens?" Mia asked.

"As soon as I can convince my doctor to sign off on my get-out-of-jail paperwork." Helen's therapist guided her into the chair. After ensuring Helen's comfort, the woman disappeared into another patient room. Helen shifted to look at Mia. "When do you get to leave?"

"As soon as Dr. Hensen agrees to close my wound and any doctor signs my discharge papers." Mia lowered herself into the chair beside Helen and swallowed her sigh of relief. She refused to look at Robyn, who scribbled across her paper notes before checking over Mia one last time and rushed off.

Helen tugged her walker closer to rest her arm on. "We both need someone to recognize we're more than capable of handling our own affairs and seeing to our own health."

"You'll let me know when you've found that person, won't you?" Mia tipped her head against the windowsill behind her and inhaled around the throbbing in her leg.

"As long as you promise to do the same," Helen said.

"Wyatt must've noticed your progress," Mia said. "Surely he wants you back home."

"My son is not the person we need," Helen said. "He doesn't believe I'm safe in my gardens."

"Wyatt wants you to give up your gardens?" Mia asked. Wyatt wanted Mia to give up on her film to focus on her recovery, as if she couldn't do both successfully.

"Insists I'm not safe in my own home now. Can you imagine? I've lived there longer than he's been alive." Helen shifted in her chair. "Wyatt doesn't believe in anything he cannot control."

Like love. Wyatt had wanted Mia to stay in Africa to discover if there was something more than attraction between them. But that meant putting her work second. Something he hadn't been willing to do himself. It also meant taking a chance on love.

But she'd vowed years ago never to risk everything for love. Her mother had loved like that and had ended up alone with only her wedding ring as proof of her thirty-year marriage. Besides, she'd witnessed her father choose between his work and his wife. There hadn't been enough love for both in his life. *You have to be willing to sacrifice for your art, Mia. It's the only way to build a legacy.* Perhaps her father was right, except there was nothing for Mia to sacrifice if she never risked her heart.

The elevator doors slid open and Wyatt stepped onto the floor, confidence and determination in every sure step down the hall toward them. Awareness fired across her nerves, straightening her spine and kicking up her pulse. He irritated her, nothing more than that. How could he take away his mother's passion and crush her like that? How insensitive was he? Keeping her mom in the home she'd bought with Mia's father on their first anniversary was Mia's priority.

But then Wyatt would've made Mia choose, too: between him and her art. Fortunately she'd fled with her heart intact and no regrets.

Wyatt nodded at her and leaned down to press a soft kiss on his mother's cheek. Mia clenched the chair arms to keep from touching her own cheek. Greetings from her ex-boyfriends had been absentminded and distant at best. Her father's greetings had included a cold cup of coffee and instructions to keep the day on schedule. Annoyed that he made her miss something insignificant like a simple kiss, she frowned at Wyatt.

"Wyatt, you never mentioned your friend was a patient here, too." Helen tugged on her robe, adjusting the silk material around her legs. "But then you never mentioned Mia when you met her in Africa either."

"You never mentioned you'd become the welcoming committee for the third floor." Disapproval thinned his mouth into a flat line.

Which would've been more than acceptable if the urge to make him smile didn't jolt Mia. Clearly, she needed a cup of her father's cold coffee and a dose of reality. She stretched both legs out as if she'd just finished an hour of hot yoga, not struggled to walk the length of the hallway without slowing to catch her breath. She needed to concentrate on her recovery, not Wyatt's lack of humor. "We're between therapy sessions."

Helen reached over, patted Mia's arm. Each tap made Mia's grin broaden as Wyatt's frown lengthened. His mom added, "There are no rules against patients visiting with each other."

But this wasn't about two patients. This was about a mother and a former something—Mia wasn't sure how to label what Wyatt and she had been in Africa. Still, she knew that hard gaze, that stiff stance from his taut shoulders to his tense hands on his hips. Wyatt had worn that same look every time Eddy had failed to follow his orders exactly. Now Wyatt leveled his displeasure on Mia and Helen. Except Mia wasn't sure what Wyatt Reid rule the women had violated.

"Was there a reason you were keeping Mia a secret?" Helen's voice was mild, as if she didn't care if she violated a rule or not.

Mia was curious, too. "Maybe he thought we'd plan to escape together."

Helen laughed. "And fly to Scotland to stroll through the fields of heather that I've always wanted to feel under my bare feet."

Wyatt's mouth opened, the smallest fraction that betrayed his surprise before he smashed his lips together.

Mia eyed him, enjoying his discomfort. "There's still more to learn about your mom."

"Wyatt is content with the mother he knows." Resignation slipped through Helen's voice.

"Certainly, your son wouldn't presume to know everything about you." Mia kept her gaze fixed on Wyatt and her voice just a notch above scolding. He'd claimed to want to learn everything about Mia one time, too. But only if Mia fit conveniently into his work schedule with little disruption to his life. "People change and grow all the time."

Wyatt crossed his arms over his chest and kept his gaze fastened on hers, the challenge clear. "People also believe they need the approval of others to feel valuable and waste their entire lives seeking that approval, which they're never going to get."

Good thing she never required or needed Wyatt's approval. She'd be waiting a long time. Maybe forever. "Everyone wants to be accepted and liked for who they are."

"But sometimes who we are isn't enough." His voice was raw, as if bruised. His cheeks pulled in, accenting that grim air around him.

Her mother hadn't been enough to keep her father home for longer than a weekend. Mia worked every day to prove she was more than enough to step into her father's illustrious shoes, despite the doubts from the network, the film industry and even her own crew. She'd prove herself, keep her promise to her father, and then she'd be fulfilled. She'd finally be good enough. And *that* would be enough. Yet her gaze locked with Wyatt's, and those slate eyes narrowed on her as if he heard the whispered denial coming from deep inside her chest. She slapped her palm over her ribs, blocking out Wyatt and disrupting the rumblings from a heart she had no intention of ever listening to.

"Well, I've had enough philosophical chit-chat for the day." Helen pulled her walker in front of her. "I don't understand why your generation can't simply say what they mean."

"We do. Your generation just doesn't want to hear it." Wyatt shifted his attention to his mom, releasing Mia from his shrewd focus.

Mia sagged against the chair as if she'd run ten city blocks, not shutting out Wyatt and keeping him from revealing truths she rejected.

"Perhaps because it's all nonsense." Helen touched Mia's arm and grinned. "Mia, I'll see you when the therapy dogs arrive later."

"Mom, you don't like dogs." Wyatt set his hands on his hips. Surprise jutted his chin forward.

"Nonsense. I had a German shepherd growing up." Helen's smile looked more girlish and young from the memory. Her voice eased into the wistful. "Smokey was my favorite pet."

"You never mentioned Smokey before." Wyatt rubbed his chin, his gaze dropping to the floor.

"You never asked," Helen countered, her voice stiff and starched.

Mia winced from the lack of lightness in Helen's tone.

Wyatt never flinched from Helen's barb. Only stuffed his hands into his scrubs pant pockets and tucked his elbows into his sides as if preparing himself to absorb more of his mom's rebukes. "Trent and I asked for a puppy every year until I left for college. Every year you said no."

"Your father told you no, not me." Helen turned to Mia. Her voice lowered, as if they'd stepped into a hushed confessional. "I'd overruled my husband on several things like the tree house, skateboards and video games. Thought I'd let him have his way with the no-dog rule. Good marriages are about knowing when to let the other one win."

Mia had witnessed only the elements of a bad marriage with her own mother: unrequited love, a stalled life and a husband who paid for the stability his absence couldn't provide.

"So good marriages are a competition, then, and not about compromise and mutual respect." The humor in Wyatt's tone soaked the sarcasm from his words as he stepped to the side of Helen's chair. He reached out as if anticipating his mom's next move.

"Good marriages are about real love, knowing what really matters to your spouse and romance." Helen gripped her walker and stood up, greeting her therapist with a wide smile. "Vicky, you've rescued me from explaining the intimate details of a good marriage to my son."

The older woman laughed and squeezed Wyatt's shoulder before assisting Helen. "Follow your mother's example and you'll have a fulfilling marriage."

Wyatt stepped back and rubbed his neck as if the idea of marriage misaligned his spine.

Mia cleared her throat, trying to break up her own laughter.

Helen turned toward Wyatt. "You'll be back for dinner." It wasn't a request or suggestion—it was a command from a mother to her son. Disobedience wouldn't be tolerated. Wyatt had more in common with his mom than Mia had first assumed. The Reid family certainly liked to order others around.

Helen shuffled down the hall, her laughter mixed with the therapist's. Mia watched Wyatt's eyebrows draw together as if he suddenly didn't recognize his own mom.

"Good thing marriage isn't on either of our to-do lists." Mia let her amusement disrupt the silence.

Wyatt faced her, his fingers tapping against

his bottom lip. "You wouldn't claim to know everything on my to-do list, would you?"

Mia's laughter fizzled like a candle in a rainstorm. Wyatt's slow smile streamed through her, spreading a warmth like the sun's first appearance after that storm.

Robyn arrived, pushing Mia's transportation to the hyperbaric chamber between Mia and Wyatt. Mia sighed, relieved she'd get to sit in the wheelchair, instead of relying on her walker and sluggish legs and muddled mind. Robyn couldn't carry her away from Wyatt fast enough.

CHAPTER FOUR

WYATT STRETCHED HIS neck and rolled his shoulders. He'd been crammed into the too-small recliner in his mother's room for too long. He should go home and stretch out in a real bed. But there was more comfort in the stiff recliner than at his mom's house.

His childhood home had been overrun by foliage and greenery, and no matter where he looked he couldn't find any old childhood memories, good or bad. The cactus terrariums replaced the kid-art shelf of awkward clay pots and smeared-handprint pictures. Oil paintings of roses and orchids displaced family photos across the hallway walls. The scent of earth and soil lingered in every room, where vanilla and fresh-out-of-the-oven sugar cookies used to fill every breath. Even the tree house he'd built with Trent one summer before fifth grade had been overtaken by vines. The house was slowly being eaten by his mother's plants.

He crumpled up another foundation application and tossed it into the wastebasket. Each scammer application etched his cynicism all that much deeper. "You'll be lucky to have even ten real applicants to choose from."

"Now isn't the time for judgment." His mom glanced up from her crossword and pointed her pen at him. "Just because these organizations don't bring medical care to an entire country doesn't make them less worthy of our support."

He'd lost her support when his brother had died. He doubted he'd ever get it back. Fanning out several applications, he waved the papers at her. "You should go through these and decide for yourself."

His mom removed her glasses and rubbed her eyes. "I'm too worn out tonight."

"Spent too much time greeting new patients and playing with the dogs." His mom was a closet dog lover. Nothing about that made sense. *Nothing.* Surely he should've known such a small personal detail about his own mother. He could recite the medical histories from his great-grandparents to his parents. Knew the family suffered from high blood pressure and diabetes and fraternal twins peppered the family tree on his mother's side. He knew the vital information and important facts. That he'd only just learned about his mom's dog history shouldn't matter. The small dose of worry stuck in the back of his throat like a partially dissolved pill that should've been easy to wash down. After all, he knew everything that he needed to about his mom, didn't he?

The click of her pen on the bedside table pulled Wyatt's attention back to his mom.

She tossed her crossword book on top of the pen. "I only met one patient, and the dog visits are good for my health. They lower blood pressure, alleviate stress and anxiety."

Maybe he should thank the therapy dogs for pulling his mom out of her death-is-coming-for-me phase and stop worrying about the things that didn't matter, like her childhood pets. "You seem more relaxed tonight."

"I owe that to Mia." The pleasure in her smile brightened her voice in the dim room.

The words on the application in Wyatt's hand blurred until all he saw was Mia's wide copper-tinted eyes and even wider smile from earlier. A smile that punched him in the gut, deep enough to leave a permanent imprint and rattle his resolve to think of her as just another patient. Now Mia made his mother happy, too. That was unacceptable. His gut twisted around that punch. "Did Mia distract you with stories of her filmmaking adventures?"

"No, she was rather closed off about her life." Helen frowned. "I'll have to talk to her more about that tomorrow."

Wyatt could hardly describe his relationship with Mia. Except from the moment he'd seen her in mud-coated hiking boots, a T-shirt splattered with blood and a fierceness in her attitude, he'd been drawn to her. Even when she'd demanded that he save her friend's life. Even when she'd defied his orders to leave the surgery area and instead positioned herself at the door like a guardian angel ready to swoop in if he failed her friend.

He wondered how Mia would describe their time in the village. He crumpled up another scam application, shooting it into the trash can, along with his wayward thoughts. Mia's version didn't matter. Nothing good came from dissecting the past. Lessons had already been learned, and he prided himself on not being a repeat offender. "Don't pry where you're not invited, Mom."

"Mia supports my desire to return home." Helen took off her glasses and folded the arms together. "I'll only be reciprocating the concern."

"She told you to move home?" No wonder

she'd made his mom giddy, telling her exactly what she wanted to hear. Wyatt struggled to keep his face impassive. How dare Mia put such impossible ideas into his mom's head. His mom already had too many impractical plans on her agenda.

"The idea that you were forcing me to give up my gardening appalled her." Helen's glass case closed with the same snap that punctuated her voice. "Mia believes a life not spent doing what you love is a life wasted."

Mia needed to analyze her own life and leave his mom's alone. Besides, one stroll through his mother's house proved his mom might've escalated her passion to an obsession. Something her new friend could surely understand after chasing her own father around the globe. The drive for the perfect film footage had consumed Carlo Fiore so fully, he had nothing else to give his only daughter. Mia wanted a father, Carlo wanted a legacy. And it looked like Carlo had won. Mia had almost died for her film. That was passion in the Fiore family and stupidity in Wyatt's mind. Still, Mia embraced her father's life just as he'd trained her to. Just as Carlo Fiore had expected. Yet Wyatt wondered how much Mia loved the reality of her life now. "You can still garden and grow your plants."

"There's hardly room for more than two plants in the single window in those places." Her frown joined the distaste in her voice. "Never mind the sunlight required for an herb garden."

"If you looked at the floor plan, there's more than one window." Wyatt crammed the stack of applications into his backpack, ramming his frustration inside, too. "It isn't a prison."

"Mia suggested that my therapists do a home visit to assess the dangers before I move back." Helen adjusted her covers, tugging the blankets up to her chin. "I spoke to both of my therapists this afternoon and offered to give them my set of keys if you're schedule is too full to accommodate such a small request."

Wyatt tapped his fist against his mouth, knocking his retort back behind his teeth. He really must thank Mia for her abundant help.

His mom lowered the head of her bed, signaling her desire to sleep and the end of their conversation.

Mia needed to stop making suggestions. Now. His mother needed to stop acting as if she came last in his life. He'd come home, hadn't he? He swung the backpack on his shoulder and kissed his mom's cheek. "I'll talk to your therapists tomorrow."

Right after he set Mia straight before things went too far and she'd written his mother's discharge and home care orders herself.

Wyatt strode down the hall and noticed the light streaming from Mia's room, not the soft night setting that allowed patients to see their way to the bathroom. But the full daylight setting that lit up the room like the noon sun across the desert. She knew the importance of sleep. A hospital room wasn't a home office, and pulling an all-night work session would set back her recovery.

She had to be awake. No one could sleep in that flood of light. After he yelled at her for working all night, he'd order her to stay away from his mother. And if he sounded like a father warning a detention-stricken boy away from his honors-achieving daughter, maybe she'd listen and get in line.

"It's lights out, Mia." Wyatt tugged on the curtain shielding Mia's bed. "As in stop working and go to..." Whatever else Wyatt might've said drained from his voice.

Several pillows propped Mia upright as if to better support her work session. Except her hands clenched the laptop like metal clamps. The deep, dark pockets under her eyes cast shadows down her cheeks. Strands of her chestnut hair poked out from her braid, stiff and crinkled, not soft and silky. Her right leg rested on top of the covers, but her foot, encased in a Bay Water Hospital sock, remained flexed, her knee locked and toes rigid as if she prepared herself to absorb the impact of ramming into the wall feetfirst.

"Working all night isn't part of your treatment plan." Wyatt reached for her laptop.

"I'm not." Her grip on the computer tightened as if someone secured those clamps. "I have to."

Wyatt checked her IVs, wondering if some sort of night terror was being caused by the pain meds. "It can wait."

"I just need to watch." Her hold never loosened. Only her wide gaze lifted to collide with his, her words toppling over each other. "If I just watch, everything will be fine again."

The terror that burned the edges of her amber eyes seared through him, spiking his own blood pressure. He hadn't ever witnessed her fear. As far as he knew, Mia dared fear to try to scare her. But in this moment, he couldn't deny that fright engulfed her like uncontained wildfire.

"You can watch tomorrow." He soothed his voice into the placating style of those hostage negotiators he'd seen on TV and tugged on the laptop, gaining some traction. She certainly hadn't slacked off with her fitness in the past two years. Of course, all those adventure and wilderness shoots didn't happen from the comfort of a jeep.

"Wyatt, press Play." Mia's gaze locked on the computer screen. Her cheeks paled as if she'd whitened her warm beige skin with bleach. "Just press Play, please."

The shiver of dread leaking through her voice crept up his spine. Time to end this and regain control. He sat on the side of the bed and shifted into her view, replacing the computer screen with his face in her line of sight. "Mia, inhale now. Breathe in until I tell you to stop." He cupped her cold cheeks in both of his hands. "Good. Exhale."

He mimicked her breathing, matching his inhales and exhales to hers. The hitch in her breath stopped after the fifth exhale. She blinked after five more inhales. Another set of five and the warmth returned to her skin beneath his palms.

"You can let go." Mia blinked, the movement slow and exaggerated, as if her eyelashes cleared the lingering fear from her gaze.

He rubbed his thumbs over her cheeks. "I'll let go when I want."

"Really, I'm fine now." Still she leaned into his touch.

The shadows finally settled back into the bruises beneath her eyes. She was better, but far from fine. "You need to get some sleep."

"I was trying to do that," she argued.

"With your laptop."

She pushed his arms away and grasped the computer as if he'd caused the crisis. "I'm being stupid. I already survived. It's not like I'll die from watching the footage."

He flattened his palm against the laptop, keeping her from lifting the screen. "What footage?"

"There's video from my accident. I need to watch it." Confidence coated her voice, yet the tremor in her fingers as she tried to open the computer gave her away.

He set his hand over hers as if he had every right. As if she was more than just another patient. "Eddy and Shane can pull out any useful footage."

"Shane already did that." She curled her fingers into a fist beneath his palm.

"Then let it alone."

"I can't." She stared at their hands. Her fingers twitched beneath his touch.

"There's no point in reliving it." If she only released her fist the tiniest bit, he could weave his fingers through hers and draw her focus back to him. He wanted to replace her fear

with something better. Something meaningful. Something worth remembering. Like
their first and only kiss.

"I relive it every night already," she whispered.

"Isn't that enough?" Couldn't he be enough?
No, he didn't want to be her anything. He
straightened and folded his arms over his
chest to keep from reaching for her again.
Or doing something absurd like giving in to
his urge to hold more than her hand.

Mia was his past. Their brief time together
nothing more than an inaccurate reading on
an otherwise normal EKG. His future involved setting up medical clinics to those in
desperate situations, not succumbing to what
was nothing more than a chemical reaction
in his body. He'd touched Mia and his brain
released dopamine and norepinephrine to
charge his nerves, trying to enhance his emotions, trying to lead him astray. Yet science
was his specialty, and any reaction to Mia,
or any woman for that matter, he controlled.

The only heart-related discussions he
planned to have involved words like *cardiac
arrhythmias*, *coronary thrombosis* and *myo-
cardial infarction*. There were no medical de-
grees in fairy tales and pipe dreams. Besides,
if love truly saved, his brother would be alive

today. Love always exacted a price, and that was a price he'd never pay again.

He shoved the clinician inside him forward and eyed her as he would any other irrational patient. "There's medicine to help you sleep. Nurses right down the hall who can administer the medicine into your IV."

"Sleep won't help me." She latched onto his arm and squeezed as if more pressure would make him understand her better. "Why can't you get that?"

Wyatt curled his fingers into fists, coiling his arms tighter against his chest like a cornered rattlesnake. Taking her into his arms and kissing her panic away had not been prescribed. Disgusted with his misplaced impulses, he didn't pause to dilute the acidic bite in his tone. "Why can't you be reasonable? Take some medicine and forget the accident."

"There is no forgetting. I almost died." Her eyes opened like a B-list horror film actress before she slapped her hand over her mouth as if trying to snatch back her confession.

"And that scares you." As it should. Finally, she recognized the risk she took, and all for a few minutes of footage for a film. No film was worth her life.

"I don't have time for this." She waved

away his comment. "I just need to get some decent sleep."

And to let go of her fear. But he wasn't her psychologist or her doctor or her *anything*. She didn't need him. Still, he never moved from the side of her bed. "So what's your plan?"

"Watch the actual footage. Set my memories straight and fall asleep like usual." She nodded, quick and bold, as if the lack of hesitation convinced them both.

Wyatt squeezed the back of his neck, trying to pinch his inner commentary back down his throat. She'd only be giving her dreams more footage to twist through her nightmares. "Isn't there a saying about how ignorance can be bliss?"

"In this case, it's a nightmare. Literally."

"May I?" He picked up the laptop and, at her nod, set the computer on the bedside table.

"I still have to watch the video." Relief softened her warning, and she relaxed into the pillows behind her.

Wyatt still had to walk away. Not look back. Instead he dropped into the chair, propped his feet on the edge of her bed and turned on the TV as if this was exactly where he belonged. He channel-surfed until he found what he wanted. "Let's try something, and if it doesn't work, you can grab the laptop and put the video on Replay for the rest of the night."

"We aren't seriously going to watch *Ruined and Renewed*," she said.

"Why not?" he asked.

"Because you live this life every day." Mia adjusted the covers around her injured leg. "Unless you like to critique the show and point out all the flaws and inconsistencies with the patients' medical emergencies and the doctors' surgical treatments."

"Except I don't get to see the buildup. What prompted these people to do what they did? Who had the common sense to take the person to the ER?" Wyatt upped the volume, trying to tune out Mia and the alarms warning him that staying any longer in her room was a bad idea. A very bad idea. "It's always good to have a change in your perspective. To see things from someone else's point of view, even if it's an utterly insane viewpoint."

Two episodes later, after an esophagus repair caused by a knife-swallowing dare and a botched face-lift performed by an unlicensed fraud, Mia slept with her good leg pressed against Wyatt's feet and her face turned toward him. Wyatt remained wide awake, rooted in the chair like one of his mother's plants. Unable to move. Or perhaps unwilling to move. He should leave. He had to leave.

Reaching for the laptop, he settled it on his lap, pressed the power button and prayed Mia had finally adopted the habit of password protection. The desktop filled the screen, the movie program already launched and no request for a password. Some things hadn't changed.

Wyatt hit the mute button on the TV sound, checked on Mia and pressed Play. Twenty too-long minutes later, he closed the laptop and tried to smother the queasiness rolling through his stomach. Resting his elbows on his knees, he inhaled, forcing air deep into his lungs to crowd the panic out of his body. Nothing in the ER or in a medical tent in Africa ever left him this raw, exposed and twitchy. All that from watching a video.

He glanced over at Mia's bandaged arm resting on top of the covers and winced at the reminder of a disoriented Mia hacking through her wet suit into her flesh with her dive blade as she thrashed around to untangle herself from the kelp and fishing line. All while running out of air. He rubbed his chest, drew another breath. Then another because he needed the reminder: he wasn't drowning. He wasn't trapped under the ocean, out of oxygen and time.

He leaned toward the bed and held Mia's good hand between both of his. The contact satisfied nothing. He wanted a reaction. He wanted her to wake up, squeeze his fingers and reassure him that she really was alive. How pathetic had he become?

Mia Fiore needed a keeper. She needed someone to watch out for her and keep her from putting her life at risk again. She needed someone to show her that she was worth more alive than dead. She needed someone to love her beyond all reason.

Fortunately, that someone wasn't Wyatt. He lived only within reason. Clearly when he was with Mia, he lost his common sense. He'd suffered a panic attack from simply watching the video of her accident. If he actually witnessed another one of her near-death incidents, he'd probably lose his mind altogether. That was an unacceptable flaw. He'd been trained to be a doctor, not a lovesick fool.

He held on to her hand, reluctant to let go. He'd forgotten how well her hand fit inside his.

Another few minutes wouldn't matter. It wasn't as if he needed to touch her to feel better. He just wanted some time to remind his body that his feet were planted on the ground, not the deck of a dive boat.

Besides, he'd be leaving soon to return to Africa. And he had every intention of boarding that plane with a sound mind and his heart intact.

CHAPTER FIVE

MIA TIPPED HER head toward the door, and delight spiraled through her stomach, making her smile fill her from the inside out. Wyatt stood inside her room as if she'd wished him there. A young girl and boy anchored him on each side, and all wore matching grins as if they'd raided the dessert bar in the cafeteria and escaped undetected. She would've joined them if they'd only asked. And that was proof of just how restorative last night's sleep had been. She'd never done silly things as a child, but the trio in her doorway tempted her now.

"Mia, I'd like to introduce you to my friends." Wyatt's mouth seemed to be late in catching up with the smile flaring from inside him. Happiness surged through his cool gaze. His movements were relaxed and easy. Clearly Mia and he needed to watch more marathon sessions of *Ruined and Renewed*, as Wyatt looked as refreshed as Mia felt. Wyatt shifted, allowing the blonde curly-haired girl gripping his elbow with one hand and a white cane in her other to move into the room. "This is Ella Callahan."

"My mom brings the therapy dogs to visit everyone here." Ella folded her cane and pushed her lavender glasses up on her nose. "I'm too young to get a guide dog, but Mom promised me when I turn sixteen, we can apply. But Mom says she'll be a working dog, so she can't come visit sick people."

Mia took a deep breath for Ella. The precious little girl spoke fast, as if she was in the final round of a timed debate. "Nice to meet you, Ella. The therapy dogs are wonderful, but something tells me I'm going to enjoy this surprise visit even more."

Ella grinned and tugged her purple sweatshirt stamped with the words *Power to the Dreamer* down over her bold-striped leggings.

Wyatt set his hand on the boy's shoulder. "This is Ben Sawyer."

Not releasing his hold on the stack of board games in his arms, Ben jerked his head and flicked his copper bangs off his forehead, revealing deep green eyes. "My dad drives the ambulance here."

Wyatt guided the pair toward Mia's bedside. "Guys, this is my friend Mia Fiore. She's the one I was telling you about who makes films."

"Cool." Ben shifted his weight and leaned forward, his gaze fixed on Mia's open wound. "What happened to your leg?" Fascination, not horror, widened the boy's eyes, as if he happily imagined every sort of grotesque reason for her cut.

"I was in a diving accident," Mia said.

"Did a shark bite you?" That wonder spilled into Ben's breathless voice.

"Not exactly. I cut myself with a dive knife." Ben's shoulders drooped, and his long sigh filled the room, making Mia want to take back the truth and confess she'd fought off a great white shark.

"Amelia got cut with a knife, too." Ella leaned into Wyatt. "Except Dr. Wyatt says the doctor had to cut her. Amelia's appendix made her sick. Ben and I have stayed in hospitals because my eyes don't work like they're supposed to and neither does Ben's pancreas. So we came to visit Amelia."

"And Dad wanted my port checked, even though Aunty Ava told him the port was fine." Ben shook his head and adjusted the board games in his arms.

"Ms. Ava would know. She was in the war." Ella tipped her chin down as if daring anyone to argue with her statement. "And she rides in the ambulance with Ben's dad."

"Dr. Wyatt told us Aunty Ava saved you on the dock." Ben eyed Mia.

The children's adoration of Ava was more than clear. Mia admitted she wanted to meet the real-world superwoman who captured this pair's love and support. "I need to meet your aunt, so I can thank her."

"I get to call her Aunty Ava even though we don't share blood or anything like that." Pride made Ben's thin shoulders straighten. "But Dad says you don't have to have the same blood to be family."

"My dad is like your aunty Ava," Ella said. 'We don't share blood either, but he's my real dad. Dr. Wyatt, do you have family that isn't family like us?"

Wyatt wrapped an arm around each child and pulled them close into his sides. His gaze locked on Mia, causing her to feel more than happiness at his visit.

He made her want to change her perspective. He made her want…

Wyatt added, "I'm starting to think it's time that I expand my family."

Right now, Mia wanted to wrap the trio in her embrace, hold on tight and demand that they tell her what it would take for her to reach Aunty status. "What are you three up to?" *And can I join in? Please.*

"Our board game tournament was halted thanks to the nurses having to do blood draws, vitals checks and other nurse things." Wyatt shuddered as if all those tests terrified him. "We were afraid they might test us, too, so we ran away and decided to hide here in your room."

Ella and Ben giggled.

"I see," Mia said. "What's your plan now?"

Wyatt checked the wall clock. "We've got a good hour before their parents come to get them."

"We have games." Ben lifted the boxes.

Ella patted the front pocket on her sweatshirt. "If you don't like those games, I have two decks of cards in here."

"I'm not sure I should play." The list of final edits and sound bites waited on her laptop.

Both kids stretched out the word *please* in unison.

Wyatt tipped his chin toward the children as if he'd dropped a challenge in the form of two adorable ten-year-old kids. As if he dared her to turn them down.

Mia swept her hair up into a bun and would've rolled up her sleeves if she had any on her hospital gown. "It's just that I really like to win, and I don't want to make Dr.

Wyatt cry when I beat him." Challenge accepted.

Ella covered her mouth with her hand, but her giggle slipped around her fingers. Ben dropped his forehead toward the game boxes and tipped his head to peek at Wyatt. The quiver in the boy's thin shoulders gave away his laughter.

Wyatt straightened and set his hands on his hips. "I'm undefeated in chess and cards today."

"Not for much longer," Mia said. "Ella, should we team up? Girls against boys for a chess tournament."

"Yes." Ben edged into Wyatt's side.

Ella grinned. "The losers have to buy whatever dessert the winners want, even if they hate it."

"Deal." Ben leaned around Wyatt to look at Ella. "Get ready to eat moldy cheese jelly beans, Ella."

"You have to win first." Ella turned her head toward her friend and frowned. "But you'll be eating beet ice cream when we win."

Ben grimaced and turned to consider Mia's leg. "Can you get out of bed, Ms. Mia?"

"I need to get out of this bed, Ben. Thanks for giving me an excuse." A quick round of finger flexes proved the numbness had lessened in her right hand. Wiggling her toes didn't grant the same results. Yesterday Robyn had steadied her more than once during her bed-to-chair transfers. She'd need help now, too, but she was playing in this tournament despite any discomfort. "Dr. Wyatt, you take the kids and set up in the visitors lounge. I'll have Roslyn take me down there."

"When the boys win, you might wish you stayed in bed." Wyatt bumped his fist against Ben's knuckles, as the boy wouldn't relinquish his grip on the games.

"When the girls win, you'll wish you'd stayed on the other ward and let the nurses run tests on you," Mia countered.

Ella cheered.

Mia waved toward the door. "Now go while you boys still have a few minutes to strategize."

"What about us?" Worry pinched Ella's eyebrows together behind her glasses.

"We're girls," Mia said. "We were born to win."

Ella brightened and set her hand on Wyatt's elbow. "I'll make sure everything is set up correctly, Ms. Mia."

"Let's give Mia some time to prepare herself to lose." Wyatt grinned and led the kids toward the door. His laughter lingered even after her door clicked shut.

Mia pressed the nurses' call button, suddenly impatient to get out of bed and begin her day.

THE EUPHORIA OF victory hummed through Mia several hours after Wyatt and the kids had departed. Mia stared at the camera bag on the bedside table. How many times had she wished for the camera to capture moments from the afternoon? The shared laughter. Ben covering his mouth to whisper the next move in Wyatt's ear, even though the boy hadn't mastered the art of the library-level whisper. Ella's mastery of the chess pieces with only the lightest touch of her fingers. And the natural ease between the trio, as if one wasn't visually impaired, as if one didn't have to pause to check his blood sugar level, as if one had always been around children. Wyatt made her think of family, yet she wasn't in the market to expand hers.

Mia picked up the camera case and set it on her lap. She wasn't about to miss the moment Wyatt and Ben bit into the beet ice cream with goat cheese swirl.

Unzipping the bag, she dug inside for the instruction manual. The digital camera weighed less than a pound and was more advanced than the ones from her budgeted days in college. Her favorite camera had stopped working on her very first trip to South America with her dad, and she'd never replaced it, preferring instead to get acquainted with his favorite video equipment. Five pages into the instruction manual, she tossed the booklet aside and gave in to her preference for hands-on learning. She wasn't changing her perspective that much.

Resting the camera in her left palm, she pressed buttons until her bed came into view on the digital screen. Settling behind the lens was as natural to her as fog in the city. All was right in the world of a city local when a downy fog blanket covered the bay and cradled the city in a cloud. All was right in Mia's world when she viewed the world through a lens. Excitement hummed across her skin. Relief rolled through her like that slow creeping fog, quieting the doubt and soothing the uncertainty. The buzz of anticipation hadn't been damaged like the nerves in her arm and leg.

"Good morning, Mia." The cheerful greeting from her wound care nurse cushioned the creaking wheels of the supply cart. Kellie checked the information board. "What's your pain level today?"

Mia lowered the camera, forcing herself to concentrate on the nurse's question. Thanks to Wyatt and the kids, she'd forgotten her numbness. She'd stopped staring at her wounds as if her laser focus would mend the cuts faster. Thanks to her unexpected visitors, she'd discovered the courage to pick up the camera. Surprise fluttered through her and fanned out into her voice, stretching out her one-word reply. "Better."

"That's what we like to hear." Kellie tugged on a pair of gloves and moved around to Mia's injured side. "Mind if I take a look?"

"What are the odds it sealed itself up overnight?" Surely her hours of sleep last night restored her damaged tissue. They'd all lectured her about the benefits of rest for her recovery.

Kellie laughed and leaned over Mia's leg to peel off the tape and dressing. "It's healing where we can't see. Closing itself from the inside out."

Not exactly the answer Mia wanted. Kellie wasn't pulling out needles and thread. Another day with an open wound and antibiotic treatment. She picked up the camera, trying to elbow the disappointment aside. She watched the efficient, deft yet gentle movements of Kellie's hands redressing her leg through the lens, sinking herself back into that feeling that all was right with her world. The same feeling she'd had with Wyatt and the kids. A necklace swung through Mia's frame.

"That one is good." Kellie tucked the silver chain beneath her scrubs and replaced her gloves. "Now let's check those stitches in your arm."

To avoid more disappointment at another slow-to-heal wound, Mia focused on the nurse. "Was that a ring on your necklace?"

"My engagement ring." Kellie tucked her glasses into her thick curls on top of her head. "Which my fiancé will slide on my finger when he returns from his deployment in the Middle East. We had a video-chat engagement."

Joy burst from Kellie via her wide smile and the glow on her face, as if her heart pumped love—not blood—through her body. But envy never filled Mia. Only a sense of contentment that her heart wasn't up for the bargaining. That love hadn't claimed her as its next victim.

Love lied and stole and misled. She'd seen that again and again with her parents. Time had moved whenever her father had returned home for a rare visit. Life and happiness like Kellie's had filled their house in those precious days. But when he'd left, everything stalled and stuttered and dimmed as if her dad had stashed the very light from her mother inside his suitcase to keep for himself.

Kellie tipped her head at Mia, her eyebrows pulled together before she rushed to explain. "It was really romantic. Hard to believe, I know."

Mia hid behind the camera lens, blocking Kellie from exposing her. The romance couldn't be denied. Mia simply denied her own heart the chance to sigh, flop over and get involved.

Kellie pumped an antibacterial solution into her hands, the white foam like cotton candy for Kellie's rainbows-and-sunshine world. "Rey got down on one knee on his side and opened a ring box. My parents snuck into my room and slid a similar ring box across the table while Rey asked me to marry him."

Mia tracked Kellie's path around her bed through the camera lens. Her heart might be banned from getting involved, but Mia appreciated the special moment. Like her father, she understood patience would capture even more. Kellie's excitement stirred inside Mia. Still, she waited, as if she stood in the plains waiting for the first sighting of a cheetah waking at sunrise.

"Five weeks, three days and eleven hours

and this ring will be on my finger and my fiancé will be home where he belongs." Kellie freed the necklace from behind her scrubs. The platinum diamond ring rested on the outside of the fist Kellie pressed against her heart. The love glowed from every part of her, lighting her like a pot of gold at the end of her rainbow.

Look for the simple moments, Mia. You'll always find magic there.

Mia never hesitated, just clicked.

"Until then, I wear it against my heart for safekeeping." Kellie tucked the necklace back inside her scrubs. "It's silly, I know, but that's love."

Mia scanned through the photographs on the screen. She had to know. Had to see if her instincts proved true. A burst of Kellie's sunshine flashed inside Mia, forcing her smile wide. She turned the camera toward the nurse. "This is what love looks like."

Kellie accepted the camera, a tremor flexing through her hands. Her mouth opened, but nothing more than a small sigh escaped. Or perhaps that was a groan.

Silence pushed back on Mia, making her twist to stretch the tightness in her muscles. She'd been caught up, too. She hadn't asked. Just zoomed in, trespassed on Kellie's memories. She'd needed to know if she could capture love in a still photograph. "I'm so sorry." Mia reached for the camera. "I invaded your privacy in the worst way. I can delete all of the pictures."

Helen edged into Mia's room, the creak of her walker preceding her arrival. She paused and pinched her cheek. "I didn't prepare myself for pictures."

Roslyn assisted Helen into Wyatt's chair.

Mia almost stopped her. As if Wyatt was returning. Coming back to sit at her bedside after he'd already spent most of the afternoon with her. Mia bit the inside of her lip, trying to tweak reality back into place. Wyatt had left. Yet his presence lingered as if he'd made a lasting impression in the room—or worse, inside Mia.

Kellie tipped the screen toward the young aide. "Look at this."

"You have to send that to Rey." Roslyn took the camera, gingerly and gently, as if she held one of Mia's mother's favorite jade figurines. "Maybe his guys can take a picture of him and you can superimpose his image into this one. It'd be like the perfect engagement photo. I saw it done on the internet, and that couple's picture went viral."

Kellie looked at Mia. "Did you just tell me you were going to delete these?"

"Mia, delete it after you email Kellie a copy. She has to have this." Roslyn walked over to Helen and showed her the picture.

"Oh, isn't that the loveliest photograph?" Helen lifted her gaze over her glasses to look at Kellie and then returned her attention to the camera. She touched her cheek as if catching the sigh that came out. "I don't know much about viral things and the internet, but this should be enlarged, framed and titled. Not deleted."

Kellie took the camera and cradled it like a baby she'd snatched away from a temperamental parent. She retreated as if she had no intention of returning the camera to Mia. "Can you superimpose images, really?"

Eddy usually made that sort of magic happen. Mia hadn't used those particular programs in quite a while, but she could try. She would try for Kellie and her future husband to celebrate their beginning. Only an end loomed for Mia. She rubbed her neck, trying to dislodge the snag of sadness. It wasn't the time to think about what happened after she finished the film. After the screening. After the final credits rolled. The last ones that would ever bear her father's name. Her throat collapsed, trapping the grief from escaping, making her voice sound as if she scraped her words against rough stone. "Email me a picture of Rey and I'll see what we can do. My gift for taking your picture without permission."

"You have my permission to reverse the aging process with your camera." Helen brushed her fingertips over her face as if removing wrinkles.

"Mine, too." Roslyn smeared a shiny lip gloss across her mouth. "If you promise I'll look as good as Kellie."

"That had nothing to do with me and everything to do with Mia. Seriously, though, thanks for showing me that I can be beautiful, if only for a moment, Mia." Kellie touched Mia's shoulder before putting her glasses on. "Now back to my ordinary self and work."

There was nothing ordinary about the nurses and staff at Bay Water and nothing special about Mia with a regular camera. *You can't do what everyone else does and expect to stand out, Mia.* "I got lucky, that's all. I'm not a still photographer."

"Get lucky again and make me look ten years younger," Helen quipped.

Roslyn laughed. "Helen, you could use your photograph for an online dating profile."

Helen fluffed her hair as if prepping for

her photo shoot, then shook her head. She frowned, but the smile in her gaze revealed her laughter. "I'm too old to love again. Besides, the young are better equipped for love's temperaments."

"You're never too old for love." Roslyn situated Helen's walker within easy reach. "Physical Therapy will be by to get you soon. They'll make sure you're ready to walk down the aisle when you meet your new love."

Kellie finished writing in Mia's chart and grinned at Helen. "You might beat your own son down the aisle."

Mia pictured Wyatt standing at the end of the aisle, a formal black tuxedo to match the serious look on his face as he scrutinized his bride like a complicated arrival in the ER. The doctor had sharpened his edges, disposed the charm and alleviated his easy laughter. Two years later, the doctor controlled the man. Except for those few hours with the kids today and last night with her.

Still, he'd made her feel safe. For the first time in so long. She'd scooted until her knee touched his feet last night, needing that connection. To someone. Eddy had his wife and soon their baby's arrival. Shane had multiple friends who happened to be girls in various cities. Although she suspected he liked his girlfriend here in the city the most. Frank had a wife of thirty-eight years and a dozen grandchildren. Mia had her father. Until she didn't and loneliness claimed her. She'd never noticed or minded her lack of a plus one until a week after her father's funeral when friends and family returned to their normal lives and Mia returned to an empty hotel suite.

But loneliness wouldn't make her race down the aisle. She had other races to run to ensure her mother's lifestyle remained the same, to build her career and the Fiore name. She'd leave the chapels and bow-tied hearts to Cupid's followers like Kellie and Roslyn.

Last night with Wyatt was a weak, not magic moment. Definitely not a walking-down-the-aisle meaningful occasion. She'd have been comfortable with the janitor sitting in the chair beside her or even her mother. She hadn't wanted to be alone. When she walked again, it'd be away from Wyatt Reid, not to. A tightness squeezed across her chest as if she'd pushed through one too many push-ups, or maybe the lies piled up against her ribs. Hardly mattered. She knew she belonged behind a camera, filming the world and supporting her mom, not standing beside Wyatt.

Kellie made one final check of Mia's bandages. "Back to the chamber in less than an hour."

Roslyn and Kellie walked out together. Roslyn suggested Rey's dress uniform for his photo. Kellie wished Mia could take his photo, too. The young aide patted Kellie's shoulder and nodded.

Mia swallowed her shout that she wasn't a still photographer. She needed to shout at herself, too. She'd almost called Kellie back to offer to do the couple's photos when Rey came home. What had come over her? Walks down aisles and still photography meant settling into one place. Establishing a home. But a home meant forsaking everything her dad had trained her to become. How many times had he told her that great art required great sacrifice? A dry sensation skimmed over her, making her skin parched and irritated, as if she stood inside a sandstorm. Mia curled her fingers into the blankets to keep from rubbing her arm and thighs to stretch her skin back out and fit into her normal world again.

Helen watched her. Her round eyes behind her oversize glasses gave her the look of a wise owl. "They agreed to let me sit in here and visit until my therapy as long as I promised not to wander off." Helen peeked around the wall toward the door as if looking for someone. Excitement quickened her words. "I saw Cinder down this hall and knew I'd miss her if I waited in my room."

"I'm happy for the company." More than that, Mia realized. Helen's presence offered her an anchor in her suddenly off-kilter world. Mia's phone vibrated. Her mom's picture blinked on the screen, tilting that axis even more.

"You're having a busy morning." Helen lifted her eyebrows and tipped her chin toward the phone.

"It's my mother." Mia opened her texts. Two more messages popped through while she struggled to reply with her left hand. "It's the first time I've slept through her morning phone call. Now she's texting, and she gets anxious if I don't reply immediately."

"She's concerned about you." Helen pushed her glasses up, as if seeing Mia better would help her understand.

Concern Mia could handle. A hug or kiss on the cheek or soothing pat on the shoulder was an acceptable expression of concern. But her mother had a way of bulldozing through concern and landing straight in the nitpicky. A kiss on the forehead became a lecture on the importance of sunscreen and dangers of melanoma. "She wants to fly from the East

Coast and I keep telling her she doesn't have to. I promised her I'd call if things became serious."

"Looks pretty serious from where I'm sitting." Helen looked at Mia over her glasses.

"It's just that the wound on my leg can't be closed until I've completed the full course of antibiotics and the doctors are certain there's no infection." Mia gave thanks every day for the doctor-patient confidentiality clause and patient privacy laws that prevented her mother from carrying through on her threats to call Mia's doctors. If her mom saw Mia's leg, she'd be hauling her to every specialist across the nation until she found the opinion that alleviated all of her concerns.

In the third grade, Mia had collided with a wall while biking and needed stitches beneath her hairline. Her mom deemed the ER doctors at the children's hospital incapable and dragged her to a series of plastic surgeons. Only the fourth plastic surgeon met her mom's meticulous requirements, and finally the needle pierced Mia's skin and the stitches went in.

"And your arm?" Helen asked.

"It's better every day." Although not improving as swiftly as she'd have preferred. Yet each day she spent in the hospital she risked her mother booking a flight. She had to heal faster. She had to heal before her mom arrived, derailed Mia's film project and rearranged Mia's life. "There's nothing my mother can do for me that she can't do from New York."

"She could keep you company. Hold your hand. Bring your clothes and necessities." Helen's eyebrows lifted as her gaze landed on Mia's hospital gown.

Wyatt's was the only hand Mia wanted to hold. Heat seared down her chest, as if she'd been caught naked. But she didn't want to hold Wyatt's hand, did she? Mia tugged at the neck of her ugly hospital gown. Had the AC stopped working? She hadn't been this hot since she'd returned to the city. "These gowns are easy for me to put on myself."

"You don't trust your friends to bring you the proper clothes." Helen sat back in the chair, her voice matter-of-fact, like a principal instructing a disobedient student. "It's why you need your mother."

Personal shopper wasn't part of the job description for her crew. The last time Mia had been good company for her mom, she'd been twelve years old and still willing to obey her mom's every decree to keep her worry from consuming her. "Did Wyatt pick out your clothes for your stay here?"

"Wyatt would've tossed me his scrubs, if he'd been here." Helen frowned and ran her hands over her silk robe as if to ensure she wasn't wearing scrubs. "I had a bag packed. Don't look so surprised. I'm an aging widow living alone. I thought I should be prepared for a trip to the hospital. The stay is more comfortable with my own clothes and things."

"But Wyatt is here," Mia said. "He came home to support you."

"On his terms," Helen said. "Now his work in the ER makes for a convenient escape."

"He loves his work," Mia said. Like her father had loved his work. Like Mia loved her work.

Helen nodded. "Above all else. I suspect your mother loves you the same way."

Mia cleaned the camera screen with the edge of the blanket, wondering when her relationship with her mother had gotten so blurry. She'd chosen to wander the world with her father rather than build a home in the city. She'd made a choice. One that made her mom uncomfortable and Mia feel guilty. Yet she'd never been enough to fill the void her father had left inside her mom, even though she'd tried until the day she'd boarded the plane to join her dad. Now she'd lost the one parent who encouraged her and questioned the love of the other.

The familiar click-click of nails on the floor announced Cinder's arrival before the silver puffball peeked his curly head into the room. Helen gripped her hands together before leaning forward to welcome the sixty-pound poodle with open arms. "There's my boy."

Mia glanced at Sophie Callahan, Ella's mom and Cinder's handler, whom she'd met earlier when Sophie came to take Ella home. She lifted up her camera. "Do you mind?"

Sophie grinned. "He's never been photographed. Have at it."

Mia retreated behind the lens and the world she understood. She aimed the camera toward Helen and Cinder, zoomed in on the paw Cinder set on Helen's good leg with Helen's fragile hand resting on top. Captured Helen going nose to nose with the poodle, her smile matching the dog's openmouthed grin. Pulled the frame wider to encompass the kindness, easy acceptance and patience between the pair. Had she ever experienced that? Even her father hadn't been convinced she'd handle the demands of his lifestyle. He'd doubted her passion and commitment even on their last, fateful film shoot together. She swallowed around that snag in her throat.

But he'd loved her, or he wouldn't have wanted her to continue his life's work. Work that she loved because she adored her father. Yet Helen's words swirled through her: *above all else*. Surely it was more than enough to just love. Still she wondered what loving above all else really looked like. And if she loved like that, what would she lose?

Sophie moved into the frame, joining the pair and disrupting Mia's thoughts. Helen latched onto Sophie's hand, the one she'd buried in Cinder's curls. The fluffy fur failed to hide the diamond and sapphire eternity band circling the pet shop owner's ring finger. Mia latched onto the distraction. The animated conversation shifted to engagements and wedding dates and flower girl dresses for Ella. A lightness swirled through Mia with every captured instance of laughter, delight and affection.

Mia even offered her own suggestions on bridesmaids' dress colors and weighed in on a fall-versus-spring wedding, all from behind the camera. She even promised Sophie she'd delete any pictures of the pet shop owner in her baseball hat.

All too soon, reality crashed into the room. Helen's physical therapist arrived along with an aide to transport Mia to her hyperbaric chamber treatment. Cinder and Sophie moved on to visit more patients. Mia set the camera down and pushed the table away as if it was responsible for her losing herself so fully she'd forgotten to check the time, think about her pain or second-guess her decisions. Even during a film shoot, she always held a part of herself back. The part that she feared exposing. The part that believed if she only wished harder from her heart, she could have everything. But wishes were for fairy godmothers and children's stories, not real life.

"Don't forget your camera." Helen motioned to the table as she shuffled toward the door. "You might find something inspiring on the way."

The aide dropped the camera in Mia's lap and rolled her wheelchair out into the hall before Mia could stop her. She ignored the camera all the way to her hyperbaric treatment. Still photography had never interested her.

Yet the return an hour later across the glass bridge that stretched over the street four stories below and connected the two hospital wings compelled her to pick up the camera as if it was her job. Two doctors raced by. The edges of their flapping white coats and feet clipped the corner of her picture of the city traffic below. Two worlds colliding.

Mia stopped clicking when the doctors disappeared through a set of automatic doors.

With antibiotics once again dripping through her IV and monitors attaching her to the bed, Mia scanned through the pictures she'd taken. Pleasure leaked through her with every picture, softening her so much she reached for her phone on the first ring without checking the caller ID. And even issued an uncharacteristic chipper greeting.

A familiar deep voice rumbled through the speaker. "Mia. It's Howard. Your father's oldest friend in the business. The one who believed in you more than your dad. Remember me?"

Mia checked the time. Her mother should've been calling. Not Howard, her agent. She smiled, praying that was enough to soften her lie. "Howard, you were on my afternoon call list."

A page for Dr. Easton disrupted the stiff silence.

"Where are you? Was that a code blue?" The boom of Howard's voice pushed the phone away from her ear.

Since she'd known Howard, he'd never talked softer than a shout. Mia clenched the phone. "Frank's aunt fell. We're in the ER."

"Frank never mentioned any family in California."

Mia closed her eyes, picturing Howard tugging on his gray beard. Confusion weaved through his voice, but never scattered his all-too-sharp mind. Pulling one over on Howard Sutton was as impossible a feat as discovering a unicorn in your backyard. Still, she gave it her best effort. "She's several times removed."

Again another pause as Howard's mental gears clicked into alignment. "Well, if you have time to lounge around in the ER, I'll assume everything's on schedule."

"We're working through the final edits now." Mia rubbed her throat, surprised she wasn't choking on the dirt from the deep hole she couldn't stop her mouth from digging.

"I promised the network the usual Fiore flair and a little extra."

Mia pushed her words out of her dry mouth. "What's a little extra?"

"Whatever you want it to be as long as it wows the network. Of course actual footage of toxic substances and pollution being dumped directly into the bay would add a nice touch of the trademark Fiore flair."

"No pressure there." Mia searched her room for the water bottle that usually sat on her bedside table.

"This is what your father always wanted for you. He's proud, Mia. So proud. I can promise you that. Just as I am."

She needed more than water to clear the clog building inside her throat. She'd only ever wanted to make her father proud. She'd only ever wanted his love. "I'll deliver like I promised."

"We can't finalize the next contracts until they've viewed this film, Mia." The rumble in Howard's voice lessened. "If you turned it in early, that'd go a long way to secure better terms for you and your crew on those new contract negotiations we'll be starting soon."

These contracts didn't include her father. These were all hers to fly or falter on alone. She hadn't planned to be all alone. Mia forced an overly cheerful note into her voice. "I'll see what I can do."

"That's my girl. I never had to track down your father. He knew not to upset my nerves."

"I'll call you soon." Mia clicked off and dumped the phone on the table like it was a venomous spider.

She picked up the camera. This wasn't the film she needed to be concentrating on. She hit the trash can icon. A box popped up asking her if she was certain she wanted to delete all. Her father had been sure. All his life he'd been confident in his choices. He'd trained her to be the same as him. She'd always wanted to be the same as her dad. To live his life. She'd chosen to live his life.

All she had to do was hit Delete. Nothing could be simpler than that. It was a button, nothing more. Nothing important like her father's life work. The work that ensured her mother had a home to live in for the rest of her life.

Her phone vibrated with an incoming call. She grabbed the phone like a lifeline tossed into a storm-tossed sea and left the trash can empty. "Hi, Mom."

CHAPTER SIX

MIA JAMMED HER fist into the cool linoleum floor of her hospital room and cursed. The very unladylike, her-mother-would-be-appalled kind of language bounced around inside her head until the searing pain engulfed her calf and pulsed up into her core, scrambling her thoughts. The bandage failed to absorb the new blood now dying her white sock crimson.

She exhaled, trying to forcefully blow the stabbing burn out of her body. The bathroom had been her destination. And why not? Helen had confessed to walking to the bathroom unassisted. Why couldn't Mia? Helen had thirty-some years on Mia, who still sported her original hip from birth. Although she suspected Helen's hip might be more stable, given Mia's legs were currently sprawled in an awkward split across her hospital room floor. The bathroom remained unused, and the blood from her reopened wound skipped her sock and dampened the floor.

Mia eyed the remote with the nurse call

button dangling from the railing on her bed. Three scoots backward and a stretch upward, she might reach it. She closed her eyes and prayed Roslyn answered the call and not Nettie. The pain stole her concentration, and battling the censure from Nettie required energy she didn't possess. Surely, she wasn't the first patient to have a lapse in judgment.

Heavy boots stomped into her room.

Mia cringed at the familiar work boots she'd followed through more than one rain forest. "Hey, Eddy. I thought you were having lunch with the guys." More familiar work boots shuffled in behind Eddy, stopping before ramming into Eddy's stiff frame. One witness was bad, but her entire crew a disaster. Only slightly less mortifying than having Wyatt there, too. She peered around their boots to look for a familiar pair of scrubs-covered legs.

"Mia." The warning in Eddy's voice drew her gaze to his. "What exactly are you doing?"

The alarm and distress in her friends' faces made her feel small and stupid, like the time she'd failed to press the record button during a rare sighting of an Amur leopard. Yet this wasn't eastern Russia, and she'd grown up since then. "Going to the bathroom, then getting the laptop. Nothing I haven't done a thousand times in my life." Frustration roiled through her. Something prickly, as if she'd sipped vinegar, sharpened her tone. "By myself."

It was a simple task. Walk to the bathroom, do her business and grab her laptop on her return. Nothing to it, even with the IV pole in tow. Nettie had released her from all the monitors last evening. Freedom was the point. Proving her independence so her mother and everyone else could back off.

Eddy's gaze skipped over the blood before he swayed and shoved Shane out of his way. "I'll get the nurse. You guys get her into bed."

Mia held up her palm, stalling Shane and Frank. "I don't want to get blood all over my bed."

"Cover up your leg." Frank tossed a towel from the bathroom at her. His trademark easygoing smile disappeared behind a frown more intense than any her father had ever leveled at her. "You're getting back into that bed."

Frank had been with her father since before Mia's birth, and he'd always been more like Mia's favorite uncle than her father's lead cameraman. He'd stayed with Mia out of loyalty to her family. Yet he'd never donned the parental mantle, even when she'd overindulged on piña coladas on the beach in Grenada. Now his disappointment with her was palpable, dislodging her thin grasp on her emotions. She wrapped the towel around her leg and foot, trying to absorb the tears from her voice. "I had the wrong socks on. These don't have the sticky bottoms."

She peered at Shane, but his impassive face offered no sympathy. Not him, too. Shane always took her side. *Always*. He was the younger brother she'd never had. The one who always teased that he wanted to be like her when he grew up. Now he looked like he wanted to be anyone but her. A shout curled up through her throat, demanding that he admit he'd have done the very same thing: take himself to the bathroom.

Eddy and two nurses rushed into the room, sweeping more censure like a dust storm over Mia. Their disapproval set Mia adrift on her own private island of bad decisions. The crowd inside her room pressed in around her and yet she'd never felt this alone, not even when she'd scattered the last of her dad's ashes over the Pacific Ocean. She collapsed back on the floor at Nettie's first prod against her leg wound. Another shout squeezed through her tense neck. Couldn't someone admit they'd made bad decisions, too? Couldn't someone hold her hand?

More footsteps pounded into the room. A page for Dr. Hensen echoed through the intercom system. A different nurse ushered her crew outside. A shiver skimmed across her skin before sinking deep into every bone. She needed her friends. Her friends held her hand to help her cross the Nile. To help her hike the crater of Kilauea. To give her strength at her father's funeral.

Her friends always stood by her. Until now. The aides lifted her onto her bed and covered her with blankets. The monitors latched back onto her good arm, her good finger. She'd only fallen. Just made a bad decision. *In a series of bad decisions*, a voice sounding like her dad chided. She sagged into the pillows, trying to shut out her father's voice and the sting from Nettie working on the gash across her arm. Her arm was supposed to be fine. She was supposed to be fine.

Yet there was nothing fine about the stabs shifting up her calf and spreading like thousands of fire ant bites across her right leg. She pushed the button to raise herself into a sitting position. She'd face the disapproval and pain head-on. Mia looked at Nettie. "Thanks for the help. Can you tell my friends to come back inside now?"

"Dr. Hensen will be here soon to see what

damage you've done." Nettie tugged off her gloves and tipped her head at Mia. "No more solo trips to the bathroom."

"I just needed the right socks."

"You *just* needed to wait for assistance." The scold erased Nettie's usual grandmotherly warmth from her voice.

"Can I get another pair of those Bay Water socks with the rubber bottoms?" Mia skipped her voice into happy and cheerful, trying to lighten the somber mood.

"Not on my watch." Nettie shook her head and opened the door, calling out to Mia's friends. "You can go in if you promise to keep her in that bed."

"I'm attached to too many monitors to move," Mia mumbled.

Nettie looked at her over her glasses. "I don't doubt you'd find a way."

Mia ignored the pain pulsing through her leg and Nettie's scorn. "Shane, hand me my laptop."

Eddy grabbed the laptop from the table before Shane. "We aren't working now."

But there was that deadline. A documentary to finish. Those contracts that'd secure their jobs for the next three years. Those contracts that'd ensure her mother's life didn't change because of her father's passing. Those contracts that'd give Mia a place where she belonged.

Without her film career, what would she have? Where would she go? Her insides ripped as if the thought of being alone carved out a void within her. Back to her mother's house wasn't an option. She'd never fit in her mom's home, even as a child. She folded her arms over her stomach, trying to keep from plunging into that hole. "The dive boat needs to be booked for next weekend."

"You aren't listening." Frank crossed his arms over his chest and leaned against the wall. "This isn't a work session."

"We're out of time." Howard had made that more than clear during their conversation yesterday. Paying her mom's mortgage wasn't happening from her hospital bed. Mia motioned for her laptop. "I have an idea for the shoot. Shane, you'll have to be in the water this time."

"You aren't planning on diving, then?" Both Eddy's tone and grip on the computer tightened.

"I'm not stupid." Mia skimmed her fingers over the bandage on her arm. The bathroom trip was a one-time lapse in judgment. "I'll watch the feed from the deck and tell you when we have the right footage."

"What you mean is you'll watch the footage when we bring it to you," Frank corrected.

"I'll be out of here before the end of next week." Mia tipped her chin up and clenched her teeth to keep from biting her bottom lip. Any uncertainty would only encourage them.

"Not with stunts like you pulled today." Eddy's frown paired nicely with his gloom-and-doom tone.

Shane and Frank nodded. When had it become three against one? As if they'd never made mistakes. She could list off any number of bad calls they'd made over the years, and she'd stood by them even when her father had railed against their idiocy. "Going to the bathroom is hardly a stunt."

"Except when you can't feel your leg and struggle to walk," Eddy challenged.

"My leg isn't that bad." Mia struggled not to give in to the pout pulling at her lips. How did Eddy know so much? Had Wyatt told him? Had Wyatt read her chart? Neither of them was even listed on her paperwork as privy to her health records.

"You're delusional," Eddy accused.

"That's harsh." Mia flinched against the pillows as if trying to deflect the truth in his words. "I'm trying to finish my father's film like I promised him and everyone else. I'm trying to make sure we have work beyond today."

"Killing yourself in the process isn't going to help anyone," Frank said.

"Walking to the bathroom isn't a death sentence," Mia countered.

"You could've cracked your head open." Shane rubbed his white-blond head as if he'd whacked his own head on the ground. "There was enough blood on the floor that it looked like you already had."

Frank and Eddy nodded like bobblehead twins. She used to be a part of their team. Now she was benched in the visiting team's dugout. "But I didn't." All three men crossed their arms over their chests and stared at her, looking like three generations of critical umpires. "Fine. What do you all suggest?"

"You concentrate on getting better and let us finish the film," Frank said.

Except she'd made promises to her agent and the network that she hadn't revealed to the guys. Commitments she would've fulfilled if not for the blood pressure cuff and IV lines trapping her to a hospital bed. The next film contracts depended on her delivering this film as promised. Failing her family and friends had never been a consideration. "We need that underwater footage, which is why the boat needs to be booked for next weekend."

"The boat is in dry dock," Eddy said.

Mia's mouth dried out like the hull of their dive boat *Poseidon*. "I promised that footage would be in the film."

Eddy dropped his chin toward his chest. Frank tipped his head back and studied the ceiling as if seeking intervention from some higher form.

Shane rubbed his chin like he was a teenager searching his smooth skin for his first beard that proved his adult status. His hand stilled and his blue eyes cleared before landing on her. "But only your father had the experience for a dive that deep."

"You were going deeper while I ascended." The accusation hardened Eddy's voice, disbelief shoved his eyebrows into his hairline and disappointment twisted his mouth into a flat line. Yet the distance between them expanded into a crater as he paced to the window. He usually moved like a swaying willow branch, loose and easy, but now, every step was stiff. Turning his back toward her, he seemed stilted and brittle.

Desperation and panic collided inside her breathless voice. "I had the shot." Yet she'd broken every dive school instructor's number one rule and left her partner. On purpose. Mia pressed her palm against her stomach to contain the guilt. Guilt only weakened her. *Nothing is ever accomplished in the safety zone, Mia.* Her father had risked. So must she. "Dad would've gotten the footage."

"You aren't your father." The softness in Frank's voice only highlighted his target.

The arrow of Frank's words pierced her core and burst the hold on her guilt. But she couldn't back down. She'd backed down before and her father had died. Guilt and grief collided, weakening her voice to a scratch. "I had to try."

"And you almost died for the attempt." Shane squinted at her as if she was a stranger he couldn't quite place.

Maybe if she'd made a different attempt her dad would be in the room, standing by her bed now. When had Eddy lost faith in her abilities? Before or after her accident? Had they all lost faith in her? The void stretched to a cavern, beckoning her to fall in. "But I didn't."

Eddy twisted around. "No boat, no more filming."

"But I have to film more." This film had to be perfect. This film kept her mom's world the same. The film proved Mia wouldn't fail her father.

Eddy scrubbed his hands through his curly hair as if trying to shake her irrationality off him. "You made promises, Mia, but we made promises, too."

Mia countered the abrasive edge in Eddy's voice, plunging her words into a frigid bite. She pointed at each of them. "Just know that keeping my word ensures you all continue to have paychecks."

"It isn't always about money." Eddy rubbed his chest as if she'd punched him.

As if he hadn't been the one jabbing at her this whole time. It was about honoring her father. Launching a career worthy of her dad's approval. Fulfilling promises. Surely Eddy understood that much. A decade-long friendship came with certain givens, didn't it? "I'll finish this film with or without your support."

"You already have everything you need in here to finish the film." Eddy handed her the laptop. "We picked up another job for the local network until you're fully recovered."

Shane straightened as Frank pushed away from the wall. Mia glanced between the men, her voice dipped below a whisper. "You're abandoning me, too?"

"Not indefinitely." Shane stuffed his hands in his front pockets and shrugged.

Frank rubbed the back of his neck. "The stakes were never supposed to be life or death."

"You and my father risked your lives on more than one occasion. I've seen all the footage." Dread dripped into her stomach.

"We got lucky every time we returned." Frank's voice stretched thin, his tone hoarse. "Until we didn't."

Shane and Frank walked toward the door. She didn't want to be on her own. She wanted her team. Her friends. Alarm slammed her words on top of each other. "But we need more footage. We have to turn in the best film with the best footage possible. I can't settle for okay because I'm too scared."

Eddy kissed her cheek. "Fear isn't always a bad thing."

Her father had never accepted her fear. He'd made her hold a venomous spider in her palm, reach into an active beehive and sleep alone in the dark all before she was ten. He'd have forced her to watch the video of her accident on replay until she conquered her terror. "If it keeps you from being who you're meant to be, then it is."

"Then you know who you're meant to be?" Eddy hovered over her from the side of the bed.

"Thanks to my dad, I've always known."

Her gaze slipped away from Eddy along with the confidence in her tone. Anyone would be insecure if their entire team walked off a job.

"Your dad always knew, but that's not the same as your knowing for yourself." Eddy tapped his fingers against the laptop. "Text me if you need help with the editing."

But not the new footage. They'd made that more than clear. She was on her own. She'd have to hire divers and secure a new boat. She had to be on that boat to prove her accident hadn't altered her life so completely she didn't know who she was anymore. Her father had accidents, but he'd never questioned where he was going or lost sight of his goals. She wouldn't either. She couldn't.

She was Carlo Fiore's daughter, who'd been groomed to continue his documentary film legacy. That had been the expectation for so long. If she stepped to the right or left, then who was she?

She shoved open her laptop and jammed her finger against the power button to stall the tremor building inside her. A tremor that had nothing to do with her injuries and everything to do with a sudden unraveling of her future.

Mia forced her shoulders back, refusing to let herself hunch over the keyboard and give in to her doubts. Being confined to the hospital was bringing out the worst in her.

The twitch of the second hand on the old, round wall clock pushed the minutes toward the night and pushed the fear inside her to the surface. Yet the moon's arrival remained several hours away. She might be alone, but not without distractions.

She stared at the empty chair. Wyatt's chair. He'd understand her need to take care of her mom. His own mother recovered down the hall. He'd returned to look after his mom. Yet he hadn't given up his lifestyle and intended to go back to his work in Africa. Mia would do the same: finish the film, provide for her mom and continue living the life of a nomad filmmaker. No wishes required.

Except the film reminded her of her final goodbye to her father. The film charged that tremor through her. She wasn't ready. Wyatt had cautioned her to change her perspective. She'd do just that tonight and tomorrow get back to work.

She turned on the TV. The *Ruined and Renewed* marathon started within the hour. Opening her email, she grinned at the new message from Kellie. Less than two minutes later, she studied the picture of Kellie's fiancé in her photo-editing program. Eddy would've known how to finesse the two pictures together within seconds. Still, she had all night to figure everything out.

CHAPTER SEVEN

WYATT STEPPED OUT of a triage room and met
the harassed gaze of the seasoned nurse man-
ager, Annmarie. "These gentlemen claim to
know you, Dr. Reid. We're an ER, not a visitor's center."

"Sorry for the intrusion." Eddy grinned at
Annmarie, his mop of curls bobbing, his tone
apologetic. "But we really are lost."

Annmarie pursed her lips and glared at
Wyatt. "We need the halls cleared for actual
patients."

Wyatt gathered Mia's friends and ushered
the group away from Annmarie. "How did
you get back here?"

"Several wrong turns." Shane grinned and
bumped his elbow into Wyatt's side. "Maybe
a cute red-haired nursing student and her
friend."

Wyatt winced. He didn't have time for their
antics. He'd already lost one patient that afternoon, and another one was barely stable.
"You really have to get out of here."

The automatic doors swung wide, granting access to a pair of paramedics. Mia's friends straightened in unison, each one running his hands through his hair as if trying to tidy up. Wyatt smiled. Ava Andrews nudged her partner, Dan, with her elbow and laughed. Again, the men shoved back their shoulders as if straining to reach their full height. As if that alone would impress Ava. He could've saved the guys the effort, but held back. Finally, Wyatt had an easy escape. "Hey, Ava, can you escort my friends out to the parking lot for me?"

Ava walked over and studied the three men. "You guys were on the dive boat last Sunday."

Eddy smiled. "You were one of Mia's paramedics."

Ava shook each of their hands, introducing herself. "How's she doing?"

Wyatt turned to head back into the bowels of the ER, but Frank's gruff voice stopped him. "If she hadn't fallen today, she might've been better."

Wyatt spun around. "Mia fell?"

"Decided to take herself to the bathroom." Frank slapped one palm against the other. "The floor decided to stop her."

"Blood was everywhere," Shane added.

Eddy rubbed his palms over his face. "Don't need the reminder."

"But it was all over, dripping off her sock." Shane spread his hands out, his glance tripping from Ava to Wyatt and back again. Delight animated his face and his words. "She could've left bloody footprints down the entire third-floor wing."

Wyatt squeezed Eddy's shoulder to distract him from Shane's imagery and asked, "She reopened her wound?"

Shane nodded, the motion on rapid repeat. "I think I saw her bone again."

Wyatt cursed along with Eddy. But the tall, lanky man shifted from one boot to the other as if he planned to sprint out of the hospital when the starter blew the whistle. Wyatt's feet remained firm, and when his shift ended he'd be sprinting up to the third floor himself. "What was she thinking?"

"She isn't." Frank shook his head, looking more like an old-time farmer talking about a lame cow he'd had to put down than a veteran world traveler. "Mia falls and then tells us she plans to get back on the boat next week."

She'd have to go through him if she wanted to get back on the dive boat. Next week or next month. The woman was fast approaching certifiable status.

"She must've hit her head," Shane said.

Wyatt agreed. It was the only rational explanation for her irrational behavior.

"Doc, can't you put something in her IV to bring back her common sense?" Frank asked.

If only it were that easy.

"She wasn't listening to a thing we suggested." Eddy snapped his fingers before pointing at Ava. "Maybe she'd listen to another woman."

Ava took a step away from the group. "You want me to talk to her?"

"Why not?" Eddy held out his hands as if that explained everything. "Women speak the same language."

Ava's partner stepped out of the bathroom and laughed. "Ava speaks her own language, and I can tell you it isn't like any other woman."

"I resent that." Ava shoved Dan in the chest. But Dan planted his boots and never budged, not even a twitch. Ava's partner owned the word *burly* from his solid six-five frame to his size-fifteen feet. If Wyatt ever wanted to feel small, he just stood beside Dan.

"Come on, be a sport. Besides, how many girlfriends do you have, Ava?" Dan asked.

"It doesn't matter." Ava pulled her paramedic hat lower on her forehead.

"She isn't your typical woman." Dan looked at the group.

"Either is Mia." Shane grinned.

That was the truth. Wyatt wasn't sure if Mia was typical anything. Perhaps if Ava joined him later, she'd keep him from tying Mia to the bed to keep her safe from herself. "I can introduce you after my shift."

"You guys are serious?" Ava set her hands on her hips and skipped her gaze from one face to the other. "You want me to talk some common sense, whatever that means, into your friend."

"She's also our boss," Shane added.

"I'm sure she's capable of making her own decisions," Ava argued.

"She wants to get back on a dive boat two weeks after she almost died." How dare that infuriating woman risk her life again while still on his watch. Wyatt forced his shoulders to relax and tried to ignore the frustration inside him. One hour until his shift ended. Sixty minutes to calm down before he saw Mia. He'd make Mia agree not to take such stupid risks until after she flew off to her next destination and out of his life.

Ava tapped her finger against her bottom lip and studied Wyatt. He'd always considered her too perceptive, something about her red hair and cat-green-eyes combination.

The smallest smile touched her lips before she said, "I'm sure she has very good reasons for taking such a risk."

Frank shook his head. "This won't work. She's already defending her. It's a woman thing."

A page called for Dr. Reid, drawing Wyatt back to his real world. One that didn't include Mia.

"I'm still going to meet her." Ava touched Frank's arm. "Now let's get you guys out of Wyatt's ER so he can get back to work."

The arrival of two patients—one with multiple stab wounds and one from a head-on collision with a semitruck—kept Wyatt in the ER two hours longer than he'd planned. At least Mia's crew hadn't sweet-talked their way back inside the ER. As for Ava, she'd taken the call for the car crash and stabilized the victim enough for transport to the hospital. Wyatt walked into the break room to find Ava slouched in a plastic chair, her long legs propped up by another chair. "Thought you preferred the night shift?"

"I do." Ava stood and tucked her cell phone into the back pocket of her cargo pants. "I took the day shift as a favor."

"Now you have the whole night ahead of you." Wyatt held the door open.

"Don't remind me." Ava glanced at her watch and groaned as if filling the night hours was a chore. "So where are you spending your nights these days, Doc?"

"There's a guest room with a queen-size bed at my mother's house." Although he slept mostly on the couch in the back porch at his mom's when he wasn't working nights. Breathing came easier out there. But he wasn't certain if the air was less clogged with the assorted floral fragrances that bombarded the house and gardens. Or because the porch had been added years after he'd moved out, and he breathed deeper without constantly searching for more displaced childhood memories.

"A bed that you aren't using," Ava accused.

"You can't know that." Wyatt smacked the elevator button and avoided looking at his friend.

"I recognize my own kind." Ava bumped her shoulder against Wyatt's. "We might have different reasons for avoiding sleep, but avoid it we do. Quite successfully I might add."

Ava had completed four tours of duty in the Middle East as an army combat medic during her honorable military career. Wyatt assumed she had more than one inner ghost that kept her awake at night, although he'd never pried into her combat history. They'd met after a massive Interstate 80 pileup that had put several area hospitals on high alert and then bonded over drinks and hamburgers at the grill across the street. "Why do you really want to meet Mia?"

"Can't I want to check up on a patient?" Ava stepped on the elevator and busied herself with pushing the third-floor button.

"As long as I've known you, you've never followed up on a patient with a personal visit." Wyatt leaned against the back wall. "What gives?"

"I used to hang the moon in Ben's eyes until he played a board game tournament with this movie lady named Mia. The same woman who has four grown men clamoring over each other to protect her." Ava pointed at him. "And one of those men happens to be you."

"What does this have to do with me?" Wyatt gripped the steel bar behind him, wincing at the distinct high-pitched note in his tone as if he was a teenage boy struggling to master his grown-up voice.

Ava smiled. "She's done the impossible and gotten under Dr. Wyatt Reid's skin."

If Ava meant that Mia burrowed under his

skin like a rash that multiple steroid injections failed to control, then yes, Mia got under his skin. He maintained his hold on the railing behind him and his mouth.

"There isn't a nurse or PA or staff employee who hasn't wanted to rattle you." Ava rubbed her hands together. "That I can promise you."

"I doubt that." Ava and Wyatt had only ever been friends. And he hadn't given any thought to the rest of the staff other than as coworkers. He strode off the elevator, not waiting for her to go first. "But thanks for the ego boost."

Ava matched his long stride with her own and counted on her fingers. "So you saved Eddy's life in Africa. Had a thing with Mia, then saved her life here in the city. Do I have the order of events correct?"

"I have to talk to those guys about oversharing." Wyatt quickened his pace down the third-floor hall. Why did Mia have to have a room at the very end? "And what's a *thing*?"

"They didn't provide too many details about you and Mia. Just mentioned you shared a thing while Eddy recovered." Ava never slowed and remained right beside him. "Care to tell me more?"

"You know more than enough already." Wyatt wondered how Mia would label their time together. A *thing* fell flat as an explanation. Their relationship had been more like one of his mother's carefully grafted plants with the prospect for unique flowers. But without the perfect conditions, both the graft and their relationship failed to bloom. "Maybe you can talk to your new girlfriend and get all the details. Isn't that what girlfriends do?"

"I suppose so." Ava stopped outside Mia's door. "But you don't think we'll be that type of girlfriends."

"Mia keeps to herself and her crew." Wyatt eyed Ava's paramedic baseball cap and cargo pants that failed to minimize her female curves. "The last time I checked you weren't a guy or a filmmaker."

"Is that what it takes to be part of her inner circle?" Ava asked.

Wyatt knocked on Mia's door and pulled back at the shrill laughter coming from inside Mia's room.

Ava leaned toward him. "I thought you said she didn't do girlie."

Wyatt shook his head. He'd never known Mia to sound like that. He walked into the room and sensed his world list like a cruise ship caught in a hurricane. Mia and her wound care nurse, Kellie, huddled over her laptop, giggling as if they were teenagers sharing their secret crushes and discussing prom dresses.

Kellie swung around with a bright smile and twin tears sliding down each cheek. "Mia is a genius. Look at this." She released another softer squeal as she picked up the laptop to face Wyatt and Ava. "Pure magic. I couldn't have imagined anything this perfect."

A photograph of Kellie cradling an engagement ring against her heart in her scrubs and a guy in full dress uniform bent down on one knee in a combat field filled the wide screen. The pictures alone were moving, yet together the image of the couple captivated. But the pride bracing Mia's wobbly smile captured Wyatt. The vulnerability in her gaze buckled his knees. How could she question her talent? This couldn't be the first time someone raved about her work.

Ava leaned toward the computer screen, her voice raspy. "It's absolutely stunning."

Kellie squealed and hugged the computer quick and fast, as if her fiancé might feel her embrace. "Wait till Rey's platoon sees this. I'll be showing everyone from the grocery cashier to the bus driver to the security guard downstairs. Everyone I can find."

Mia laughed, the sound artificial like one of those canned sitcom laugh tracks. Carlo

Fiore had wanted his work shown to everyone, as often as possible. Wyatt always assumed Mia wanted the same: to leave her imprint worldwide. But Mia looked uncomfortable. Her hands fluttered in front of her as if she reached for something to ground her. Wyatt stepped forward, but the footboard on her bed blocked his progress like a caution sign alerted drivers on the highway to stop. He stopped, too. His medical training wasn't required to treat Mia's distress. Her gaze landed on him and stuck as if he was some sort of anchor. He stuffed his hands in his pant pockets to keep from reaching for her and tethering her to him.

Kellie handed Mia the computer. Mia's fingers wrapped around the laptop. Wyatt curled his hands into fists, denying that he'd rather have her fingers wrapped inside his. The laptop commanded her focus. Her composure dropped back into place, her strikes on the keyboard firm. "It needs a few more adjustments, then I'll email it to you. Now go." Mia shooed Kellie away. "You have other patients who need you."

"I'm off." Kellie grinned from the door. "But you should know I'll be bragging about you all the way to the bus stop."

"It was nothing." Mia typed on her computer and refused to meet Wyatt's gaze.

He smiled, liking the idea that she wasn't as composed as he thought. That she knew he'd seen her vulnerability and cursed him.

Mia frowned at the screen. "Wyatt, if you came to yell about my bathroom trip, you can leave right now."

Wyatt cursed her right back. Five minutes inside the woman's room and he wanted to kick Ava out. He wanted Mia all to himself. He wanted to erase Mia's doubts and give her his support. He wanted to convince Mia of her talent. He was becoming as irrational as Mia. "I wanted you to meet Ava Andrews. The paramedic who saved you last Sunday."

"You're Ben's aunty Ava." Mia snapped her laptop closed and reached to shake Ava's hand. "I thought there was something familiar about you when you came in. Your eyes. I think, I remember your eyes."

Ava pointed at her thin oval glasses. "I lost my contacts again, so it's back to the glasses for the weekend."

"No, I remember your voice. It was so calming while I was a total mess." Mia leaned around Ava to look at him. "Wyatt, you could learn something from Ava."

"I'm not there to soothe my patients." Or

Mia. He paced toward the window. "I'm there to save their lives."

"Ava does the same, and all with a soothing tone," Mia countered.

"About your bathroom stroll today." Wyatt kept his attention on the view outside her window and smiled at her quick inhale.

"Your mom takes herself to the facilities all the time by herself." Mia's fingers tapped against her laptop. "I should be able to do the same."

"I should've known." He never stopped the irritation from leaking into his voice. "You two need to be separated."

"This isn't kindergarten, Wyatt." Mia glared at him. "We can talk to whomever we like."

Wyatt moved closer and reached for the bandage on her leg. Mia slapped his arm away. "Kellie just redressed that. Don't touch it."

"How far did it reopen?" Wyatt studied the wrapping.

Mia ignored him and looked at Ava. "What do you do when you aren't answering emergency calls?"

"That's pretty much my life." Ava jammed her hands in her jacket pockets, rocked back on her steel-toe boot heels and let her gaze wander between Wyatt and Mia. A smile curved her lips like she'd just figured out the details about Mia and Wyatt's so-called thing.

He'd inform Ava whatever she thought was wrong. Completely wrong. "Ava can shoot better than ninety-nine percent of the men in the army. There's a rumor she's taken up fencing, although her partner, Dan, and I haven't been able to confirm that yet." Wyatt crossed his arms over his chest and stared back at his friend. "And I saw you walking down Pine with the therapy dogs last week."

"Wyatt, you're not her doctor or her nurse. Leave her leg alone." Ava pushed Wyatt away from the bed and rubbed her hands together. "Now that we're alone, I need some insider information to win the staff pool."

Wyatt set his hands on his hips and stared at her. "You were complaining last week about your losing streak and vowed to quit betting."

"But I can win this one and turn my luck around." Ava pointed at each of them. "Because I have access to you both."

Wyatt crossed his arms over his chest. "What does this have to do with us?"

Ava raised her hands as if cheering for her favorite sports team. "The bet is you guys."

"What did I miss?" Mia scowled at Wyatt as if he'd instigated the whole thing.

"I have no idea what she's rambling about."

Wyatt held his hands up, palms out. "Eddy and the guys wanted her to talk to you."

"What's Eddy have to do with this?" Mia copied Wyatt and crossed her arms over her chest. Her gaze darted from Wyatt to Ava, as if uncertain whom she needed to watch more.

"Your boys wanted me to talk some sense into you." Ava brushed that aside. "We can get to all that after you tell me what you guys are to each other."

Wyatt scrubbed his hand through his hair, wondering if he pulled hard enough would he also yank words back into his voice. He'd rather handle an intoxicated, belligerent patient or read through his mother's applications. He shifted his gaze to the blank TV, wishing for a cue card from a TV producer. This was one of those impossible questions like a girlfriend asking if her skirt made her look fat.

"It's a simple question." Ava paced around the side of the bed. "Are you friends, ex-lovers, secret lovers, frenemies? Although I'm not getting the whole frenemy vibe."

"That's private," Mia said.

The grit in Mia's voice relaxed Wyatt. Here was the Mia he'd expected: the one closed off from everyone around her, except her crew.

She'd opened up to him the other night. But that confession was terror-induced, nothing more.

"But now I'm curious about what you've been telling the staff, Wyatt," Mia said.

She dropped her computer on the table. The thump pounded up Wyatt's spine, tensing into his shoulders. Wyatt backed away from the bed. "Nothing. I swear."

"You do know this is a hospital, right? We're all trained in observation. Words aren't really needed." Ava shook her head, her mouth twisted in disappointment as if they were trainees who floundered with the basics. "Other than the ER, Wyatt spends more time on this floor."

"His mother is a patient down the hall," Mia countered.

"Who also spends a lot of time with you," Ava said to Mia. "Which hints that you guys are more than friends."

"I just met Helen this week," Mia argued.

"Yet you're already on a first-name basis with her." Ava nodded as if she'd won that volley.

"Okay. We need to leave," Wyatt said. "I didn't bring you up here for this."

Ava planted her feet. "No, you brought me up here to lecture Mia on her poor choices and lack of common sense." She looked at Mia, her smile somber. "Their words, not mine."

Mia nodded, as if not surprised by the lack of support from the guys. But their opinion stung. Wyatt saw that much in her gaze. Even her rapid blinks couldn't stall the tears filling her eyes.

He hated the hurt on her face, hated more that she believed he lacked any faith in her. Hated that his detachment kept her safe. He lashed out, "Wanting to get back on a dive boat two weeks after a near-death accident is beyond stupid."

"My father's life work isn't stupid," Mia whispered. "Honoring him in the only way I know how isn't stupid."

Wyatt slumped forward and covered his face with his hands. Where was the rewind button? "Dying is not the way to honor him. But it definitely is the way to join him."

Ava touched Mia's shoulder, giving her silent support. Now it was two against one. No way could Ava with her kind eyes and calming voice have broken past Mia's defenses in less than ten minutes. She'd come upstairs only for the information to win a bet. He'd wanted to check on Mia after her fall. A concerned doctor looking out for a patient.

But there was another part of him that

wanted to know if Mia had looked for him last night. Were the dark circles under her eyes from her fall or another sleepless night? It'd taken every bit of his willpower to pass by her room last night. He'd forced himself to step onto the elevator and go home, where he'd tossed around on the couch and stared at the ceiling, trying to extract Mia from his mind.

Now he watched her retreat as if she needed to guard herself from him. The one who only wanted to protect her. Same as he protected all his patients. That lie detector inside him blared, knocking his world sideways.

Mia tipped her chin up. "You should go see your mother. You missed dinner with her, and I'm sure she's probably worried."

Ava scowled at him and stood beside Mia as if she'd become the woman's champion against Wyatt. As if the two women were longtime friends. As if Mia opened her inner circle to strangers and outsiders all the time. But that circle was closed to Wyatt. He should prefer that. He should want exactly that.

Yet his steps slowed near the doorway and he waited. Waited for Mia to ask him to come back. Waited for his own mouth to spill the truth: he wanted to sit down and hold her hand. To find comfort with her after losing a patient today. To find that balance only she seemed to give him.

But no words came. Only the hum of the AC propelled him into the hallway.

Wyatt walked into his mother's room and smiled for the first time all day. Her nose was once again pressed against her tablet screen while she muttered about faulty technology. Finally, some place that made sense.

"Mia sent me the pictures she took today, but they're the size of an ant's postage stamp." His mom thrust her notepad toward him. "As if Mia's camera screen hadn't been hard enough to see."

Wyatt opened the pictures and swiped through the images of his mother with a gray standard poodle. Images that might've been simply sweet if not for the punch to his own gut. There with that dog he saw his mom, the one from his childhood who'd soothed a scraped knee with a soft touch and kissed his cheek after she sang him the good-night song. Her smile offered acceptance, her touch kindness and love. No judgment glinted in her eyes. He rubbed his forehead as if that would make everything clearer. "Mia took these?"

"Yes." Helen smoothed her hands over her blankets.

Those were the hands she'd tucked him in

with at night as a child and the same ones that had pounded on his chest when he'd told her about Trent. The ones that had held him close as a boy and shoved him away as an adult. How had Mia brought out the mom he'd once known? The mom he missed. He wanted to hate Mia for the reminder.

She added, "Her film crew gave her a camera to keep her distracted. But those are more than a distraction. She's talented."

Wyatt couldn't argue. He gave the tablet back to her and watched her face soften again as she scrolled through the pictures. The sun had long since set, and no trick of the light brought back the mom from his memories. He missed her. Missed her comfort. Perhaps more so tonight when he could use that very comfort now. But that was Mia's fault, too, for jarring him out of his emotional lockdown.

His mother set the tablet on her lap and used her fingers to enlarge a picture. Her smile stretched wide. "I told her it was a rooftop garden."

He kept his voice mild, hoping his mom might stick around for a while. "The hospital doesn't have rooftop access for patients or visitors."

"Your neighbor across the street." Helen pointed to her window but kept her attention on her notepad. "You need to tell the tenants to add a cast-iron plant and ostrich fern, as they will thrive on the rooftop with little care."

Wyatt walked over to the window and looked at the apartment building across the street. "I'm not knocking on their door to pass along plant advice."

"Why not?" Surprise shifted across her face. "It's the neighborly thing to do."

"We aren't neighbors." Despite his mother's cheerfulness, he still wasn't about to talk plants with strangers across the street. He motioned to the picture. "Besides, it feels strangely like spying."

"It's spying, but with the intent to be helpful, so it's perfectly okay."

That utter nonsense was clearly Mia's doing. Blaming Mia fit better than his guilt over hurting her. But Mia had to hear the truth. She had to stop risking her life.

Helen never allowed the silence to settle between them. "If you haven't finished going through the applications, you don't need to bother."

"Why?" Wyatt turned around to face her, noting the rather pleased look on her face.

"I've made other arrangements."

"You put the foundation on hold?" Wyatt

asked. Finally, his mother took his advice. Maybe they'd turned a corner away from the tension and spite.

"Mia agreed to help me sort through the applications and decide who to give money to."

Mia again? Mia knew about the local wildlife, but that hardly made her an expert on the subject of viable local charities. She'd never called San Francisco home. Even now, her residency here was temporary until her next documentary called her away. That his mother needed Mia, too, jabbed a spike of irritation through him. "Mia has to concentrate on her recovery."

"She promised I wouldn't be interfering with her therapy," Helen said. "She's always so willing to help."

More praise for Mia. Annoyance splattered through him like the mud puddles he'd used to jump in as a kid after his mother warned him not to get his clothes wet. When had his mother last sang his praises? He couldn't remember. He also couldn't deny that Mia's pictures of his mother captured the mom he remembered from his childhood. The mom he missed. He'd been tempted to email the photographs to his personal account. But those were only snippets of time. Like now. He was only fooling himself. There was too much pain, too much anger, too much blame between them to bring the past back. He had to live in the present and not waste his time wishing for something else. Like memories his kid self might've altered to make them seem happier than they were.

Not that it mattered. He was about to launch himself back into the tension pool that stretched between them, but he couldn't help it. Life wasn't lived in still photographs. Life was messy and difficult and hard. And often those were the good days.

He'd bet his return ticket to Africa that Mia encouraged his mother to move back to her family home. He'd bet a return flight that his mother confessed with tear-filled eyes how much her house meant and how much her own son, her own flesh and blood, couldn't understand that simple fact. "Did you get the flyers I left on the bathroom shelf last night?"

"There's a garbage can in the bathroom, too."

"You can't keep tossing this discussion in the trash."

"There's nothing to discuss." Her voice hardened along with the lines around her eyes. The mom from the pictures disappeared as if she'd only been a trick of the moonlight or his faulty memories. "I've made my decision."

He'd had the best part of his mom as a child. That had to be enough. "You'll want to visit each place before you make any final decision."

"That won't be necessary," she said. "I'm more than familiar with the place and location. I've resided there for more than forty years."

"How about this," Wyatt said. He scooted his chair closer to her bed, smoothing the irritation from his voice. "What if you picked one of these centers as a backup plan?"

"I have a perfectly fine house," she said. "I don't need a backup plan."

She needed a reality check. How was he supposed to give her that? Clearly Mia needed one of her own for putting unrealistic ideas in his mom's head like a fairy who sprinkled pixie dust to fix the world's problems. "There's nothing wrong with backup plans."

"Then you must have a backup plan for Africa," Helen said.

"It's not the same," he countered.

"You expect me to uproot my entire life to move into an assisted living center. Change everything I've known so that you can be certain I'm safe." She yanked on her covers. "Well, I want to be certain you're safe. You're my son after all. And your living in Africa doesn't make me feel safe. Certainly, you've planned for this contingency."

Wyatt dropped his head into his hands and stared at the faded floor tiles. Africa wasn't up for debate. His mother's living situation was. "Your therapists might not recommend letting you move back into the house after their home visit next week."

"I've spent countless hours with my therapists. I know their minds."

The therapists knew Wyatt's mind, too. Their decision would be medically determined and one based on his mother's safety, not their friendship. They also knew that Wyatt intended to leave the country after his mother's discharge and she would need more than the neighbors' unreliable help. Weariness drained his willingness to continue this fight. He had to get a decent night's sleep. He doubted he'd find that at his mom's house or in the recliner here in her room. Doubted he'd find any rest at all tonight. "We'll see when we get the report next week."

"Don't forget to bring in those applications. Mia and I can take care of that foundation business over the next few days."

That was so not happening. Mia didn't even know the particulars about the foundation. He wasn't even certain how much his mother had outright. There wasn't an endless stream of money, and she certainly couldn't fund every charity just because they asked. His mom had to live, too. And that required money, whether she moved into an assisted living center or back home. "You don't need to invite strangers into the family business. I'll take care of the applications like I promised."

"I didn't realize Mia was a stranger," Helen said.

"She certainly isn't family." He didn't know what Mia was. Or what he wanted her to be. He jumped out of the chair and paced the floor.

Helen pressed the nurses' button. "I'd like to use the bathroom and prepare for bed."

"Mia mentioned you've been taking yourself to the bathroom without assistance," Wyatt said.

"It isn't polite to share confidences with strangers."

From the perturbed bite to her tone, he assumed he was the stranger his mom referred to.

His mom welcomed the aide with a big smile that dismissed Wyatt. He strode down the hall and slowed at the nurses' station. Left took him to Mia's room. Right to the elevators. He turned right.

CHAPTER EIGHT

MIA PUNCHED HER pillow into submission, wishing she could slam thoughts of Wyatt out of her head, too. Sunlight peeked around the curtains, highlighting the empty chair beside her bed. Wyatt never returned last night. Never dropped into the chair to watch *Renewed and Ruined*. Never came back to apologize.

He hadn't promised to return. Yet Ava had been certain Wyatt would come back, and so anticipation had kept her awake and waiting. She smashed her fist into the pillow again, calling herself every kind of fool. Only a fool lay awake, staring at an empty chair, wanting to make Wyatt understand.

Only fools got involved. That stopped this morning. She vowed she'd no longer treat the third floor as her own personal social center as if she was starved for friendship. She was starved for a decent night's sleep, as she was fast becoming nocturnal like a bat, except she never slept the daylight hours away in her roost. Catnaps had become her new norm, quick, brief and anything but rejuvenating.

Her last good night had been with Wyatt three nights ago. But he had a job and life that didn't include being her personal dream catcher or confidant. With her father, they'd been too busy completing their projects and developing new ones to indulge in conversations about inner secrets and dreams and stories from the past. Why was she looking for that now? A few hours with Ava and one photograph for Kellie hardly constituted lasting friendships; the women were acquaintances at best. Besides, the women worked for Bay Water Medical. Their job descriptions included being kind and courteous to every patient and family member.

Her sleep problem was clearly job-related. Confined to a hospital bed, with an IV line and monitors, prevented her from working herself into exhaustion. She just needed to focus more on her work, stop occupying her mind with all these trivial distractions, and the sleep would fall into place. Like usual. Like always.

I've worked too hard for my daughter not to be great. You need self-discipline and dedication, Mia. You need to do what needs to be done, even when you don't feel like it. Okay, Dad, she got it.

Mia adjusted her bed and propped her computer on her lap. She needed to review the edit list with Eddy. Her finger paused on the power button. Her crew had walked out yesterday. Left her on her own. Surely that wasn't permanent. She'd never meant to chase her friends away. They'd come around. They had to. They were a team. Teams didn't quit on each other. Mia rubbed at her arm, trying to wipe away the same chill she used to get when she'd been five years old, huddled under her bedcovers, hiding from the storm winds that scraped tree branches against the metal siding on their house, making her believe a wicked witch clawed up the wall to snatch her away.

But she'd grown up, even enjoyed thunderstorms. Her guys would realize she was right once they watched the footage. Fiore productions hadn't earned its name for boilerplate films and mediocre products. The rare footage had earned Fiore Films awards and acclaim and additional contracts. Her father had never accepted ordinary, in himself or his daughter. Fear wouldn't drag her into the average category now.

Mia booted up her laptop. Time to watch the footage from Sunday's accident. She glanced at the air vent and brushed that shiver off her skin again. The film wasn't going to finish itself. This was about more than her and her fear. She had her mother to consider. If she wanted this life, she must embrace it, even the uncomfortable parts, like the near-death experiences. *Fiores aren't built for comfort zones, Mia.*

Mia flexed her fingers over the keyboard. Risk had inspired her father; he'd thrived on the impossible. And those near-death experiences were dares he'd never turned down. Before every challenging shoot, he'd look at Mia over his glasses, his gaze alight with energy and enthusiasm, and say: *Don't die wondering, Mia. Always take the risk.*

She hadn't almost died wondering. She'd almost died panicking. Unlike her father. She'd seen the footage from his final film about a drug cartel's underground role in human trafficking. Even after the two gunshots in his abdomen and leg, his camera had remained steady. If only she could cut the threads of panic inside her. Stop the spike to her pulse. The fear would've disappointed her dad. That was the last thing she'd ever wanted to do: disappoint the man who'd nurtured the artist inside her.

Mia opened her accident footage and held

her breath, trying to plug those panic holes inside her lungs that let the air leak out and the dread seep in. She hesitated; reliving the accident messed with her head. Yet finishing this film severed her last real connection to her father. After the credits rolled, an *In Memoriam* tagline would be her final goodbye to her dad. She rubbed her chest, digging her fingers into her skin to disperse the ache already expanding against her ribs. She wasn't ready. Would she ever be ready?

A soft knock on her door stopped her from pressing Play. The golden Lab bumping its tail against her door loosened that cinch inside her. Yet the irresistible little girl holding the dog's leash scattered that loneliness inside Mia. But she'd vowed not to get involved. Not to be distracted. "Good morning, Ella. Who do you have with you?"

Ella's smile filled her entire face, displacing all the emptiness inside the room. "This is Gretel. Hansel is out in the hall with Mom, but he needs to go home."

"What happened?" Mia leaned forward, trying to see into the hallway.

"Hansel decided to let Mom know he didn't feel well outside your room." Ella wrinkled her nose. "I tried to tell her in the elevator, but Mom said all elevators smell bad because strangers are crammed together and worried about getting stuck. She says hospital elevators are the worst."

Mia cleared her throat to break up her laughter. "I kind of thought the elevators around here smelled rather clean."

"Me, too." Ella checked her path with her cane and took three large steps closer to Mia's bed. "That's what I told Mom."

"Ella, did you make sure Mia wasn't sleeping?" Sophie rushed inside. She touched Ella's shoulder and eyed Mia's computer. "We don't want to bother her."

"I whispered her name and Ms. Mia answered." Ella pushed her glasses up on her nose and lifted her chin. "She wasn't sleeping—she was typing."

"I definitely wasn't sleeping." Mia smiled at Sophie. "Ella isn't bothering me at all."

"Sorry, I'll be right back." Sophie disappeared into the hallway.

"You were typing, weren't you?" Ella rubbed Gretel's head, and the dog leaned into her leg for even more attention.

"I was." Mia closed her laptop and set her computer on the table. *Where's your discipline and dedication, Mia?* Paused, but just long enough to enjoy a moment with Ella. Her heart already hurt less after only two minutes with the little girl. Maybe she could find some of the courage Ella embraced and finally type *In Memoriam* into the script. "I'm putting together a song list for the hyperbaric chamber. I have to lie in there for an hour, and it's quite boring."

"You could listen to a book."

"I've never listened to a book before."

"I love books." Ella's enthusiasm rushed through her words. "Mom can't get me new ones fast enough. I listen to them anywhere and everywhere, except in school. The teachers get mad when we don't pay attention to them."

"Teachers are like that. Ella, do you think you can help me find a book to listen to in the chamber?"

"Definitely." Ella nodded, her blond curls bouncing against her small shoulders in approval. "Do you like fantasy books? Fairy-tale stories or ones about the Greek gods or adventure books? I don't like scary books, but Ben does, so we can ask him."

Mia rubbed her neck, debating about telling sweet Ella the truth about her poor reading habits. "I usually read magazines."

Ella touched Gretel's head as if she needed to balance herself. "This might take a while, Ms. Mia. Can Gretel and I sit down?"

"There's a recliner straight in front of you and right beside my bed."

Before Mia could offer the little girl assistance, Ella extended her walking stick and settled into the chair. Gretel stretched out on the floor beside Ella's boots. "I think Hansel's stomach got sick again."

"Sounds like it," Mia said. "You guys okay hanging out with me?"

Ella nodded yet chewed on her bottom lip. "But Gretel likes to sleep on a bed. Someone chained her to a light pole in the Market district in a lightning storm. Hard, cold floors make her scared."

Mia scooted over and patted her bed. A graceful leap brought the golden Lab next to her. Gretel curled up against Mia's good leg, rested her head on her thigh and tracked Mia's movements with big, soulful brown eyes. Ella put the footrest up on the recliner and settled into the leather chair as if she was at home, making Mia forget her priorities and reset her inner timer.

Sophie walked in and surveyed the scene. A chocolate Lab sat down beside her and rested its head against her thigh. "Evie is coming to get Hansel and take him home. I need to meet her downstairs."

"I can wait here with Ms. Mia." Ella stuffed

her hands inside her sweatshirt pocket. "She told me I could."

Sophie tugged on her ponytail. "It might be a little while."

"I don't mind. Ella agreed to help with an important task." Mia rubbed behind Gretel's ears, earning a tail wag from the gentle dog.

"Well, everyone does look pretty comfortable." Sophie leaned across the bed and took Gretel's paw as if they'd concluded a beneficial business agreement. "Gretel's looking for her forever home. Aren't you, sweet girl?"

"You're adorable, Gretel, but I'm not your person. Not your forever home." That emptiness tapped on Mia's shoulder as if anxious to take up residence again. She cuddled closer to Gretel. A lot of people lived full and happy lives without a forever home. She couldn't think of any one particular person other than herself, but she was certain they existed. Her father's work fulfilled her. She knew nothing about forever homes and had no inclination to change herself to fit into one.

"Everyone needs a forever home." Ella's voice was matter-of-fact. "My mom can find you one, Ms. Mia. She's really good at it. She gave me one."

Sophie kissed Ella's forehead, her smile wobbly and her gaze tender. "I'll be back soon, then we'll bring Amelia the new art book and gel pens like I promised."

"I know." Ella hugged Sophie as if she'd never doubted for one minute that Sophie wouldn't keep her promise.

Mia wanted to have the type of all-in, 100 percent faith in herself like Ella had in her mom and her world.

Ella added, "Mia needs a book. And then Gretel needs a family."

Everyone deserved a family, even if it was made up of four-legged friends. That was what Ben and Ella had explained during their chess tournament. Mia agreed the golden Lab needed a family. A picture of Gretel: her face smashed against Mia's leg, eyes wide from the bliss of being petted that'd capture the attention of multiple forever families. That'd bring in adoption applications by the dozens. Framing the dog in her mind's eye, Mia considered submitting her own application. But she wasn't a forever kind of person. Still Mia reached for her digital camera. "Ella, I have an idea how we can help find Gretel a home, but I'd need to take a picture of you and Gretel together."

"My dad takes pictures in secret," Ella said. "It's his job."

"I always ask first." Mia turned on the camera and checked the settings.

"Can you make me look pretty in a picture?" Ella asked.

Sophie stopped in the doorway and turned around. "Ella Marie, what have I told you?"

"Pretty comes from the inside." Ella lifted her hands, palms out, as if that would make Sophie understand better. "But, Mom, you told Ms. Ava that Ms. Mia would make her look pretty in her pictures."

Sophie rubbed her hand over her face. "Maybe just talk books until I get back. Mia, I can explain later about Ava."

"And take a few pictures?" Hope stretched out Ella's words.

"Not too many." Sophie urged Hansel to stand up. Hansel tipped his head back at Ella as if he'd rather curl up in the chair with her. "We don't want to wear out Mia."

"We'll be fine." Mia waved Sophie out the door. "Go do your dog duty. We got this."

Books downloaded, and Gretel's adoption photos stored, Ella settled back into the recliner, Mia adjusted her pillows and Gretel stretched out on the bed. "We need to discuss the next game challenge. How do you propose we beat the boys again?"

Ella rubbed her hands together and launched

their lengthy, funny conversation that continued until Sophie strode into the room, a black-and-white collie at her side and Ava behind. "We heard you two laughing when we stepped off the elevators."

"Ella, your mom made me jog down the hall because she wanted to find out what was so funny." Ava set her hands on her knees and drew a deep breath.

"We're building a strategy to beat Ben and Dr. Wyatt at the next game challenge," Ella said.

Mia grinned. "I like Ella's style. She likes to win, no matter what it takes."

Sophie smiled. "She gets it from me, I'm afraid."

"The boys will be eating sweet potato ice cream before the week is out," Mia predicted. Ella giggled, her shoulders twitching.

"Did you find a book for Ms. Mia?" Sophie asked.

Ella nodded and tried to chew away her grin.

"We bought five," Mia said. "We couldn't decide on just one."

Sophie shook her head.

"And we took pictures." Ella bounced in the recliner, making the chair rock. "Now Ms.

Ava can have her picture taken, too. I bet Ms. Mia makes her look like a princess."

Ava pointed at the fabric headband covering her red hair and yoga pants. "I'm afraid I left my princess clothes at home with my glass slippers."

Mia studied Ava's flawless, porcelain skin, her symmetrical eyebrows with natural arches, her slightly imperfect mouth adding visual interest. She was long arms and even longer legs, all wrapped in muscle and strength. Her subtle, understated beauty made her approachable, relatable. Ava wasn't a supermodel or centerfold, but to Mia that made her a perfect subject for a photo shoot.

Ella tugged on Ava's hand. "Ms. Mia says it's not about your clothes. She says pictures work the best if you act natural. So that's what I did."

Ava tucked a curl behind Ella's ear. "How did you do that?"

Ella shrugged. "I just did what I always do."

"And that worked?" Ava asked.

"You have to see the pictures. Ms. Mia told me they were perfect."

Mia turned on the camera and handed it to Sophie to let her scroll through the pictures of Ella and Gretel.

Ava tweaked her nose. "Because you are perfect, Ella-bell."

"Nobody is perfect." Ella's voice lowered into the wise and thoughtful tone of an enlightened philosopher. "But you can be perfectly you."

Sophie looked up from the camera screen. "Where did you hear that?"

"Ms. Mia." Ella's voice turned matter-of-fact, as if it should've been obvious.

Sophie nodded at Mia, her smile grateful, before she pointed at the camera screen. "Can I have these pictures?"

"Sure, I'll email them to you," Mia said.

"Let me see." Ava took the camera and scanned through the photographs. "Post these on your website and social media pages, Sophie, and you'll be flooded with applications for Gretel." She tugged on the leash in her hand and the collie came forward. "Pepper's turn now. She needs a forever home, too."

"You have to be in her pictures, Ms. Ava." Ella's tone was firm like her grip on the armrests. "I was there for Gretel. You need to be there for Pepper."

Ava shrugged. "I'm not looking for a forever home."

"Neither was I." Ella grinned and relaxed

back into the leather. "But it makes the dogs more comfortable in front of the camera."

"Is that so?" Ava set her hands on her hips and frowned at Mia.

Mia timed her nod to match Ella's and pinched the edge of her lip with her teeth to keep from smiling. Ella was a powerful force and definitely difficult to deny.

"Okay, but this is for Pepper. It's not my photo thing for Dan." Ava pointed at both Sophie and Ella, waiting for their agreement.

"There's a photo thing?" Mia eyed Ava. Something like eagerness ping-ponged through her. She'd been re-creating her father's vision for so long. But the still photographs would be her creation, her vision.

"Ava lost a bet with her partner, Dan," Sophie added. "I was going to take the photograph of Ava with my phone for her to pay up, so to speak. But last night I saw the picture of Kellie and Rey online, and I knew we needed to ask an expert like you."

"Mia has better things to do than take my picture." Ava's disgruntled tone pulled her mouth into a deep grimace.

"You want me to photograph you?" Mia asked. These women wanted to include her. When was the last time Mia had been included in something not related to one of her

father's films? When was the last time someone had sought her out for her and not to gain
access to her dad? Mia glanced at Ava. "But
don't you have a photograph to use?"

"Not one that Dan will accept. He says I
have to be smiling, at least." Ava's displeasure lengthened the last two words.

"She needs a photo for a calendar," Ella
volunteered.

"Not yet." Ava slid onto the floor as if her
misery dissolved her resolve and coaxed the
docile collie into her lap. "But I lost the bet
and I have to give Dan a photo and bio that
he can submit to make me a candidate for this
local hero charity event."

Mia raised an eyebrow at Ava. The woman
clearly had difficulty turning down bets.

"An event that includes putting together a
calendar of everyday local heroes and local
celebrities to then sell to raise money for the
children's diabetes organization." Sophie
walked over to the recliner, picked up Ella
and settled her on her lap in the chair.

"We have to raise money for kids like Ben."
Ella pulled Sophie's arms tighter around her.

Sophie's enthusiasm trampled over Ava's
pique. "Ava needs a great photograph from a
serious photographer."

"I'm a documentary filmmaker." Mia repeated her statement inside her head. Any step off the path felt like a betrayal to her father's memory and all he'd done for her. She'd indulged too long with these women. It wasn't about her art, it was about her father's vision for a better, kinder world. It was about providing for her mother.

"With obvious talent." Sophie opened the engagement picture on her phone and flashed it at Mia. "Not just anyone can do this. Kellie already has over a thousand hits and well over five hundred shares. It's going viral."

Ava hugged the collie and whispered, "I don't want my picture to go viral."

Ella leaned over the side of the chair. "But then everyone will know you. Don't you want to be famous?"

Ava reached up to set her hand on Ella's cheek. "I have everything I want right here with my friends and family."

Mia felt the same: accepted and protected by these folks who were little more than strangers. She wasn't a professional photographer, only collecting simple snapshots of the present. She made important films like the one waiting to be finished. Films with messages and calls to action: to save the wildlife, uncover large-scale corruption or shine a light on illegal and toxic pollution of the oceans and waterways. Yet she couldn't stop herself from giving this memory color and texture for her to relive anytime with only a quick scroll through her photos.

Mia understood the woman's desire to protect her privacy. Still, Mia wanted to capture Ava on film. She'd head back to her real life and the real world that Ava and Sophie and Ella weren't a part of soon. But first she'd discover if her picture of Kellie was simply luck and good timing or something more.

Sophie gave Mia the thumbs-up sign. Mia reached for her digital camera, set the camera to her eye and asked, "What was Dan's side of the bet?"

"He bet me that he could beat my best score at the shooting range. I bet I could beat his best 10K time." Ava hugged Pepper as if the dog could relate. The collie kissed Ava's cheek, gaining Ava's full attention. "But he cheated."

Sophie laughed. "He did not. You lost fair and square."

"Never run a race you can't win, Pepper. That goes for you, too, Ella." Ava grinned.

"Speaking of winning, how do Ava and I get in on this girls-against-boys game tournament?" Sophie asked.

Ava nodded. "Yeah, we want to be included, too."

Mia clicked, adding to her Ava photograph collection. "Ella and I are open to expanding the team, aren't we, Ella?"

"Maybe." Ella giggled. "We need to know how you plan to win and what things you'll make the losers eat."

And like a local wanting fall to linger longer and keep winter's chilly gusts and rain out of the city, Mia extended their conversation. That loneliness remained outside her room while these women were with her. The empty ache inside her dulled to a twinge with every minute they stayed. Mia wanted more time with them. "Give us your best ideas."

No one held back. Food suggestions and game ideas bounced off the walls as if they were part of a game show audience shouting out answers to the contestant on stage. Sweet potato cupcakes made the list, but the dark chocolate coconut avocado ice cream failed as Mia and Sophie decided it actually sounded good. Mia was certain their laughter could be heard down in the ER. Through the laughter and conversation, Mia kept snapping photographs. She'd taken too many pictures already, yet couldn't seem to stop herself from adding more.

Mia's phone vibrated on the table beside Sophie. "Do you want to answer that?"

Mia glanced at the time on the camera screen. Her mother was fifteen minutes late for her afternoon check-in. "No, it's fine. Just my mom."

"You should get it, then," Sophie said.

"Moms don't like to be kept waiting," Ella added.

"This is her afternoon check-in." Mia adjusted the lens and checked the settings. "We texted this morning. She'll call again tonight. Once before dinner and one last time before she goes to bed."

"She isn't here?" Ava adjusted Pepper on her lap, shifting the dog's paws to force the collie to lie down across her legs.

"She lives in New York." Mia widened the frame to include Pepper and Ava. "I told her not to fly all the way out here."

"My mom would've flown from the other side of the world." Sadness washed over Ava's face, dulling the glow of her skin. "There was a time nothing I said would've stopped her."

"It wasn't easy convincing her to stay home," Mia confessed. But now she could tell her mother she'd spent the afternoon with friends. Surely that would prove she was on the mend and not in need of her mother's on-site support.

"You're fortunate to have mothers who care so much," Sophie said.

Mia swung the camera to Sophie sitting with Ella. The shadows from the rim of Sophie's baseball cap only enhanced the hopelessness in her gaze, yet the firm set of her mouth hinted at an inner determination. Suddenly, Mia wanted to know more about these two women. To share confidences and life experiences. She stumbled as if tripping into some new world, unable to keep herself from getting involved. But it was only for now. This one time. This one moment.

AN HOUR AFTER the laughter faded and her room settled back into its usual quiet zone, Mia pressed Play on her voice mails and clicked through the pictures from the day. The boom of Howard's voice over her phone jarred her inner calm and burst her happiness into shards. The caller from earlier hadn't been her mother.

Worse, Howard wanted to let her know about a few minor changes to the schedule. Minor because Mia had told him she was ahead of schedule during their last conversation. And she knew how much they needed to impress the network. Therefore, Howard had agreed to move the screening party up three days. Mia was to call if there were any conflicts.

Only her current status as an in-patient and the lack of a film crew and her inability not to get involved were a problem. Other than that, she had no conflicts.

CHAPTER NINE

WYATT STEPPED OUT of the path of an oncoming gurney and reviewed the notes from the triage nurse for his next patient. The halls remained rather empty for a Sunday evening. No gurneys lined the wall with patients waiting for a treatment bay to open. He would've preferred standing room only in the ER. More patients delayed the end of his shift, postponing his debate about the merits of heading to the third floor.

Yet not even the steady stream of patients the last ten hours had been enough to shake off his strangely insistent compulsion to apologize to Mia. He'd never apologized for attempting to save someone's life before. He supported Mia's wanting to honor her father, but preferred that she find a different method, specifically something that wouldn't put her own life at risk. He understood the very real need to honor the memory of a loved one. But he also knew that nothing brought a loved one back. *Nothing.* Yet the emptiness and torment of the loss lingered. Impossible to outrun. Impossible to disown. As reliable as the aging process in every living thing.

Things were better as he'd left them with Mia. He'd said how he felt, what he'd meant. Mia's hurt feelings were out of his control. Perhaps now she'd stop and think. Besides, Mia would be leaving soon anyway, and if she continued with her risk-taking adventures, her departure might be more of a permanent nature. He'd hate for his mother to suffer another loss. He'd leave everything alone and concentrate on what he did best: patient care.

Wyatt stepped into the last ER bay. "Mr. Price, I'm Dr. Reid. Can you tell me more about your pain?"

"It's gone." Mr. Price stretched his arms wide as if waking from a well-deserved nap, preparing to take on the world. "The nurse gave me that drink and it's gone."

"What drink was that?" Wyatt asked.

"A minty concoction in one of those little paper cups." The forty-something Gen-Xer secured his long hair with a rubber band, the tousled and unwashed mass looking like a final ode to his grunge roots.

"Have you had this type of pain before?" Wyatt asked.

He scratched his fingers through his scruffy

beard, from his cheek to his chin, as if requir-
ing extra time to consider Wyatt's question.
"Only after I eat onions."

"What did you have for dinner tonight?"

"French onion soup from the Chophouse
in the Heights. One of the best menus in the
city."

Wyatt pinched the back of his neck, trying
to draw the irritation out of his voice. "Onions
give you heartburn and yet you ate French
onion soup."

"It's a staple when you're feeling sick." Mr.
Price smoothed his hand over the ugly hospital gown as if he straightened a pencil-thin
tie down the front of his dress shirt during an
important sales call. "I'm trying to limit my
red meat intake."

"Were you feeling sick today?" Wyatt
moved to the side of Mr. Price's gurney and
pulled his stethoscope off his neck.

"Not particularly."

"But you came to the ER." Wyatt set the
stethoscope in his ears and listened to the
man's heart.

"Had to see you."

"Because of your stomach pain." Wyatt
dropped the stethoscope around his neck,
reached for the clipboard to write his order,
then looked at Mr. Price.

"No, because of the Piping Plover Mission," the man said.

Wyatt pressed his pen against the clipboard. On the other side of the curtain, codes blasted over the intercom system and the staff hurried by. But Wyatt was stuck in the general ER section with the nonurgent patients. Or in Mr. Price's case, the pretender who kept Wyatt from his real job treating the real emergencies. "Excuse me?"

"Sent in the application to the Reid Family Foundation, but we haven't seen a check." Mr. Price tossed his hospital gown behind him and reached for his dress shirt as if he wasn't sitting on a gurney, but in a leather chair in a corner office. "We're going to get a check, aren't we? Takes money to save the piping plover."

"I'm sure it does." But his mother's money wouldn't be doing the rescuing. Wyatt wondered if Mia even knew what a piping plover was and where it made its habitat. He'd bet it wasn't in San Francisco and that the smooth-talking Mr. Price had never seen one beyond a photoshopped picture on the internet. "I'm afraid I can't comment on affairs of the Reid Family Foundation."

"Of course you can," he said. "You're the

one in charge. That's what the attractive lawyer told me outside the cathedral this morning."

"You go to church?" Wyatt asked.

"When necessary. And it was necessary this morning to see the lawyer about my application." He leaned forward as if imparting insider-trading secrets. "You might want to consider different legal counsel. She's poor at responding to phone calls."

Because Lacey Thornton had more important business than Helen Reid's foundation. Not to mention it was Sunday. "Mr. Price, I'm here to treat your stomach pain, not hand out foundation money. I'm going to order an EKG and blood work just to make sure everything's good with your heart, then we'll work on getting you out of here. You're going to want to follow up with your primary doctor about your recurrent heartburn." And Wyatt was going to need to follow up with his mother. When exactly had he taken over control of her foundation?

"It's just those onions," he said.

"Stay away from onions and see your doctor." Wyatt stepped around the curtained wall, handed the orders to the nurse and took another clipboard from her.

"Got another special request in the second bay." Annmarie set her glasses on and scanned his notes.

"Special request?" Wyatt asked.

"Laceration across her right arm." The nurse grinned. "Says a barbed wire fence caught her. Doesn't remember her last tetanus shot."

"And she requested me?" Wyatt said.

"Used your first and last name," Annmarie said.

"Any mention about what she was doing near a barbed wire fence?" Wyatt asked.

"Rescuing a lame goat from a slaughterhouse." Annmarie looked at him over her glasses. "Showed me pictures of her rescues this week. Seems like the real deal."

Mia probably knew all about farm animal rescues and slaughterhouses. She'd encourage the woman to continue her good deeds for the abused animals. Still, Wyatt couldn't allow foundation business to interfere with his job.

Three wound irrigations, two plastic surgeon consults and a serious case of poison oak later, Wyatt stalked the hallway toward the nurses' station. "Please tell me there haven't been any more special requests."

"Three more." Annmarie checked her computer monitor. "You're quite popular tonight."

Or cursed. None of his "special request"

patients had true emergencies. Each one could've waited to call his or her primary care doctor in the morning. But treatment at the Bay Water ER was only a side benefit. Their real purpose: press their cases to receive funding from the Reid Family Foundation. He had no doubt the next three patients waited with similar agendas. "My mother's foundation is popular tonight. Give them to Becker."

"He's prepping for a possible OD burn victim's arrival," the nurse said. "Five minutes out."

"I'll take it," Wyatt said.

"You have patients waiting." Annmarie rolled back in her chair and crossed her arms over her chest.

"They're not real," Wyatt argued.

Annmarie tipped her chin down and looked at him over her bifocals, one eyebrow arching into her salt-and-pepper hair. Annmarie's tenure in the ER extended over three decades. Wyatt doubted there wasn't much the experienced nurse hadn't encountered and as such had a limited tolerance for nonsense from both patients and staff.

"Fine. They're real people," Wyatt corrected. "Just not sick."

"You haven't seen them." Annmarie stared him down.

"But you have and you know I'm right." Wyatt squeezed all the charm he could into his smile and voice. Fortunately, Annmarie liked him. "Give me this one. I'll stay past shift."

She tapped her finger against her pursed lips. "Dr. Becker mentioned that he wanted to leave early."

"Give Becker my patients and tell him to leave after that." Wyatt lost his smile and pleaded. "I cannot take another sob story about the struggles of a nonprofit. I need real medicine, or it's going to get bad. My medical degree is slowly being erased with each of my so-called special request patients."

"Cut the drama and get outside. I'll find Dr. Becker." Annmarie shoved him toward the ambulance entrance. "You'll owe me for this."

"Anything." Wyatt rushed toward the doors. "Name it and it's yours."

"I'll get back to you." Annmarie flicked her wrist, waving him away like a pesky child. "Now go save a life."

Even late-night diners had long since finished their desserts and after-meal drinks when Wyatt finally left the ER. The arrival of multiple critical patients pushed his medical training to the forefront and shoved aside any thoughts about his special request patients and unspoken apologies. The lives of the fifty-five-year-old woman with severe chest pain, the grandfather with left-side paralysis and speech impairment and the twenty-something who'd OD and suffered severe burns from an accidental apartment fire commanded his full attention and demanded his focus. There was no place else he'd wanted to be the last few hours than in the ER.

He stepped off the elevator onto the third floor. Even the cleaning crew had finished mopping the hallways. No doubt his mother had fallen asleep during the late-show monologue as was her nightly habit. He walked into the talk show host's laughter and his mom's sleepy welcome. "You're awake?"

"I wanted to see that nice actor from that superhero movie," his mom said. "And I'm a bit too excited to sleep with so much planning to do."

"Does that planning include sending your nonprofit applicants to my ER?" Wyatt asked.

"I only called Lacey to talk to her about the changes," Helen said. "I know nothing about your ER patients as you don't ever talk to me about your work."

He wasn't getting sidetracked by the pitiful tone or dejected voice. She knew that there were patient-doctor privileges and confidentiality laws. "What changes?"

"That you agreed to take over all aspects of the foundation. I passed that information to Lacey early this morning."

He'd agreed to cull through the applications, not run the foundation. He opened and closed his mouth, but nothing emerged.

His mom covered a yawn with her hand. "I'm rather relieved to give the foundation over to you, Wyatt. I need to concentrate on planning for my upcoming discharge."

Discharge? They hadn't decided where she'd be headed once she left the hospital. "The home visit isn't until next week."

"The therapists' schedules changed. I know my address and the location of the spare keys." Not at all perturbed by his stilted silence, she lowered the head of her bed and added, "I busted my hip, Wyatt, not my mind."

His mind might've exploded. Right there in the middle of his mom's room where he stood like a lost tourist who'd missed the last ferry from Alcatraz.

"In case you're curious, the house passed the evaluation." She lay back and pulled the covers to her chin, a peaceful and all-too-satisfied smile on her face. "I'm free to go home."

That meant Wyatt was free to return to Africa. Free to get back to his life. Why wasn't that same peaceful satisfaction in his mom flowing through him? They both were getting exactly what they wanted. Adjusting the covers around his mother was easier than adjusting his attitude. "It's good I have the next three days off. We have a lot to do."

"I don't suppose they'll release me first thing in the morning." She yawned again. "No matter. It's enough that I'm going home."

Enough for her. Too soon for him.

Wyatt closed his mom's door and pulled out his cell phone. Two texts to Lacey Thornton confirmed his mom's claims. His mother had informed Lacey that Wyatt was handling the foundation's affairs. She'd also thoughtfully added that any inquiries regarding applications and fund dispersals should be directed to Wyatt indefinitely.

He'd refused to hand over the applications to her, and she'd let him know her opinion without a confrontation of harsh words or insults. It wasn't an acceptable solution. Nonprofit owners and directors couldn't be clogging up the ER to get to Wyatt and their perceived foundation payouts. Not to mention the time wasted by the skilled ER staff taking care of those noncritical, deceiving patients. The disruption couldn't be tolerated.

He couldn't stop his mother's discharge, but he could fix this problem. Tonight.

He glared at the light streaming from underneath a certain patient's door. No surprise there. The surprise was that he wasn't online right now booking his flight to Africa. Checking out of his childhood house that had been transformed into the unrecognizable. Getting away from the reminders of his brother and how he'd failed him. He should be running down the hall at the chance to go back to the relationship his mom and he preferred: one of distance and surface talk.

Except he'd seen a difference in his mom with Mia. One more thing to blame on Mia. She'd made him want the impossible: a mother-son relationship, not based on anger and blame.

He skipped the knocking-on-the-door part and simply plowed into Mia's room. His backpack thumped on the floor, announcing his arrival. Yanking the chair closer to the bed, he sat down, stacked his hands behind his head and propped his feet on her bed.

"Don't get comfortable." The light from her computer screen highlighted her frown. "You're not staying long."

"Were you going to sleep?" The sarcasm in his taunt poked at her.

She flinched but kept her focus on her laptop. "I need to work."

He wanted her attention. He deserved her attention for all the trouble she'd caused him. He dropped his feet on the floor and leaned his elbows on his knees. "I can help. We can watch your accident video together."

"No," she snapped.

"You watched it, then."

"No."

He'd have missed her quiet response and the vulnerable quiver across her lips if he hadn't been so close. Fear still gripped her and sleep still eluded her. He might've offered encouragement if she hadn't sabotaged his plans to move his mom into an assisted living center. He might've held her hand if she hadn't reminded him of the mother he once knew. He might've comforted her if she hadn't messed with his emotions. Instead he unzipped his backpack and pulled out a thick envelope.

"No, I don't want to talk about it." A definite bite cooled her words.

Now that satisfaction streamed through him. He'd bet her irritation with him matched his annoyance with her. He tossed the envelope on her bed and grabbed Mia's laptop, instead of her hand. "This doesn't look like underwater footage. It's too furry."

"That's Pepper, one of the therapy dogs." Mia reached toward him.

Wyatt leaned away, pressing back into the chair. "When did therapy dogs become your work?"

"It's nothing." Except the way she strained forward as if trying to rescue a kitten stranded on a high tree branch challenged her claim.

"Be careful of your stitches. You don't want to loosen those."

She slumped back into her pillows and stared at the TV as if the blank screen revealed the exact location of the lost city of Atlantis. Yet she glanced at him more than once without moving her head, just a quick shift of her gaze that etched her frown deeper. The more he pried into her photo album, the more she withdrew into herself: her arms folded across her stomach as her body sank farther into the pillows.

Wyatt kept scrolling. The contrast of a fisted hand against the unbending metal of the waiting room chair absorbed him: Was it the hand of a frustrated doctor who lost a patient or that of a grieving family member cursing fate's cruelty? The running footsteps of the hospital staff trapped in the same frame with a patient's still bare feet grasped the idea that time both stopped and flew inside these walls. The compassion of an arm around a patient's shoulders, the laughter shared among nurses offering each other a moment's relief, the empty gurneys and quiet monitors prepped in anticipation of new arrivals: she'd captured the very essence of hospital life with grace, poignancy and humor. He clicked until the black-and-white collie's openmouthed grin filled the screen and set the laptop on her bed. "These are really good. Sophie could give a free picture when the dog gets adopted."

"How long have you known Sophie?" Finally, she looked at him, her gaze curious, no longer guarded.

He stepped further into the safe topic, but decided they'd discuss her photographs soon. She had talent and a gift that he doubted she recognized. "I met Sophie through Ava right after I got back. Ava helped Sophie get her therapy dogs into the Bay Water Medical system. They're neighbors and like to nag me about working too much or pester me with plant questions."

"You didn't inherit your mother's green thumb?"

"Hardly." He needed no more proof than the number of wilted plants in his mother's nursery, desperate for her return. Her gardens would rejoice in less than forty-eight hours. If only his doubts quieted and his concerns dissolved. How would his mother be safe at home? How could he leave her? How could he not? "And stop encouraging my mom."

"How exactly have I done that?" she asked.

"You showed her the picture of the rooftop garden across the street." He motioned toward the drape-covered window.

"She wanted to see it."

"Did she also want you to talk to the residents there about the need to put ostrich ferns in their garden, or was that just a request for me?"

"Wow, she thinks an ostrich fern will survive up there." Mia's head tipped as if she considered the merits of ferns.

"Not the point."

"What's the point? That you don't support your mom's hobby?"

"It's more than a hobby. A hobby implies several dozen plants scattered around the house and patio." Wyatt shoved out of the chair and paced around Mia's bed as if searching for a lost contact or his own focus. He wasn't there to spill his issues, yet his mouth kept rambling. "She has an infestation. Plants everywhere inside and out. If it isn't a plant, it's soil mixtures, spray bottles, pots, vitamins and seeds. It's an obsession and she's a fanatic."

"I've heard from the staff that her gardens rival the best city parks."

Wyatt shrugged, bumping his opinions out of the way. "Just stop taking pictures of the neighbors' plant life."

"That'll be easy." Mia stretched her arms in front of her and grinned.

The same satisfied delight as his mom's curved through her face. Wyatt pressed on his stomach, as if that would stop the pit from opening inside him and stall her next words.

"I'm getting discharged in the next day or so."

He dug his fingers into his stomach, trying to wrap his hands around everything before it escaped him completely. First his mother and now Mia. Yet he'd done his job and watched over them while they were in the hospital, treating them like any other patients. He wanted Mia to move on with her life. He wanted to move on with his. After all, he had impactful and meaningful work to finish in Africa. This had always been the plan. Why wasn't he ready, then, to let go? "I thought you disliked still camera work."

"Where did you hear that?"

"Your father."

"I haven't forgotten what my real job is." Her smile disappeared inside her terse tone. "And when did you talk to my father?"

He raised his hands, palms out at the accusation in her voice. "He liked to walk after the camp bedded down and the fire died. He'd ask me to join him."

"He never invited me." She smoothed out her covers, as if that would straighten out the past. "Not once."

Confusion shifted through her voice, but sadness made her shoulders slump forward. Wyatt had more one-on-one time with her father than she'd had. Why wasn't he surprised? Mia had her father's attention when it involved shot angles, reels and lighting. But she'd loved her father, and stomping all over that with his opinions wasn't fair. "You were usually in the chair beside Eddy's cot."

Her nod was too weak. She didn't believe his excuse for her father's oversight. He hadn't convinced himself. There was little good in changing the memories she carried of her father. The past needed to remain as it was. Picking up the large envelope, he shifted her attention and his. "Since you aren't sleeping or really working, I could use your help."

"No." She tipped her chin up and stared at him.

He wanted to smile. He'd have been disappointed if she'd agreed right away. After all he'd never apologized for the other night, not that he was going to. He'd pried into her personal photographs and dented her memories of her father. Yet she hadn't kicked him out of her room and he hadn't disconnected his unexplainable desire to be near her. "You agreed to help my mom."

"You aren't your mother." She set the computer on her lap, keeping her attention away from him.

"Thanks for noticing." He leaned forward and placed the envelope on her keyboard. "Seriously I need your help sorting through the applications for her foundation."

"It hasn't been at the top of your to-do list." She scowled at the envelope as if it was an unwelcome stain on her favorite shirt. "What happened?"

His mother happened. Chaos in the ER happened. Mia happened. "It just has to get done quickly, and I can't do it alone."

"You and your mother could go through them together. You don't need me."

That was true. At least he wanted it to be true. Because needing Mia complicated his entire life. Needing Mia involved a part of him he'd sworn never to risk again. He denied the whisper that it was already too late. He pulled an application out of the envelope and stuffed his wayward thoughts inside. "We don't exactly see things the same way. Here's an application from Steve's Wishing Well. I call it a scam. Mom would say every wish deserves to be granted."

Mia laughed.

And everything inside Wyatt released. Only one other person had ever been able to cut through his inner restlessness and make him believe everything would be all right: his brother. Yet Wyatt had failed to calm Trent's anguish. His love for his brother had blocked the doctor inside him from seeing the truth of Trent's condition. Love had lied and everything hadn't been all right. That was a truth he'd do well to remember right now. In this moment. With Mia.

Mia read over the application from Steve's Wishing Well and shook her head. "Your mom has a soft heart."

"And I don't." A soft heart endangered those closest to him. He need only stand at his brother's grave for proof of that. He held up his hand to stall her response and any more discussion of hearts. "I'm the practical cynic who wants to make sure his mom doesn't bankrupt herself with her philanthropy."

"Give me half." Mia held out her hand. "We'll separate them into legit, scams and questionable."

His frank words jarred her cooperation and confirmed his suspicions that Mia cared for his mom.

The scam pile grew out of proportion to the other piles. Wyatt wasn't surprised.

Mia stacked her last one on the questionable pile and sat back. "There are hardly any legit ones in here."

"Same for me," Wyatt said. "Now what?"

Mia handed him her laptop. "We search the questionable ones online."

He kept his arms tucked against his chest. "It's your computer."

"It's your mother." She placed the computer on the rolling table and nudged it toward him before leaning back in her bed. "Besides, my eyes are tired of looking at the screen."

He wasn't tired of being with her. He traced the evening from the moment he'd stormed into her room, ready to argue with her about all her wrongdoings, to now, with her relaxed against her pillows and something very close to contentment skimming through him. "What happens next?"

"You let your mother write checks to the legitimate charities of her choice."

He didn't want to talk about his mother. He wanted to talk about the impossible. "I meant after your discharge?"

"I go back to the Fog City Hotel, room 442, and my film. My schedule is going to be tight with work and therapy sessions." Mia cradled her head on her good arm and stared at the ceiling. "There won't be time for anything else."

That contentment faded at the warning laced in Mia's tone. He sensed she'd stepped back behind her camera lens already, distancing herself. He wanted only to break through that barrier and get back to where they were less than five minutes ago. "My mom wants to show you her gardens."

"I'll do my best to visit her," Mia said. "But I can't make promises."

"Have you broken too many promises already?" Like him. He'd vowed to save his brother. Vowed to return to Africa. Vowed to remain detached and indifferent with Mia.

"I make it a habit to keep all of my promises," Mia countered.

"You've never broken a vow?" Wyatt scrubbed his hand over his mouth. Hadn't he vowed not to do this? Vowed to keep their interactions on the surface like all of his successful relationships. He excelled at doctor-patient exchanges.

"No." Mia stared at him. "But you don't believe me?"

"I don't." His blunt reply made her recoil.

But she recovered. Her reply curt and abrupt. "I'm not sure I care what you believe."

She lied. He saw how much she cared in the pinch around her eyes. He smiled, pleased he wasn't alone. He cared too much, and that irritated him, making him want to harass everyone closest to him. And right now, that someone was Mia. "There's no one, nothing that would make you break your word? Would you break your promise not to swim again to save someone from drowning?"

"I'd never make that promise in the first place."

"Bad example," he said. "Would you give up your film work and your dad's legacy for true love? For the chance to be the happiest you've ever been?"

"I'm the happiest working on documentaries." She kept her focus trained on the ceiling.

"How do you know if you've never been in love?" he challenged.

"I've seen what love looks like." She lowered her gaze to his. "I'm not sure my mom would call it the happiest time of her life."

"But would she tell you it was worth it?" Wyatt held her gaze, refusing to let her retreat.

She countered with her own attack. "What about you? Ready to risk everything for love?"

"I'll leave that to someone else." He broke the connection and sat back, looking toward the window while he withdrew.

"Too scared?" she taunted.

"Too practical." He shoved the doctor inside him forward. "I refuse to let anything interfere with my work."

"Love is an interference?" she asked.

"Most definitely." He'd admired the brother who had taken the punches with him when Wyatt had instigated the fights in their teenage years. He'd adored the brother who had rescued him when he'd gotten sucked into the undertow at the ocean one summer vacation. He'd respected the brother who stood by their father during his battle with cancer so Wyatt could concentrate on medical school. He'd loved that brother and failed to see the man with the personal demons. Just as his mother loved her son and refused to reveal just how far past rock bottom Trent had truly fallen. Wyatt blamed love for his failure.

"We're quite the match," Mia said. "Both unwilling to put anything above our work."

Except when he was with Mia he didn't want to put his work first. That made her dangerous to his well-being and his heart. "It's as if we were made for each other."

"Good thing we don't believe in romance and all that."

He never said he didn't believe. "Why's that?"

"We'd only hurt each other for our work, and that'd turn our love into resentment."

"That's depressing and cynical."

"I prefer reality over fantasy," she said.

"What's our reality?" he asked.

"I get discharged tomorrow or the next day and finish my film. You return to your aid work in Africa after your mom is settled into her home," Mia said.

Simple. And right. Another goodbye. But something stuck in his chest like a spike, or perhaps it was Cupid's broken arrow. He tossed the last of the applications on top of the laptop and slouched in the chair, sliding down until his head hit the chair back. "This would be so much easier if she'd donate to a rehab center in Trent's name."

"Have you talked with her about that?" Mia asked.

"There's no talking with my mom," Wyatt said. "When her mind is made up, there's no changing it."

"Seems like a Reid family trait." Mia yawned and turned on the TV, switching the channels until she landed on *Ruined and Renewed*. "You should work on that."

He became less like his mother with every hour he spent with Mia. He'd never changed his mind so many times in his entire life than he had since Mia's gurney landed in his ER. If only he knew what he wanted, he might make up his mind.

CHAPTER TEN

Roslyn pushed Mia's wheelchair into the patient pickup area outside the hospital entrance. Mia gripped the plastic Bay Water Medical bag on her lap and wished she'd taken a few extra minutes to dry her hair. The wet strands dampened the scrubs top Ava had loaned her to match her scrubs pants. Ava thought the scrubs would work better over her bandaged leg and arm, and she'd been right. Mia had already asked Ava if she could borrow another pair.

A silver extended-cab truck pulled up to the curb. Wyatt jumped out of the driver's side, opened the passenger door and focused on Mia. "Your chariot awaits."

Mia tried to ignore Wyatt in his jeans and casual T-shirt. The everyday wear for every man worldwide and yet she was never more aware of the man inside the clothes than she was now, with Wyatt. She tightened the strings on the worn scrubs, knotting her unwanted reaction to Wyatt deep inside her.

She'd been discharged, but her mixed-up emotions about Wyatt hadn't remained back in her hospital room. Still she was fine and didn't need Wyatt. "I called a cab."

"We weren't putting you in a taxi." Roslyn touched Mia's shoulder as if to reassure Mia that she'd never fail her.

Wyatt shrugged. "Besides, my mom insisted I drive you, and you don't want to upset her."

Helen cared about her. Mia couldn't disappoint the kind woman, could she? "You can just drop me off out front of the hotel."

Roslyn settled Mia in the front seat and placed the Bay Water bag on Mia's lap. Wyatt dropped the camera and laptop bags in the back seat. The aide made sure Mia was comfortable, gained Mia's promise to visit, then sprinted inside. Mia clutched the plastic bag with her few personal items inside as if it was her only link to her favorite place in the world.

Wyatt tugged the plastic bag from her grip and set it on the back seat. "Everything okay?"

"For now." Mia ran her fingers through her damp hair. Wyatt's gaze sharpened, and her fingers tangled in the wet strands. "Did you plan this?" Now she sounded like they were something more. Like people who made plans together. Even her brain was scrambled.

"I told you I'd be checking up on you," Wyatt said.

His one-sided smile suggested he knew he made her uncomfortable. No nurse or tech would interrupt them. They were alone together. Really alone. She tugged her fingers free, trying to release the snag from her throat, too. "Well, you can see I'm fine."

Wyatt yanked on his seat belt. The buckle snapped into place with a soft click before he reached for her. He curled a wet strand of hair around his fingers and brushed his thumb across her damp cheek.

He'd done the same thing in Africa when she'd stepped out of the river exhausted and spent after too many days and nights at Eddy's bedside, willing him to open his eyes. But Wyatt had used both hands, wrapping her hair around his fingers before tugging her closer and covering her mouth with his. Their first and last kiss. Their only kiss. But she remembered. Every vivid, tender detail. He did, too. She saw the memory in his slate gaze and heard it in the hitch of his breath. Would it be the same? Or something more now, like an antidote for that void deep inside her? Did she want to know?

He shifted, her hair still trapped in his hold, but his gaze collided with hers, locking everything inside her in place. She wanted to know.

A small smile drifted across his face. "You should dry your hair. It isn't good to be walking around with a damp head."

Mia blinked. Her world slammed into place. She yanked her hair free and leaned away, back into her reality. The one without Wyatt and kisses. The one with her film crew and documentaries. "That's an old wives' tale."

"There's some truth in many old wives' tales." Wyatt tipped his head toward the windshield. "Besides, it's supposed to cool down tonight."

"It's good that I'll be spending the night in my hotel room working." Alone. Like she preferred.

"Eddy and the crew going to join you?" he asked.

"Not tonight." No one would be there to interrupt her. Eddy had texted her before her breakfast had been delivered to tell her the guys were still on their job with Shane's contact and apologized for not welcoming her home. But this wasn't a homecoming, and any fanfare would've been wasted. Frank had followed up with a text about the boat still being in dry dock for at least another week. That left her with her laptop and too many hours to edit the film and prove to herself and her crew that she needed more new footage.

"Still haven't kissed and made up with your boys?" Wyatt asked.

"It's complicated," she said. Like her feelings for Wyatt.

He sped through the city. Everything outside her window blurred. Unfortunately, things weren't much clearer inside the car.

Wyatt turned right toward the financial district. "There's nothing complicated about wanting you to be safe."

There was everything complicated about her crew's defection, from almost derailing the final film to ruining future contract negotiations to wiping out her father's legacy. Not to mention their lack of faith in Mia shook her own resolve. Although the worst of the fallout involved her mom and Mia's failing to uphold her promise to her father. But Wyatt's shoulder wasn't hers to lean on. "Helen seems to be handling herself fine at home."

"That's what she tries to tell me." Wyatt weaved around the parked cars that made the road more like one lane than two.

"Why can't you believe that your mom is fine? That I'm fine, as well?" Mia nodded, telling herself she was fine. She didn't need him looking after her. She didn't want him filling any voids. "That we can take care of ourselves."

"Because you're both too reckless and too stubborn to be left on your own."

"I know what I want, and I'm willing to work for it. There's no shame in that."

Wyatt pulled into the turnaround in front of the Fog City Hotel and eyed her. "Do you really know what you want?"

She wanted to return to her normal life. To not be woken up in the middle of the night for a vitals check or blood draw. To not hear doctor pages and not smell the sanitized antiseptic-scented air as if even the cleaning agent had been disinfected before use. She wanted Wyatt to kiss her. No, that wasn't right. She shoved the truck door open. "I want to get to my room and put my leg up."

"Then let's do that." He opened his door and hurried around to help her.

Mia left Wyatt near the three-tiered fountain with her bags and the dancing cherubs splashing water over the tiers. She needed to get a new room key from the front desk. She'd lost her original room key somewhere between the boat and ambulance ride to the hospital.

The guest services representative, Clara, clicked several keys on her keyboard, tilted her head at her screen and shifted only her eyes toward Mia. "You've been checked out."

"That's not correct. I've been in the hospital and I'm back now." Mia lifted her wrist with the hospital band and shook her arm. "I just need a new key to my room."

"But you checked out of your room." The woman tapped her computer screen with a manicured nail.

"Then I'll check into another one." Mia fumbled for her wallet. Her phone vibrated on the marble counter. Call me in capital letters filled her phone screen. She couldn't deal with her mom. Another text filled the screen: Now.

The nail tapping stilled. "We're booked."

"There isn't one open room in this entire hotel?" Mia asked. Panic vibrated through her in tune with her mother's texts. She had to have a room. She had to have a place to stay.

Her mom continued her texting blast as if she was marketing the sale of a lifetime to thousands of mobile users. Ten minutes or I'm booking a flight.

"I'm sorry." The woman's smile barely reached to her upper lip as her gaze narrowed on Mia's phone. "But we have your luggage and final invoice."

Her mom followed up with her next volley: Nine minutes. I talked to Eddy so I know you're at the hotel. Mia glanced at the envelope with her name scrawled across the front with an invoice for a room she'd spent only two nights in. There was no apology letter or coupons for her troubles. Just a quick dismissal as Clara, the ever-efficient guest services rep, waved the next couple waiting in line over, displacing Mia to offer real guests her services. A doorman set Mia's suitcase in front of her and wished her a good evening. Mia rolled her luggage over to Wyatt. Her phone vibrated again, alerting her to her mother's countdown.

She could deal with only so much at one time. Mom, we can video chat tonight. Of course, it wasn't that easy. Mia sent four more texts confirming the time before her mom was satisfied. She tucked her phone into the front pocket on her scrubs top and faced Wyatt. "Sorry, it's my mom."

"What's wrong?" Wyatt asked.

"There are no more rooms." Mia sank onto the marble ledge of the cherub fountain and propped her leg up on her suitcase. She ached, deep into her bones, from the wound in her shin up to her skull.

"But you have a room you checked into." Wyatt towered over her, his gaze shifting from the front desk to her.

Mia flexed her foot, hoping to stimulate

some circulation. Weariness washed over her like the water over the edge of the fountain behind her. "I've been checked out of that room."

"What now?"

"I need to find another hotel." In a minute she'd begin her search. Ten more ankle rolls and she'd feel like running. Okay, maybe a slow jog. Or perhaps a stroll. But she'd move.

"Come to my mom's." Wyatt crouched in front of her.

When she opened her mouth to argue, he took her hands in his, squeezed her fingers and rushed on, "Just for dinner. You need to eat and put your leg up. She has Wi-Fi. You can book a new hotel room from there."

Mia glanced around the crowded lobby. A handful of guests waited to check in at the front desk. Several more lingered at the concierge desk. The happy-hour crowd from the bar and grill had spilled into the lounge area. Latecomers were hard-pressed to find standing room only. The splash from the fountain behind her failed to dim the laughter and boisterous evening conversations. This wasn't the quiet she'd craved. There was something more intense about the loneliness of being alone in a crowd.

The throb in her leg pounded up her spine,

settling like a fist in her neck. She wasn't ready to be alone. That weakness irritated her, weaving an ungrateful edge through her tone. "I appreciate this."

"It's nothing." Wyatt picked up her camera and computer bags, then grabbed the handle of her rolling suitcase. "It's not like you're moving in."

"A few hours will be more than enough." Surely, she'd find a room quickly. Then she'd stop wanting to fall into Wyatt's arms. She'd stop wanting Wyatt's embrace to support her and his words to convince her everything would be fine. Clearly her brain had been checked out with her hotel room. She followed Wyatt outside. Perhaps the slap of cold evening air would snap her common sense back into place.

Wyatt opened the truck door and dropped her bags in the back seat. "You can pay me back by helping me with my mom. She wants to go over the foundation applications and start writing checks."

Mia collapsed into the still-warm leather seat. "But there weren't any suitable organizations to donate to."

"I already tried to tell her that." The strain in his voice clashed with the distress on his face.

She'd claimed the situation between herself and her crew was complicated. But things between Wyatt and his mom made her issues look like nothing more than a few misspelled words on a contract. "You think she'll listen to me?"

"I'm praying she'll listen to you." Wyatt closed her door and walked to the driver's side.

He slowed his driving through the city as if he was content not to arrive home too quickly.

Mia looked out her window. Lights glowed from empty offices, dotting the sides of the buildings like stars in a country sky. The bus carried one passenger to the deserted bus stop. An older couple conquered the layers of their thick coats to stroll arm in arm. A gentleman guided his miniature poodle to one of the trees planted inside the cement sidewalk. Several women, still in their staid business suits, spilled out of a cab, their bright laughter bouncing through the darkness. Night had descended yet the city never really slept, the pulse simply slowed. Much like Bay Water Medical. There was comfort in that. Like the comfort of sitting beside Wyatt now.

She'd be even more content if he held her hand. Or her. She folded her hands together in her lap. She really needed to find a hotel room.

Wyatt turned down one of the established residential streets and pulled into a narrow driveway.

Mia studied the Craftsman bungalow with the front porch that begged for a swing. Tree branches draped over the fence in front of the truck as if reaching out to greet newcomers. She'd never considered settling into a house, but imagined a lovely home like Helen's would be perfect. Even from the truck, something special surrounded the house as if the ground carried Mother Nature's blessing. "You grew up here?" She heard both the awe and jealousy in her voice.

"Built a tree fort in the backyard and played hide-and-seek in the street." Wyatt leaned across her and opened her door.

Mia imagined the boy inside the man racing through the neighborhood and acting like a pirate in the tree house. A child's dream. Couches covered in sheets and lampshades wrapped in plastic anchored her childhood, making mud pies and collecting fireflies had been prohibited. Her childhood home looked as if it waited, suspended in time, dust-free under the protective coverings, until a new family moved in to give it life again. Stepping onto the porch, she understood why Helen re-fused to leave. She'd refuse to leave as well if she called this place home. "How'd you ever leave?"

"Easy." Wyatt wiped his shoes on the wel-come mat. "I went to college and kept on moving from there."

Always moving. Always running. Mia gripped the patio post. "This would call me home."

Wyatt studied her arm wrapped around the post as if he'd never seen the intricate detail in the woodwork before. "Careful, you're sound-ing like someone who wants to put down some roots."

"I'm just appreciating your childhood home." Mia tipped her head against the post and stared at him. "Nothing wrong with that."

"Good to know things haven't changed." He opened the door, motioned her inside.

Mia paused in the doorway and looked up at Wyatt. The sleeve of her scrubs brushed against his shoulder. The slightest shift and she'd touch him. A little more and she'd be close enough to kiss him. "Have you suddenly found your roots?"

He set his fingers under her chin, tipped her face up to his. His thumb stroked across her cheek. Back and forth as if he tried to rub his warmth into her chilled skin. Only each caress stirred something deep inside her, something deep inside her heart, pulling her closer to him.

He shifted, closing the distance to less than a breath away. "You know me better than that."

"You're right, then." She moved into the entryway, instead of into his embrace. That warmth disappeared. "Nothing has changed."

Yet her heart tripped over itself being so close to him again. Her breath threatened to hitch. And a whisper wound through her, hinting that everything had changed.

THE TAP OF a cane on the hardwood floor pulled Wyatt's attention away from Mia.

His mother wrapped her greeting in a warm hug for Mia before touching Mia's damp hair. "You really shouldn't be wandering the city with a wet head. Wyatt, let our houseguest come inside where it's warmer."

"Our what?" Wyatt cleared his throat.

Mia had stood in the middle of the hotel lobby like a homing beacon. Her eyes had been damp from trying not to cry, yet resolve had firmed her chin as if she'd dared him to comfort her. He'd wanted to draw her into his arms and do just that. He'd wanted to fix everything for her. She'd made him want to cross a boundary. A boundary like the one his mother just trespassed across.

"Scrubs seem to be a new fashion trend. I must've missed that update while I was in the hospital." Helen took in Mia's attire and frowned. "Mia will be staying with us in the second guest room. It's nothing."

What was between Mia and him was nothing. Nothing more than an awareness. Nothing unusual about that. They were two healthy adults after all. He'd closed off his heart. Avoided the messy emotions. Preferred his life like this. He flexed his fingers. A small stretch and he could wrap Mia's hand inside his, tuck her into his side, hold her close. Would she stay? Annoyed at the appeal, he blurted, "Why would Mia stay here?"

His mom gripped her cane with both hands and gaped at Wyatt. "Because there are no rooms at her hotel."

"How would you know that, Mother?" Wyatt asked. Why did he still want to pull Mia into his side as if it was his right, his responsibility to take care of her? And his awareness of Mia was supposed to be a passing urge, not a consistent, ever-present one.

"Mia's crew and I decided Mia shouldn't

stay in a hotel all by herself. It's not right," Helen said.

Mia's smile didn't reach into her eyes, even when she pushed her mouth wider as if not wanting to be rude in front of his mother and watched him. "Didn't you know, Wyatt?"

"Of course he didn't." Helen waved her hand and turned away from them. "Wyatt wouldn't have cooperated. I talked to Eddy and we worked out the details. Eddy promised to speak to your mother, as well."

"Eddy?" Mia repeated.

"Such a kind soul." Helen walked down the hallway. She never turned around as if already certain they'd follow. "Eddy promised to send me an announcement when the baby is born."

Mia dropped into one of the antique kitchen chairs Wyatt had always considered too small and too fragile. Yet Mia looked like she belonged there, as if she'd always claimed that chair and brightened that spot. "Has my mother booked her flight?"

"Eddy told me that she will if you insist on staying at a hotel." His mom patted Mia's shoulder. "You should book a room with two double beds. That way you'll each have your own sleeping space."

"I've stayed alone before," Mia said.

Wyatt moved the chair beside Mia and motioned for her to prop her leg up on it.

His mom nodded at him as if she approved and then pulled out the chair next to her for him to sit in. "Mia, you won't stay in a hotel after spending ten days in the hospital."

"But we can't force Mia to stay with us if she doesn't want to." Wyatt shook his head as if that would dislodge the panic creeping through him. He'd only invited Mia over for dinner and to use the Wi-Fi. Mia living in the same house was never the plan. Ever. He agreed Mia needed to find a new place to stay, but not here, with him and his mother. In the guest bedroom right beside his.

"But we have the space. And you won't need to worry about my being alone." His mom rubbed Wyatt's arm like she used to when his father scolded him. Only now, her touch encouraged his dread, not calm.

"I couldn't impose," Mia said.

No, she couldn't. She wouldn't. Wyatt wouldn't allow it. She'd already imposed enough on his dreams and intruded into his thoughts during the day. Now having a thin wall separating her from him would be an even bigger imposition.

"Nonsense." Helen waved her hand, brushing aside Mia's weak argument.

Yes, it was nonsense. Total nonsense. Mia had to find different living quarters far away from Wyatt and his peace of mind.

"We'd love to have you stay here, wouldn't we?" His mom's smile bloomed wild like one of her rare burgundy hibiscus flowers before she jabbed her elbow into Wyatt's side.

Wyatt nodded like when he was seven and she'd nudged him to behave in church. "But don't think you can raid my closet for clean scrubs." Satisfied with that warning, he walked to the refrigerator and pulled out a soda. He was going to have to shut down his awareness of Mia if he wanted to get her out of his system.

"Wyatt, that's absurd," Helen said. "Mia has her own clothes. No one wants your scrubs of all things."

"I do have a full suitcase. I just didn't bring it inside," Mia said.

No, she brought only herself into their home, and that was more than enough. She'd make an imprint in the rest of the house same as she'd claimed her seat at the kitchen table. The only answer to this home invasion: work more. His body revolted, the grumpy side reminding him that he wasn't a superhero, and rolled that no-sleep-induced nausea through him for incentive. He needed to recover.

Maybe he'd survive more shifts if he channeled his superpowers at least until Mia was gone.

"Wyatt will get your things after dinner. Now that the sleeping arrangements are settled, we can eat." His mom moved over to the oven and waved at Wyatt. "Help me get the lasagna out of the oven. Mia, dear, the plates are in the cabinet near the sink."

By the second serving of lasagna, the conversation circled around favorite dishes, unwelcome spices and underappreciated proteins. He swiped a slice of Italian bread from Mia's plate, and she stole a cucumber from his salad as if they'd shared dinner at the table every night. Like a typical family. He kept waiting for Trent to stroll in, fill his plate and inject his always-entertaining commentary. Any minute his father would call out his arrival and kiss his mom's cheek.

But that was the past. He hadn't lived in the past ever. He had to get out. Dad wasn't coming home soon. Trent was gone. Yet he kept glancing at the door, waiting, hoping.

Mia snuck a bite of his slice of caramel fudge cheesecake his mother had ordered from the Whisk and Whip Pastry Shop. He slid his plate out of her fork range. "Get your own."

"I just wanted a bite." Her napkin failed to hide her wide grin.

His mom picked up his plate and handed it to Mia. "We've always served our guests first."

"She didn't want any." Wyatt shook his head and sliced another piece.

Mia lifted her fork, loaded with another bite of his cheesecake. "It's really hard to resist."

So was she. He leaned back in his chair, his fork and his nostalgia untouched. Nausea rolled through him as if he'd worked seven nights straight without sleep. This wasn't real. This wasn't his everyday life. He had to stop the charade before he believed this was normal. Before he wanted this. He stood and grabbed the thick envelope from the kitchen counter. Time for a reality check.

He tossed the envelope with the foundation applications on the table. "There's a serious lack of genuine organizations in this pile. Mia and I looked through all of them the other night."

His mom ignored the envelope and finished her dessert. "Then the ad needs to continue to run."

"The ad is only going to bring in more of the same." Wyatt shoved a bite of cheesecake in his mouth, hoping to smother his frustration with chocolate decadence.

"I have an idea. I did some research on grassroots nonprofits in the city." Mia pulled out the pile of applications and unfolded a piece of paper on the top. "I thought Wyatt and I could visit several to get a feel for their causes and how well they're run and report back to you, Helen."

His mom dabbed the corner of her mouth, folded her napkin and set it on her dessert plate as if signaling the wait staff that she was finished.

"When do you want to go on this little field trip?" Wyatt pushed his half-eaten dessert away. Heartburn, not chocolate bliss, seared through his stomach.

"Aren't you off the day after tomorrow?" Mia asked.

Not if he could help it. His body revolted, demanding downtime. Demanding time to shut his mind off. "This might come as a surprise, but I do have things to do on my day off." Like sleep.

"I'm only asking for a few hours." Mia dug inside the envelope. "We'll keep it well-rounded. Here's one that rescues senior animals. One that promotes urban revitalization with a green infrastructure. And one that assists foster and homeless kids as they transition into adulthood." Mia aimed the research at him. "You can't disagree with helping older animals and kids. The Tree Rally speaks to Helen's passion."

Wasn't it enough that she was invading his home? Making him wish for impossible things? Now Mia wanted to take his time, too. The walls from the corner he'd been backed into jammed his spine straight. "There's an easier solution. Mom, you could buy the naming rights on an in-patient drug rehabilitation center. I have colleagues building one near Napa. They're looking for investors now."

His mom set her glasses on the table and scooted the application pile closer as if building a barrier between them. "Why would I do that?"

"To honor Trent's memory." Something she'd neglected to do at Trent's funeral.

His mother touched her cheek and ear, as if to make sure her skin still covered her bones and her skeleton hadn't been exposed. "You can't expect me to fund a drug rehab center."

Wyatt jerked out of the small kitchen chair, paced the hardwood floor, stomping the quaint air out of the evening. "Mia knows the details of Trent's death."

Helen stiffened, from the flattening of her

mouth to the rigid set of her shoulders to the tense grip on her glasses. She hardened like quick-dry cement.

Her silence was like an invitation to fill the dead air with his torment. One he accepted, letting his words lash out, unchecked. Unfiltered. "Relax, Mother. Lightning hasn't struck the Reid family because someone else knows the truth. It won't be a secret I take to my grave like you expected."

His mom swayed back as if absorbing the impact of his words. Then she straightened, prepared to launch her own counterattack. "You told me strangers weren't allowed into family affairs. Just last week in the hospital. That's what you told me."

Wyatt gripped the chair back and dropped his chin to his chest. She used his own words against him. That he could take. Her constant deflection wore him out. "When are we going to have a real conversation?"

"This is quite real, as was our conversation in my hospital room about Mia's being involved with the foundation applicants." She tapped her glasses on the application pile like footsteps down a dead-end path.

"Stop it, Mom. Just stop." Wyatt stepped away from the table. "Stop turning the focus from what matters."

"It matters very much that you've let strangers into our affairs." She touched Mia's arm. "It's not personal, my dear."

"Nothing's ever personal." Wyatt lifted his arms over his head, then dropped them to his side. "But that's the point. How long do we need to pretend to be a loving, supportive, giving family before it becomes true? Clearly we haven't pretended long enough."

Mia rose, drawing his attention. She was calm, and if he walked to her, he believed she'd comfort and support him. All the things he'd wanted his mother to be after Trent's death. He held up his hand to stop Mia's retreat. "No, stay. You should know the truth. Know that the best thing you could've done was walk away from me in Africa. Because the Reids are fakes."

His mother's fingers curled into a fist. He didn't doubt she'd slap him if she could reach. It wasn't necessary. He ached already, deep and gnawing and consuming. "Deny it, Mother," Wyatt taunted. "We're also experts at denial."

"Wyatt James Reid, lower your voice and leave." His mother rubbed her forehead.

"Not until we talk. Really talk." Wyatt spoke softer, but kept the demand in his firm tone. "For once."

"You've done quite enough of that already." She set her hand on her stomach and refused to look at him.

"That's it?" Fury and anguish collided inside him. He hated the reminder that he'd never have another dinner with his brother. Despised himself for wanting to retreat into the past. Loathed himself for not walking away as if a tornado of torment swept him up and demolished his world. "That's all you have to say?"

"What else is there that you haven't said?" Helen asked.

"What about Trent? Let's talk about your son. My brother. The one whose laughter I miss every day like a lost limb. The one I couldn't save. The son you wish stood here right now, instead of me." He stormed around the kitchen, his words wreaking more damage. "Let's talk about selling your house, as your neighbors aren't reliable caretakers when I leave. Let's talk about putting Trent's name on the rehab center to save someone else like we couldn't save Trent. Let's talk about anything, except your precious plants. Because your plants don't matter."

His mother rose and slapped her palm on the table to steady herself. Mia jumped up and wrapped her arm around his mom's thin waist.

The whip of Mia's voice lashed through his tirade. "Wyatt! That's enough." She guided his mother toward the hallway. "I'm taking Helen to her room."

Wyatt cleared the table, wanting to smash the china plates over his own head, crack his common sense loose. He'd never unloaded like that. Never on his mother. And in front of someone else. In front of Mia. He jammed the plate under the water, letting the heat scald his skin and burn away his regret. How could he attack his mom like that? When had everything gotten out of his control?

He loaded the last of the plates into the dishwasher and returned the kitchen to its usual spotless state. If only he could simply wipe away the damage he'd caused like the crumbs from the table. But there was too much worry about his mother after his departure. Too much unresolved pain. And so much indecision. He needed sleep. Real sleep. He needed to return to Africa and escape his life.

He walked out onto the sun porch and sank into the sofa. The air was oppressive out there, too. He was like a weed in his mother's garden that had to be yanked out. He'd killed more plants than he saved, disappointing his mom further. He should get his phone out and search flights. But he stayed where he was, staring out into the dark garden.

Mia sat next to him on the sofa. "She's in bed. Resting."

"I'm better in Africa." He belonged with strangers and patients, not loved ones. Ironic those were the people he failed every time. "I shouldn't have pushed. I'm a doctor. I know better. I need to know better."

"She's your mother."

"Which is why I needed to be better." He set his head back on the couch. "You're better with her than I am." He was better with Mia, too.

"She's hurting, too," Mia said.

"Thanks to me." Wyatt ran his hands over his face. "We can't share the same space without taking each other out at the knees. I should've stuck to plants and watering schedules. Shut my mouth. I just wanted…" The family he'd once had. The mom he'd once loved and who'd loved him. Without resentment. Without obligation. Without blame.

"What did you want?"

"Doesn't matter." Wyatt shrugged. "This is what we have now. It needs to be enough."

"She's your only family," Mia said. "She loves you."

"I love her, too," Wyatt said. "Because I love her, I'm going to stop."

"Stop what?"

"Stop wishing for something we never had." He raised his head and looked at Mia. He needed to be plucked from the garden. But Mia, she needed to be planted. She fit. "My mom would really like it if you stayed in the guest bedroom." He'd really like that, too. If only for the help with his mother.

"Sure." Mia bumped her shoulder into his, then plucked at the collar of her scrubs. "Besides, you've got a closet full of scrubs that I can raid while you're at work. It seems I'm becoming partial to this sea-foam color."

Wyatt closed his eyes, but all he saw was Mia in his scrubs. He shoved his eyes wide and stared at the ceiling. "What happens now?"

"We change our perspective." She set her hand on his leg, the gesture one of comfort and encouragement.

Wyatt slid his hands under his thighs. He wanted to hold her hand, pull her in close. But he'd just vowed to stop wishing for things he never had. That included Mia. "There isn't a TV out here."

"We'll work something out." She smiled and kept her hand on him, kept the connection. Until her phone rang and pulled her away from him.

That was for the best. Besides, his perspective needed to be fixed, not changed. He needed to go back to when he was detached and everyone close to him was safe.

A video screen opened on Mia's phone. "Mom, I'm at dinner. Can I call you later?"

Wyatt leaned toward Mia, wanting to put a face with the soft, dignified voice coming from the phone.

"But you told me you were free all night," Mia's mom said.

"Something came up." Mia tried to shove Wyatt away with one hand and hold the phone steady with the other.

He scooted closer, pressing his leg against hers, not even pretending he wasn't listening in. He still hadn't gotten a good view of Mia's mother.

"That seems to be happening quite often." Disapproval was thick in her voice.

Good to know he wasn't the only one suffering from mother disapproval syndrome.

"Mom, back up." Exasperation quickened Mia's words. "All I can see is your nose."

Wyatt swallowed, but his laughter escaped. Mia slapped her free hand over his mouth.

"I'm just trying to get a better look at you," her mother said.

"Why?" Suspicion stretched the one word out. She freed Wyatt to touch her hair and cheek.

"You might be taking too many of those pain pills," her mother said.

Wyatt saw only her mother's dark gaze, narrowed on the screen as if to better see into her daughter's mind.

"I've been reading all about people who've gotten addicted to their pills. You can't be too careful." The worry was there in her sharp inhale.

"Mom, I'm fine." Mia gripped the phone with both hands as if she gripped her mother's shoulders to ensure she heard Mia's slow and precise explanation. "I'm having dinner with friends."

"What friends? Eddy and the boys are working late." Her mother backed away from the camera but appeared preoccupied looking at herself.

Wyatt grinned at the faces her mother kept making at the camera, as if she sat in front of a mirror in her bathroom.

"I'm with Helen Reid and her son, Wyatt. We met at the hospital." Mia's grip on the phone never relaxed. "I know Eddy told you about Helen Reid."

"I know about Helen, but not her son." Her mom stopped making faces and zoomed herself back into the lens.

"He's a doctor. Dr. Wyatt Reid."

"Doctors can be psychopaths, too, Mia." Her voice dropped to the conspiratorial level of a thief plotting a heist. "Or suppliers of too many pain pills. I've read all about that."

"Wyatt isn't..." Mia lost her words.

Wyatt wondered when he'd last seen Mia flustered. Her head shook in small, quick motions as if she discarded every response that popped up. He slid the phone from Mia's grip. "Hi, Ms. Fiore. I'm Wyatt Reid."

"You're quite handsome." Her mother's voice lifted with renewed interest. "Mia, is he good-looking, or is it this screen?"

Wyatt nudged Mia with his elbow and faced the phone toward Mia.

Mia kept focused on her mother and sighed as if handsome men offended her. "Yes, he's as good-looking as he seems."

"Well, isn't that lovely. Put him back on." Mia's mom transitioned from accusing Wyatt of being a psychopath to welcome-to-the-family mode as easily as other people brushed their teeth. She tucked chin-length black hair behind her ear and smiled, open and pleasant. "When did you two first meet?"

"It was several years ago in Africa." Wyatt intended to put her at ease. His error was obvious when her eyebrows pulled in and her lips pursed. A look eerily similar to his own mother's whenever Africa was mentioned.

Mia's mom recovered with a quick brush of her hand over her face that returned her soft smile. "Well, you're not there now, are you?"

"Not right now," Wyatt agreed.

"Eddy explained that your mother graciously offered to let Mia recover at her house. Will your bedroom be close to my daughter's room?" her mother asked.

"Not too close." Wyatt grinned, forcing his laughter back behind his teeth. The proper Mrs. Fiore probably wouldn't want to learn from him that her daughter was sleeping in the room right next to his.

Mia curled farther into the sofa, as if trying to sink between the cushions, and slammed her hands over her face.

"She'll want to move back to the hotel, I'm certain." Her frown reflected her displeasure. "You'll keep her there, won't you? Until she's fully recovered."

"Absolutely," Wyatt said. "But you might prefer talking to my mother. She can give you all the details you'll want to know about Mia's recovery."

"My daughter isn't very forthcoming." Her mother shook her head. "You should know that up front."

Mia tried to snatch the phone away. Wyatt stood and held the phone out of her reach.

"I appreciate the insight," Wyatt said.

"Forewarned is forearmed," her mother said. "I'd very much enjoy speaking to your mother, Wyatt. What a kind gesture. My daughter should've made the offer."

Mia shook her head at him and made the motion of slicing her throat with her hand. Wyatt ignored her and rattled off the phone number.

"Do you think she'll be available to speak in the afternoon?" her mother asked.

"That's her favorite time of the day," Wyatt offered.

"I'll call her in the afternoon, then. Could you put my daughter back on the screen?"

"Sure. Pleasure to meet you, Ms. Fiore," Wyatt said.

"It's been mine, as well," her mother said.

Wyatt handed the phone to Mia. "Mom, I'll call you later."

"There's no need." Her mother's voice was cheerful. "I don't want to interrupt your evening with your friend. I'm certain Ms. Reid will have all the information I need. Sleep well."

"Night, Mom." Mia ended the video chat and tossed the phone on the coffee table. "That was awkward."

Wyatt picked up Mia's hand and squeezed her fingers. "They need each other. Trust me on this."

They both leaned into each other. That didn't mean they needed each other. Wyatt studied their joined hands, appreciated how they fit together. Something inside him unwound and he settled into the couch with the night blooms and Mia. For the first time in a long while, he felt like he belonged.

CHAPTER ELEVEN

MIA CARRIED A cup of coffee out onto the porch, her camera hanging from her shoulder. The wrinkled blanket and indented pillow confirmed Wyatt had slept there. She'd stayed with him for a long time, her head on his shoulder, her mind filled with the nighttime scents from the garden. She couldn't remember ever being that content. That peaceful.

But dawn arrived, along with clarity in the form of multiple texts from Howard. Followed by her mother. Nights with Wyatt, no matter how tranquil, weren't permanent. Those kinds of moments belonged to the ones who wanted love and believed in forever. She'd awakened to a cold, empty guest room where sleep had mostly evaded her. She'd rolled over and picked up her camera to distract herself.

Helen called a good-morning, informing her that Wyatt had left for his meetings before disappearing deeper into the gardens. Mia followed, hoping to walk away from the memory of holding Wyatt's hand. How was something so simple, so mundane, also so special? She wrapped both of her hands around the coffee mug, seeking the same warmth she'd found in Wyatt's touch. What was wrong with her? Fortunately, she intended to be out of the house for most of the day. Perhaps when she returned, she'd have Wyatt and her feelings tucked back where they belonged: separated and sequestered.

She found Helen near the fountain, rounding one of the hedges with a large pair of shears, and grinned, happy to focus on the older woman for a little while.

"The boys were very rambunctious kids, full of extra energy. I'd stand in the kitchen at the window and imagine a retreat. A private place where I could collect my thoughts and gather myself." Helen waved her shears to encompass the bench and fountain before hacking off a dead branch. "Now I have such a place, and I find I don't want to hear my own thoughts."

Mia had been having a few too many unwanted thoughts herself lately. If only she could take a pair of shears to her own thoughts. "Where did you find peace?"

"In the bathroom like most mothers." Helen paused, the memory drawing a sweet smile to her face. "Wyatt and Trent would stand outside the door, whispering and waiting."

"Waiting for what?" Mia asked.

"An audience." Helen laughed. "Their antics worked best when they had someone watching and witnessing the brilliance of their imaginations."

"What did they do?" Mia asked. She pictured Wyatt as a boy: free with his laughter and his hugs. She wondered if the man, guarded and haunted by his grief, could be like his childhood self again.

"If I stepped out of the bathroom and received twin bear hugs, I knew I wasn't going to approve," Helen said. "If I came out and they each tugged on a hand to get me to hurry, I knew they'd built something I had to see. Most often, the hugging and hand pulling were intertwined."

Mia set her coffee on a paver and aimed her camera at the tree house, imagining a young Wyatt climbing the ladder with a pirate sword and his brother. Vines and tree branches wound through and around the tree house, embracing the structure as if preserving the memories contained within the wooden walls. "They built the tree house."

"With their father, when they were older." Helen stared at the tree, her voice wistful. "It was the last thing they'd all built together. I even contributed, sewing blankets and pillows."

The last remnant of Helen's family together. That the tree house endured for so many years despite the weather and the elements spoke to its strength and resistance. "Did they sleep up there?"

"As often as possible," Helen said. "I had the perfect view from the kitchen window to keep an eye on them. They never knew. I'd stand there until they fell asleep, then rest on the porch in case one of them needed something."

A mother watching over her children. Only a shout away. Always within reach. "Did they come and get you during the night?"

"Every time they slept out there." Helen laughed. "It was easier back then to make everything right again. A hug or promise that it was only the wind and not a dragon trying to climb inside to eat them. Or a quick late-night snack to calm an empty belly."

"Wyatt wanted the snack, didn't he?"

"How did you know?" Helen asked.

Every time he'd visited her in the hospital, he pulled something to eat from his backpack. "He never outgrew that habit."

"We've not shared a late-night snack in

many years." A weariness shadowed Helen's smile. She attacked another bush with her shears. It seemed with every clipping that drifted to the ground, her melancholy slipped away, too. "I believe I've done enough wandering down memory lane for one day. What are your plans today?"

"I'm heading over to Sophie's store, the Pampered Pooch, to drop off the photographs of the dogs needing forever homes." Mia captured a few more photos of Helen. She looked from the display to Helen, wondering if Helen looked pale or if her settings were off. "Then I have a meeting with a contact at the shipyard across the bay."

"You've a full day." Helen stared at her gardens and waved with her shears. "I'll be tidying up out here."

And she'd be alone with her thoughts. Perhaps Mia wasn't the only one in need of a change of setting. Besides, she hated the idea of Helen's being alone, especially after last night. She wasn't certain, but Helen had appeared to be suffering from more than Wyatt's harsh words when she'd tucked the older woman into bed. "Would you like to come with me to Sophie's?"

"What about your meeting?"

Mia checked her watch. "We'll have plenty

of time to swing back here before I head over to the Ferry Building."

"I think an outing might do me good." Helen ran her hands over her gardening apron and smiled, color brightening her cheeks.

Mia nodded, pleased she'd suggested it. "You'll get to see Gretel and Hansel. They're good mood boosters."

"Let me just put some things away and freshen up." Helen gathered her gardening tools into a wheeled wagon.

"I'll do that and you can head to the house." Mia grabbed the handle on the wagon and pointed it toward the nursery.

"Thanks, dear." Helen grabbed her cane. "Everything takes a bit longer these days."

Mia ended up taking longer than Helen to get ready. She'd debated over the easiest way to carry the digital camera with her. The bag was bulkier than she preferred, but strapping the camera around her neck made her feel too much like a tourist. Finally, she repacked the camera bag to fit her wallet and phone. Set for her afternoon business meeting, Mia held the taxicab door open for Helen in front of the Pampered Pooch.

Her fingers twitched to pull out the camera and snap pictures of Sophie's quaint store tucked within one of San Francisco's more tree-lined streets. Across the street, the café with the three outdoor tables caught Mia's attention. The bridal boutique with two wedding-attired figures in its window shared an alley with the bar and grill, its sign tilted and rusted. Row houses and newer apartment buildings jostled for curb space with businesses tucked into every retail space. Mia could spend an entire day walking the city block and most likely not discover all its secrets, and she loved that.

Mia pushed on the door to the Pampered Pooch, admiring the paw print Open sign.

"Welcome to the Pooch, ladies." Ava grinned from a doorway in the back near the checkout counter. She gestured to two round fluffy gray cats resting on each of her shoulders. "I have to say my goodbyes to Rio and Banjo. They're off to their forever homes this afternoon."

An older woman, with white-gold hair and an intricately tied paw print scarf, leaned around the computer on the checkout counter and introduced herself as Evie Davenport, then added, "The cats have been fostering with Ava for the last month."

"If she'd adopt, she wouldn't need to put herself through these routine goodbyes." Sophie nudged around Ava and patted each cat's head before hugging Helen, then Mia.

"Fostering is all I can manage." Ava rubbed her cheek against one of the cats.

"She's afraid of long-term commitments," Sophie teased.

"I'm committed to senior animals that need love to learn to trust again. It would be selfish to give all of my love and affection to only one long-term pet."

"Who said anything about a pet?" Sophie laughed.

"I prefer the company of my four-legged fosters." Ava walked over to Mia, as if needing the support. "I see no problem with that. If Sophie wasn't so in love, she'd agree with me. Love distorts a person's perspective."

Mia agreed with Ava's outlook on love. But she had to admit love looked better than fantastic on Sophie. She pulled her camera from the bag and focused on the pet shop owner.

"Okay, ladies, it appears that Daisy is an umbrella cockatoo, according to this website." Evie stopped typing and smiled at Ava. "The bird needs a foster mom, Ava, and your place is empty now."

"Not for long." Sophie rearranged cat toys on one of the end caps. "I got a call about two brother dachshund puppies found in a Dumpster this morning. They should arrive tomorrow afternoon."

"I'll have my place puppy proofed by tonight." Ava carried the cats toward the back door. "Sorry, boys, I need to get ready for my new arrivals."

Mia zoomed in on the gray cat nestled against Ava's neck, then shifted to Helen's slow approach toward the oversize birdcage beside the checkout counter. The umbrella cockatoo spread its wings, revealing a bald patch on its chest. Dingy came to mind when Mia studied the bird, its white feathers seeming to be covered in a layer of dust. A tender smile softened the lines around Helen's eyes.

"I didn't know you took in birds." Helen placed her hand flat on the cage and whistled to Daisy. Tilting its head, the bird stretched its wings, revealing drab yellow feathers underneath, before it edged slightly closer to Helen. Helen whispered, "Aren't you a pretty thing."

"Brad and Ella took in the bird." Sophie walked to the other side of the cage. "Told me if I said no, I'd be showing favoritism to animals with fur. And didn't everyone deserve a second chance at a happy life?"

"Everyone deserves a second chance," Evie agreed. "But with our lack of knowledge on large-bird care, we might not be the second chance Daisy wanted."

Sophie jammed her hands in the back pockets of her jeans and eyed the bird. "I'm trying to locate a bird sanctuary."

"Daisy needs to sing to the flowers and trees." Helen whistled again, more breathless and low, trying to coax the bird even closer.

"Except I don't have any greenery around here." A lean black-and-white cat wove between Sophie's legs. She picked up the cat. "I have fur and parrot predators."

"I have a garden and flowers that will remind Daisy of home," Helen said. "Maybe her feathers will grow back."

Mia lowered her camera and stared at Helen. "You want to bring that bird to your house?"

"We've the empty corner on the sun porch, beside the window, and it doesn't get drafty there." Daisy finally edged close enough to touch Helen's palm with her beak, as if to say, yes, I choose you, too. Helen kept her hand still and her voice soft as if she'd suddenly become a bird trainer. "Daisy could look out and sing to her heart's delight."

"This is the same sun porch that Wyatt sleeps on most nights." The same porch Mia spent most of the night on, holding Wyatt's hand and leaning on his shoulder.

"He'll have to share." Helen's firm voice enforced her resolve. "Or move back into the guest bedroom like a proper guest."

Except it was Wyatt's home. He shouldn't be treated like a guest in his mother's home. Was that why Wyatt slept on the couch? Mia reminded herself to ask him.

Sophie handed the lean black-and-white cat to Ava, asking her to take him back to the kennels. Running her hands over her jeans, she faced Helen and the birdcage. "Do you have any experience with large birds?"

"None." Helen talked to the bird. "But neither did Daisy's former owners, judging from her appearance and dreadful cage. I'd chew my feathers out, too, if I had to live in a cage with nothing more than two pretend branches."

Evie adjusted the computer monitor, leaned forward and read aloud. "Cockatoos are affectionate and fun. They bond to their owner but get depressed without a lot of attention. They need to eat leafy greens and fresh vegetables and fruits along with the occasional nuts."

"I'll have someone to share my vegetables from the garden with." Helen stepped behind the counter and stood beside Evie. She pointed to the computer. "What does it say about toys and cages?"

Sophie took off her Pampered Pooch baseball cap and ran her hands through her hair.

Mia tucked her camera inside the bag on her shoulder and moved next to Sophie. She kept her focus on the two older women chatting together. "Can Helen really take Daisy home?"

"She can," Sophie whispered. "But should I let her? She knows nothing about large birds. Then again, neither do I."

Mia studied the bird, which looked as if it curled in on itself, its beak tucked into its chest and its feathers plastered into its sides. "Daisy seemed to like Helen. She touched her palm."

"That's more than she's done since we got here." Sophie rocked side to side like a shortstop anticipating the next pitch. Or the next move from the two older women.

The pair were now shoulder to shoulder, nodding and frowning in unison at whatever they looked at on the computer. Helen pointed at the screen and told Evie to add it to their shopping cart. The women shared a laugh and continued shopping. Mia smiled, liking the glow radiating from Helen's face.

"I think Helen is taking home Daisy and Evie approves."

Sophie adjusted her hat back on her head as if she'd reached a final decision. "Helen, this would only be temporary until I can locate a reputable sanctuary."

Helen told Evie to add the swing to the cart and shrugged at Mia and Sophie. "We might need a larger cage."

Evie nodded and typed away on the keyboard. "The food bowls really should be off the floor of the cage."

Helen added her agreement while she dug through her purse and pulled out her wallet. "Let's place the order."

Mia leaned toward Sophie. "I'm not sure she heard you."

Helen looked up, and her happiness bounced around the room like a hundred colorful bouncing balls released inside Sophie's store.

Sophie sighed beside Mia. "How can I refuse her now?"

"Everything for Daisy's new cage will be here tomorrow." Helen wrapped one arm around Evie's shoulder and hugged her. "We can have a welcome-home party for Daisy on Saturday."

Sophie rushed to the counter and touched

Helen's shoulder. "It's only until I find Daisy a suitable sanctuary."

Helen patted Sophie's hand. "Of course, dear. Now Saturday, you have to bring Ella and Brad. I'd like to meet Brad, finally. Evie, you must come, too."

Ava returned from the kennel area . "What have I missed?"

"Well, you're just in time for the official invite to Daisy's homecoming party." Helen leaned on her cane. "Bring your partner or, even better, a date."

"I'll check with Dan and leave the date part to someone else." Ava lifted her eyebrows at Mia.

Mia shook her head and retreated a step.

Evie rubbed her hands together. "Helen told me about Mia's film crew. Have you met them yet?"

"Yes, they're all very nice and all very attached to their significant others." Ava held up her hands and pointed at Mia. "What about Mia? She's single, too."

Mia retreated down the aisle, away from the older women, yet she couldn't stop her smile from breaking through at the thought of watching Evie and Helen play matchmakers. She checked the time on her phone. Panic erased her grin. How had it gotten so late?

How could she have forgotten her work? "I need to catch the ferry for a work meeting across the bay."

"Convenient excuse," Ava teased. "But you won't have a meeting on Saturday, and they can do their matchmaking on you, instead of me."

Helen linked her arm through Ava's. "Can you help me outside, dear? I don't want Mia to be any later for her meeting."

Mia waved to the others and opened the main door. Outside on the sidewalk, Helen smiled at them both. "You are aware we can play matchmaker to more than one person at a time. We might be old, but we can still multitask."

Ava helped Helen inside a cab and spun around to hug Mia. She embraced her friend and knew exactly why she'd lost track of time in the pet store. Mia liked being with these women, liked being a part of something that wasn't film related, but rather friends simply enjoying each other's company. But work and real life demanded her complete focus. Distractions like friends and rescued umbrella cockatoos couldn't be accepted.

Already the loss of her new friends stirred sadness through Mia. She added extra cheer to her voice, hoping Ava wouldn't detect her distress. "We're younger than Evie and Helen. We just need to stick together on Saturday."

"Deal." Ava laughed and shut the door to the cab.

Mia sat next to Helen and gave the driver Helen's home address.

Helen interrupted, "We must head straight to the ferry station so you won't miss your meeting."

"Are you sure?" Mia had promised to take Helen home, but they'd stayed too long at Sophie's. Her contact at the shipyard would only be there for another hour.

Helen nodded and settled into the stiff vinyl seat. The cab pulled into traffic.

"You don't have to bring Daisy home." Mia touched Helen's hand. "Sophie would understand if you got caught up in the moment." She'd gotten caught up in the moment.

"I want Daisy and she wants me." Helen squeezed Mia's hand.

Helen's weak, clammy touch pulled Mia's attention to the older woman. "Are you feeling okay?"

"Fine." Yet Helen kept her gaze directed straight ahead. A pinch creased into the lines fanning out from Helen's eyes. "Is it far?"

Mia held on to Helen's hand. "Not too much longer."

"You'll be in time for your meeting?"

"Yes."

"Then everything is all right." Helen dipped her chin as if convincing herself, too.

Except Mia wasn't certain all was right with the older woman. Mia tried to study Helen without being obvious. She wanted to believe Helen, yet alarms sounded in the back of her mind.

"My phone keeps vibrating. Can you see who it is?" Helen handed Mia her phone. "If it's Wyatt, could you call him? I'm not prepared to take him on right now."

Mia spent the last minutes of the cab ride texting with Wyatt. Each text upbeat and confident: yes, they were fine. No, they didn't need anything. Yes, his mom ate. She never mentioned the bird adoption. Helen had to confess that on her own. Though guilt pressed in on her like a third passenger squeezed in the back seat of the cab.

But she had nothing concrete to tell Wyatt about his mom. Clammy hands hardly qualified as an emergency. She peeked at Helen and managed another quick survey as the cab slowed by the curb in front of the Ferry Building. Helen had been fine, more than fine in the pet store while she'd purchased a new home for Daisy. Mia hurried around the cab to assist Helen. She checked Helen's hands for tremors. Set her arm around Helen's waist in case her legs wobbled and she lost her balance.

"I'll wait over there." Helen used her cane to point at an empty black cast-iron bench. "You get our tickets for the ferry."

"Are you sure you want to go with me?" Mia settled Helen on the bench and stepped to the right, then the left in front of the older woman. She studied Helen from several different angles, trying to decide if the light inside the Ferry Building dulled Helen's skin or something else.

"It'll be lovely." Helen lifted her glasses and rubbed her eyes. "I've not seen the city skyline from the water in years."

Mia tipped her head and chewed on her bottom lip. Excitement drifted into Helen's smile but failed to push color into her very pale cheeks. "I'd take you home, but I'm supposed to meet a source for the film in less than an hour."

"The fresh sea air will do me good." Helen nodded toward the ticket area. "The line is getting longer. Don't forget my senior discount."

Mia carried the tickets and a bottle of water back to Helen. After she took several sips and a tinge of pink returned to Helen's cheeks, Mia pulled her camera from her bag to check her remaining storage. She'd taken more pictures than she'd expected to at the Pampered Pooch. She'd planned to give Sophie the photographs she'd already developed, not take another series of pictures. She clicked through several photographs of Ava's foster cats and sighed at her reluctance to hit the delete button. Pathetic. When had she become such a sap for run-of-the-mill senior house cats? "Sophie is going to love these."

Only a slight hum came from Helen.

Mia glanced up and dropped the camera in her lap. Helen's forehead rested in the palm of her hand. She touched the older woman's frail arm. "Helen?"

"It's nothing, dear." Helen straightened and gripped her cane with both hands. "I just exceeded my activity limit today."

"We should leave," Mia said.

"Nonsense," Helen argued. "I'd like to sail today."

But if something happened to Helen, Mia wouldn't forgive herself. Wyatt wouldn't forgive her. "Helen, what's really going on?"

"I'm old and lack the stamina I once had." Helen added a frown as if to let Mia know she didn't care for her impertinence.

Mia wanted to believe the older woman. The meeting with her new contact would give her the footage to finish the documentary. Her deadline approached in less than six days. Tomorrow was field trip day with Wyatt. Friday included doctor's appointments and more hyperbaric chamber time. The weekend wouldn't allow her to capture the boatyards' toxic substances leaking into the bay and contaminating the water. She had to make this meeting. Today. "Are you sure?"

Helen nodded, but seemed less than sure.

Mia could leave Helen at the ferry docks in Harbor Bay, join her contact and return within the hour. What harm could come? But emergencies offered no preparation time. Only a few minutes had passed before the first shot from the drug cartel had been fired in her father's direction in Costa Rica. Only a few more minutes had ticked by before her father had suffered the lethal damage from two of those bullets. She should've left the Pampered Pooch sooner and kept her camera in her bag where it belonged. Helen would be home now if she'd kept to her plan to drop off the pictures and leave. She knew better than to get involved. Clearly, she hadn't been thinking, but that had to stop now.

Helen touched Mia's leg. "I promise not to

disrupt your meeting. I know how important your work is."

Mia squeezed the camera. She'd promised her father the very same thing years ago when she'd first joined him in the Amazon rain forest. She'd vowed she wouldn't be a disruption to his life's work. Vowed she'd prove herself to him. Vowed her father would discover her worth as an apprentice and a daughter.

She'd gone so far as to talk off her symptoms of a severe viral infection to appease her father a week after her arrival. She'd lied about her temperature, downplayed the chills and aches, vomited in silence. All to keep herself from being a disruption to his precious film schedule in the Amazon rain forest. Of course, medical aid hadn't been within easy reach out in the rain forest. Still, her dad had concentrated more on his filming than his ill daughter. *Work always takes precedence, Mia.*

She stuffed the camera into the bag, zipped the cover and zipped the taunt of her father's voice.

Helen refused to admit something was wrong, too. Yet Mia knew Helen wasn't holding back the truth about her condition because of Mia's work. No, Helen had other motives that Mia guessed involved Wyatt.

The boarding announcement echoed inside the building. Mia rose and helped Helen stand, steadying the older woman against her side. *If you don't put our work first, Mia, someone else will steal the attention. And you'll wither away with your art all alone.* Mia guided Helen toward the main entrance, blocking out her father's censure with every step.

"This isn't the way to the boat." Helen's steps slowed.

"My leg is starting to ache," Mia lied.

"Why didn't you say something before?" Helen glanced over and frowned. "You need to get home and put that leg up. We've been walking too much today."

Mia helped Helen into the cab and slid inside beside her. Mia covered twice as many miles walking during one day of shooting not less than a month ago. The problem wasn't with the number of steps she'd taken today. The problem was whether those steps led her in the right direction. And why the right direction suddenly felt so wrong.

MIA SET A stack of cookbooks on the oval patio table next to the nursery. Helen adjusted the wide brim of her teal sun hat and rubbed her hands together. Leftover lasagna and a long afternoon nap had restored Helen's color and revived Mia. She had meant to go to her bedroom and work on the film. After a hot shower, she'd propped her leg up, leaned into the padded headboard and promptly fallen asleep. The laptop had rested in sleep mode on the pillow beside her. Mia used Helen's request for help with the cookbooks as an excuse to linger and make sure the older woman had been right about simply overtaxing herself that morning.

"I had a wonderful chat with your mother after my nap. She's such a lovely lady." Helen tugged a cookbook from the middle of the stack. "She wants to see you."

"We talked on video chat last night." Mia took the digital camera off her shoulder.

"It's not the same."

It was better. "It's less frustrating for both of us."

"Perhaps." Helen flipped through several pages. "But that doesn't make it right. After all, you're family."

Family that was closer because of the distance between them. When they got in the same space, their relationship fractured. Much like Wyatt had said last night after his argument with Helen. "We don't see things the same way."

"Your mother understands you better than you know," Helen said. "She only wants the best for you."

Her mom believed it was best for her to run Mia's life. "She believes my art should be a hobby and would prefer it if I joined the *real world* with a regular nine-to-five job."

"She recognizes your talent." Helen looked up from the cookbook. "She showed me several of your photographs hanging in her bedroom."

"Those had to be from high school. I haven't sent her any still photographs in a very long time." Mia adjusted the pot of Sweet Peas she'd carried out from the nursery and angled the camera to frame the small wooden trellis and several white and purple blooms.

"That's a shame," Helen said. "I'm sure she'd love new ones to add to her collection."

Mia's collection remained on a film reel now. And the pictures she collected on the digital camera weren't for sharing. "She'll have to watch the documentaries now."

"She has a special shelf for all of the Fiore films," Helen said. "She showed me that, too."

Surprise pulled Mia's focus from the flowers. She looked across the table at Helen, waiting for the older woman to tell her that the special shelf was nothing more than the garbage can, but she was silent. Given her father's travels and film schedule and his absence from home, Mia never understood why her parents hadn't divorced; they'd lived separate lives far longer than they'd lived as a couple. How could that be a happy marriage? How could that be love? And yet, she knew her parents had felt deeply about each other. "My mom can add a new film to her shelf soon."

The final film from her father. Mia's last connection to her dad. Her mom's connection to her husband lived on in the two-carat ruby wedding ring she'd simply transferred to her right hand after his death. Her mom had always told Mia that her love for her husband would fade only when the blood-red color drained from the stone. At his funeral, her mom had kissed her ring, touched his casket and whispered, *The fire inside the stone still burns as it always will. For today, tomorrow and forever.* Her mom had her ruby ring and her dad had his films, and neither had each other. What did Mia have?

Mia settled back behind the camera lens and captured more photographs of the Sweet Pea flowers, trying to click away the thought that perhaps her parents' baffling marriage was better than being truly alone. Mia moved from the potted flowers to the garden oasis, stepping on and off the pavers for different shots. Helen returned to her cookbooks and occasionally called out a recipe for Mia's approval.

At the fountain, Mia settled as if the water washed her insides clean and cleared her thoughts. She returned to the table and sat across from Helen.

"The more you push your mother away, the more permanent the distance becomes." Helen handed the *Six Ingredients or Less Cookbook* to Mia. "And the pain becomes the new normal."

"I'm not pushing her away." Mia opened to the middle of the cookbook.

"You haven't asked her to come here," Helen countered.

"Her life is in New York, where she wants it," Mia said. "Traveling is too stressful. She worries too much already. Add in a six-hour plane ride and she could implode."

"She'd fly for her daughter." Helen tapped her finger on the hardcover of her cookbook, as if to drive her point home. "That's a mother's job."

"We don't have a typical mother-daughter relationship." Mia scanned several recipes, the words blurring together until all she saw was her mom's face the day she'd boarded the plane to work with her dad.

"Even more reason not to push her away." Helen's voice sounded as if she'd swallowed something bitter.

Mia reached across the table and squeezed Helen's hand. "Wyatt doesn't mean to push you away."

"No, he wouldn't do that," Helen said. "But my son and I have settled into the distance. It's our new normal."

"But you can change that." Mia clutched Helen's hand between both of hers.

Helen closed her eyes. "It's not as simple as building a bridge. As one reaching for the other. That would be nice, but it isn't to be. There's too much lurking in the cavern between us, waiting to swallow us in its depths."

"It cannot be that hopeless," Mia said. One argument couldn't sever a lifetime of connection. Besides, hopeless would be if she failed to pay her mother's bills. The tragedy would be in failing her father.

"You've a kind heart, my dear. You've brought sunshine into my old heart, and for that I'll be forever grateful." Helen set her other hand on top of their joined ones. "Now we need to decide on dessert for Saturday."

But Mia's so-called sunshine wasn't enough

to take away Helen's pain of losing both of her sons. Yet Mia struggled for how to help the older woman, who hadn't hesitated to take Mia into her home. "I have it on good authority that Daphne's On the Corner offers the best salted caramel brownies in the city."

"I'm sure their brownies can't be as deliciously decadent as the peanut butter cheesecake brownie made at the Whisk and Whip," Helen argued.

"Shall we have a taste-off?" Mia asked.

Helen leaned her elbow on her cookbook, rested her chin in her palm and grinned. "I'm listening."

"We could ask everyone to bring their favorite brownie, homemade or store bought. We'll all taste and vote on the best."

Helen tapped her fingers against her cheek, but excitement swirled in her gaze. "What does the winner get?"

"Beyond bragging rights." Mia sat back and drummed her fingers on the armrest. "The winner gets all of the leftover desserts."

Helen and Mia laughed and shook hands.

"This looks like a bet being made." Wyatt studied them from the porch. The screen door shadowed his face, but not the hesitancy in his voice. "Do I want in on this?"

Mother and son hadn't spoken all day. Mia

knew, she'd asked Helen. "You already are in on it."

"We're having an open house this Saturday night." Helen kept her gaze on her cookbook and missed the surprise and flutter of pleasure across his face.

"You've not had one of those in quite a while." Wyatt dropped into the chair beside Mia and set two pairs of scrubs on the table for her. "What's on the menu?"

Helen beamed at his interest in the party and listed several recipes. He added two of his favorites before Helen said, "Appetizers and dinner are settled. Now back to the bet."

Mia recognized Wyatt's olive branch of supporting his mom's Saturday gathering, but she planned to tell him later that it was a decent start, but not nearly enough. Still Wyatt's interest made her bounce in her own chair. "We're having a taste-off."

"Dessert based," Helen explained. "You need to buy or bake your favorite brownie. We're all going to sample and vote on the best one."

Wyatt leaned back in his chair and eyed them. "That's too easy. The best brownie is the skillet brownie from Rustic Grill. There's no need for a taste-off."

"Well, I disagree." Mia leaned toward Wyatt. "So get your fork ready."

Wyatt pushed back into her personal space. "I'm always ready."

But for what? This was about dessert, yet the glint in his slate eyes felt like sunlight reflecting off a polished knife cutting right through her. Flustered, she fought to break their connection. "Are you off tomorrow?"

"Yes." The interest in his gaze tangled her insides.

She struggled to put more than a wheeze into her voice. "Then we can visit those non-profits we discussed."

She expected Wyatt to decline or argue or pull away. But he wasn't through being accommodating. And the smile he sent Mia was anything but distant. "Tell me what time and I'll be ready and waiting."

If only she knew what he was really waiting for.

CHAPTER TWELVE

MIA SWUNG HER makeshift purse—the camera bag with her wallet inside—onto her shoulder and followed Wyatt out to his mom's car.

Wyatt started the car and looked at her. "Do you have your list?"

Mia pulled a folded piece of paper out of her scrubs pocket. She'd come to rely on the front pockets on her scrubs shirts, carrying everything from her cell phone to pens to cloth cleaners for her camera screen. "I have four like we agreed."

"I have the same," Wyatt said.

"You made a list of nonprofits to visit today, too?" Impressed that Wyatt might be coming around to her ideas, she covered her confusion with praise. "You really are sorry for making your mom cry."

"I wasn't trying to make her cry." Wyatt backed out of the driveway. "And my list isn't nonprofits."

"The focus today is to help your mother," Mia said.

"We are," Wyatt said. "We're finding her people to give her money to as well as finding her suitable living quarters."

"She has a fine place to live now." Mia crossed her arms.

"Fine for now. While we're there." It wasn't long before he pulled into the curved entryway of Sunrise Manor Care. "But we're both leaving soon. Then her home won't be fine."

"Why can't you see that she's better right where she is?" Mia asked.

He reversed into one of the visitor parking spots and shoved the gear into Park. "Why can't you admit that having a backup plan isn't a bad idea?"

Fine, she'd allow Wyatt his backup plan. She definitely didn't need or want one. But first she'd prove to him that Helen had recovered and a plan B was unnecessary. She released her seat belt and rubbed her stomach, certain the jabs were only her irritation at Wyatt. She had nothing to be guilty about. Helen's minor setback seemed to have been nothing more than a lack of sleep or pushing herself too hard. Why read more into the event than necessary?

Yet she wasn't a trained medical professional. Wyatt was. And she should tell him. Let him decide if his mom should see a doctor.

She'd do just that if Helen slipped up in the next few days before the party. Mia frowned at the drab building that looked like a cross between a dilapidated elementary school and a jail. "I'm not going inside."

"Yes, we are." Wyatt opened his door and turned to look at her. "I need your help. If you like one of these places, my mother will listen to your opinion. It's just a backup plan."

That's what he said to gain her cooperation. Yet she knew he'd move his plan to the top of the list at the first opportunity. She wasn't giving him that chance. Mia walked through the parking lot. "There are not enough visitor parking spaces."

"You can't be serious," Wyatt said.

Mia pointed at the handful of empty spots. "People drop their loved ones off here and never come back. Otherwise they'd need more spaces for visitors."

"Or their families live in the city and walk or take the bus to visit." Wyatt yanked on the main entrance door, his exasperation more than obvious.

Four minutes later, Mia buckled her seat belt to keep from giving Wyatt an I-told-you-so grin.

"Don't say anything," Wyatt muttered and

shot out of the parking lot like someone pulled the fire alarm.

The center had been even more depressing inside with its dark entrance and lack of welcoming staff. Wyatt hadn't made it past the front entrance before he'd sprinted back to the car. Mia grinned. "We're going to the Tree Rally now. It's on the ocean side of the park."

"Fine." Wyatt clenched the steering wheel and glowered at a red light.

Mia happy-talked right over his surly mood. "The Tree Rally has planted more than one thousand trees in the city and helped residents start neighborhood gardens throughout the county. Their mission is to plant nature among the cement."

Wyatt nodded, but his expression was contained and tight as if he'd been given a shot to lock his jaw in place.

"It's the perfect cause for your mother." Mia opened the Tree Rally's website on her phone and read more about the nonprofit to Wyatt.

Twenty minutes later, Mia crumpled up the solicitation letter from the Tree Rally and jammed her seat belt in, wishing she could jam her frustration into the metal buckle, as well.

Wyatt grinned beside her. "Am I the only one who sees the irony?"

Mia pushed on her sunglasses and leaned her head against the back of the seat. "I saw it just fine."

"It's just they're an organization that brings greenery to the city. But then they want donations primarily to build an office building." Wyatt chuckled and pulled out into the traffic. "A big cement structure without one tree on the property."

Mia clutched her forehead. "You can stop talking."

"Their business is trees." Wyatt laughed. "Except when it's not."

"What's next on your list?" Mia tried to change the subject and ignore Wyatt's delight that she'd also picked a less-than-desirable nonprofit.

Three hours later, Mia brushed crumbs from her avocado chicken sandwich off her scrubs pants and leaned back in the wrought iron chair outside the deli, wondering how such an imperfect morning could transition into this. A perfect slice of city life: the blend of businessmen and women with tourists and locals made for a swarm of people, conversations and agendas. Some strolled, some raced, others teleconferenced and a smattering lounged under the trees, content to watch the world pass by. So much life, so much vibrancy from the window shoppers at the jewelry store to the couple arguing at the bus station to the woman scattering bread crumbs for the pigeons.

If only Wyatt's list of assisted living centers and Mia's list of nonprofits had been perfect like Mia's view.

Across from her, Wyatt offered advice to his coworkers in Africa between bites of his BLT and typed one-handed on his notepad. Mia swiped a potato chip from his plate, smiling when he glanced up. She offered her plate of raw vegetables to him in exchange. He dunked a chip in her ranch dressing instead and ended his call.

"Sorry about that," Wyatt said. "I have an idea."

"We go back to your mother's applications from her newspaper ad and you forget about moving your mom to an assisted living center." Mia snapped a carrot in half.

"Not quite." Wyatt crunched on a chip and eyed her.

She recognized that look in his eyes, the one that made her want to lean in and pull away at the same time. Her breath lodged in her throat.

"You search out three assisted living centers." Wyatt picked up his phone. "I'll find three nonprofits and we'll visit them this afternoon."

"Why?" She was supposed to spend only the morning with Wyatt. This wasn't a full-day excursion. If she spent more time with Wyatt, she might be tempted to discover more about him. She should be finishing her film.

"We failed on our own lists," Wyatt said.

"You should never have put a living center without a garden or apartment planters on your list," Mia challenged.

"Same could be said for you. Do we need to talk about the goldfish toilet bowl rescue?" Wyatt swiped his finger across his phone screen.

They never needed to discuss goldfish and toilets ever again. "Fine. I'm certain I can pick out more appropriate living centers that your mom would like."

"But you doubt I can choose nonprofits?" Wyatt asked.

"You don't have an open mind," Mia said. "You're biased to your own agenda."

"I could say the same about you," Wyatt challenged.

"I don't have an agenda." At least not one she wanted to share.

"Why didn't you tell me about my mother?" he asked.

"I'm not your mother's informant." Mia covered her inner turmoil with a defensive tone. What had he found out that she'd been privy to? "Uh, she's a grown woman. If she wanted to tell you, she could have."

"My mom likes to tell me what to do with her plants." Wyatt dunked more potato chips in her ranch dressing. "In case you haven't noticed, we don't exactly share."

"You should work on that," Mia suggested.

"It is what it is." Wyatt shrugged and chewed the last bite of his sandwich.

"That's it?" Mia asked. "You accept it? Do nothing to change it?"

"I've tried."

"Not very hard."

"Look, all I'm saying is that you should've told me." Wyatt crumpled up his napkin and dropped it on his empty plate.

But she didn't really know anything for sure. She suspected, but that wasn't the same as knowing. How dare he put her in this position. If he'd only learn to talk to his mother, Mia wouldn't be in the middle. "Helen's an adult with a sound mind, Wyatt. She can do things on her own."

Wyatt grabbed two carrots from her plate and shook them at her. "You should've stopped her."

Mia relaxed her grip on the table. She couldn't have stopped his mother's health blips the past few days if she'd wanted to.

Wyatt continued between bites of carrot. "Or talked her out it."

He wouldn't be casually chomping on her carrots if he suspected she'd withheld medical information about his mom. "How was I supposed to do that?"

"Easy. Tell her no," Wyatt said. "Tell her that she knows nothing about birds and their care. That she can't possibly care for a bird when she can barely take care of herself."

He'd learned about the cockatoo. This she could handle. "But she can take care of herself," Mia challenged. "She is doing just that. Quite well."

"We're living with her."

"But not catering to her every need."

"She hasn't been alone," Wyatt countered. "Even now, Robyn and Nettie are touring her gardens and having lunch with her."

"She can handle herself." Mia stood firm. Helen was fine. Mia wasn't lying to him. Helen and her own mother were where they wanted to be. In their own homes. "You have to believe in her."

"I believe we'll keep her safe while we're

there," he said. "I also believe a pet bird is nothing but a liability."

"Why do you have to be so negative?" Mia asked.

"I'm realistic," he countered. "The bird is one more thing I'll have to deal with."

What he didn't add was: when he checked his mom into an assisted living center. Mia stared at him. "I'm going to prove you wrong about your mom and Daisy."

"Right now, we're going to prove to each other that we can pick nonprofits and locate suitable assisted living centers." Wyatt tossed their plates in the trash and headed toward the car. "Where to first?"

Three hours and five stops later, Wyatt slid into the driver's seat and bumped his fist against Mia's. "I want to move in there."

Mia laughed. "Any place named Bright Heart Sanctuary had to be visited. Can you imagine how your mom could transform their solarium and outdoor garden?"

"She'd have a purpose." Wyatt grinned and started the car. "Like Charlie at the Next Stop—Success Village. He pulled me aside to ask me if he could join our aid work in Africa. Can you believe that?"

Mia had watched Wyatt and Charlie in the corner, their heads together while Wyatt scribbled across a piece of paper. Charlie had grown up in the foster care system and now faced life on his own. Fortunately, Next Stop—Success Village provided Charlie the resources and help to find the right path for him. For a small nonprofit, its impact on every child's life in the program was impressive and touching. It wasn't influencing thousands of lives like her father had often preached art must do to be a success. However, the lives Next Stop touched were forever changed for the better. Mia found something powerful in its message. "What did you tell Charlie?"

"I gave him my phone number and told him I'd talk to my partners about a summer internship as long as he finished his freshman year at the city college." Wyatt turned into the traffic. "We're going to meet up for lunch next week and talk about his degree options."

Surprise widened Mia's eyes behind her sunglasses. Wyatt hadn't hesitated to get involved in Charlie's life. Now he'd leave an impression on Charlie, possibly guide his future in a direction the boy had never considered. Mia had always preferred to remain behind a camera lens and follow her father's lead. Yet she wondered if she shared her passion her way, would she impact someone's life? She wouldn't risk uprooting her mom's entire life.

Her father's plan worked, she just needed to follow it. "Does this mean you're feeling better about local nonprofits and ready to let your mom write a few checks?"

"My perspective has definitely changed." Wyatt reached over and grabbed her hand. "I need to thank you. I couldn't have found those care centers without your eye for the details. I only looked at the quality of the medical care provided without considering the living quality and comforts of the apartments and rooms."

Mia squeezed his hand. "I have to say I liked the window boxes outside the apartments at the Gracious Living Village. I even wanted to get in on their social calendar. Their residents are more active than most twenty-somethings."

Wyatt nodded. "One more stop?"

"Last one on the list." Mia kept her hand inside his, suddenly wanting to hold on to the afternoon and Wyatt.

"We made a good team today." There was nothing confused or bewildered about his tone. Just a matter-of-fact statement.

They were good together. But one day seemed more like a lucky distraction than something to open her heart to and change her direction for. She'd held his hand a few times and shared several lonely nights in his company. Nothing earth-shattering or sweep-her-off-her-feet consuming. But he'd seen her fear and stayed by her side. He'd introduced her to new friends and accepted her into his home. And even encouraged her picture tak-ing, always wanting to scroll through her most recent photographs and pick his favor-ite. But that was nothing more than what a proper friend would do. Eddy had visited her in the hospital and given her the camera after all. Except she'd never wanted to hold Eddy's hand. She'd never wanted to get closer to her friend, whether by sharing secrets or a sofa. She'd never wanted to kiss Eddy like she did Wyatt. She slammed her eyes shut and pressed back into the headrest. She needed more than the pliant leather to knock some sense into herself.

Wyatt turned and checked the navigation on his phone. "I haven't asked how the cham-ber treatments are going."

Mia inhaled, focusing on Wyatt's casual question instead of the not-so-casual quick-ening of her pulse. "I finally figured out how to pop my ears without the technician's as-sistance. I could be done with the sessions as soon as next Friday." There, she'd put a deadline on whatever this was between them.

She'd have no reason to linger in the city without treatments or her documentary. That gave her nine days to kiss Wyatt. She rubbed her free hand across her scrubs, praying Wyatt wouldn't notice her suddenly sweaty palm inside his.

"Can you fly?"

She could kiss. What was wrong with her? "That depends on my doctors. Howard already informed me that I can take the train to the film location for the next documentary. It's in Canada so no planes required." But goodbyes were required.

He nodded and pulled into the parking lot for Still Wagging Sanctuary. "Then everything is coming together for you like you wanted."

"Looks like it." But everyone knew that looks could be deceiving. And she wasn't sure what she wanted. She jumped out of the car and lunged away from Wyatt and her impractical thoughts.

Wyatt held open the door and guided her inside with his hand on her lower back. A sigh left her lips, and she paused. She'd never reacted like this before. She opened and closed her own doors, walked into rooms alone and capable. But she couldn't deny she liked being beside Wyatt as if she was more than his friend. She stepped forward, out of Wyatt's reach, to shake hands with the director of the Still Wagging Sanctuary.

After a tour of the place, Mia suggested they rest for a moment. She sat and invited Bessie, a twelve-year-old beagle, into her lap. "Evie is still with your mom, so we don't need to rush."

"She is?" Wyatt sat across from her, seemingly content to linger awhile longer with the dogs needing new homes.

"They're still working on the perfect location for Daisy's cage and gathering supplies." Mia adjusted Bessie across her legs and used her camera to take a close-up of her sweet face. She shifted the camera to Wyatt, noted his frown and hesitated. "Let your mom have this. It's the happiest I've seen her. Don't ruin that just yet."

"It isn't my mission to make her unhappy." A bulldog bumped into Wyatt's leg and flopped down, content and happy.

Mia clicked, capturing the pair and repeating the director's words from their interview. "Part of senior care is nurturing and loving through every stage, even the difficult ones."

A medium-sized mixed breed with blue eyes like a husky and the floppy ears of a Labrador stretched out along Wyatt's leg. "We're talking about my mom, not an old dog that needs to be rescued from being put down."

But the principle was the same. Helen and Wyatt were still in their difficult stage. "This is about letting your mom rescue a parrot destined for a similar fate. The director mentioned that the owner and senior animal save each other. Maybe it will be the same for your mom and Daisy."

"Daisy? That's the bird's name?" Wyatt stroked one hand over the mutt's stomach and the other over the bulldog's back.

"Fitting, isn't it?" The mutt's smile from Wyatt's petting pulled out her own.

"Not the word I'd use."

"Let Daisy stay until after the party." Mia clicked more pictures. She'd ask the director if she'd like them for their website. "If bird caring proves too stressful for your mom, we can return Daisy to Sophie's store." She had no idea if Sophie had a return policy on pets. And she also knew Sophie wasn't equipped to keep a parrot like Daisy.

Wyatt coaxed a basset hound with a limp over to him as if building a dog barrier to block out Mia and her bird support.

"It's only two days away," Mia added. "Daisy arrives Saturday. She can be returned to the store first thing Monday morning if needed."

"You'll take care of the return?" Wyatt asked.

"Me?" Mia lowered the camera.

"I've crushed her enough."

"But you're the one who wants the bird gone."

"You agree with me. It's too much right now."

Mia shook her head. "I only ever agreed to your idea of a backup plan."

"But you liked the Gracious Living Village," Wyatt said. "You even wanted to get in on their social events."

"That doesn't mean I think your mom should move in there tomorrow." If it was Mia's choice, she'd allow both of their moms to remain in their own homes until they decided to move. "Stop trying to get me on your side."

"What happened to the good team we made?"

They'd only ever been on opposing teams. Sure, they'd been on the same side today, but that fit their own agendas. Teams had the same goals, worked together to achieve them. Wyatt and Mia had different goals, and if they worked together, one of them would lose.

CHAPTER THIRTEEN

WYATT WASHED THE empty shrimp platter, soaked the chicken casserole dish and cleared the last of the dinner things from the kitchen table. The dessert tasting would commence as soon as he located Mia and his mother. The three of them had spent the day prepping food, cleaning the house for Daisy's homecoming party and arguing over the details for the dessert taste-off.

Wyatt suggested placing name cards in front of each dessert and letting everyone write down their favorite on a piece of paper. Simple and easy. Mia and his mom had nixed that idea, then concocted an elaborate plan on how to number the dishes and cast votes, claiming no dessert would have an unfair advantage.

The preparations had continued into the afternoon with more laughter and more ideas about napkin color, plastic or china and formal seating or free-for-all. The afternoon swept into the evening with the arrival of their guests and the donning of their hosts' hats. The three of them had maneuvered through the kitchen, prepping platters and fixing drinks as if they'd been entertaining friends and family together for years. The air of loneliness inside the house had been replaced with welcoming hugs, shared laughter and caring friends. And with the night's arrival the harmony continued.

The gift for the hosts was books, pamphlets and printed pages of bird advice all attached to a bird accessory. Wyatt shook his head at the counter overflowing with bird snacks, bells, ropes and other toys. He paused in the doorway leading to the sun porch, sipped his drink and felt his smile reach into his eyes. Friends filled the house, not needy neighbors, but people genuinely interested in his mom, her gardens and her welfare.

His mother sat on the sofa between Evie and Sophie. Brad, Sophie's fiancé, waited in the corner, his hand resting on the fifty-two-inch black metal birdcage on wheels. Sophie read instructions from her notepad about proper placement and wheel locks. Brad shifted the cage toward the windows and earned protests from all three women. Brad scratched his head and scanned the room as if looking for the nearest emergency exit.

Dan stepped in from the gardens and Brad pounced, calling Ava's partner over for assistance, or perhaps Brad wanted to shore up his defense against the women's determination to build the perfect home for Daisy. Brad positioned Dan on the other side of the cage then noticed Wyatt. "We could use your help, Doc."

The desperation in Brad's voice made Wyatt return to the kitchen and grab another drink. He handed the cold drink to Brad. "I've got host duties to see to. The dessert challenge won't set itself up." Wyatt toasted both Brad and Dan with his glass. "Besides, you guys look like you have everything under control here."

"That's convenient." Dan grabbed Wyatt's drink and finished the rest in one swallow.

Wyatt punched Dan on the shoulder and headed toward the door leading to the gardens. "What kind of host would I be if I shirked my duties?"

"There's usually payback for this," Dan called out.

Brad nodded in agreement. "Something like you have to host the next poker night."

"Or get tickets to the baseball game," Dan suggested.

Brad nudged Dan with his elbow. "For the doubleheader."

"I'll see what I can do." And he meant it. Wyatt stepped outside, realizing his mother wasn't the only one with new friends. The laughter and happiness in the air blended easily and seamlessly with the scent of his mother's gardenias and jasmine plants. He paused on the pavers leading into the garden and rubbed his chest, wondering why everything seemed to feel right inside him. Wondering how he could hold on to the feeling a little while longer.

Maybe it was the way the gardens lit up as if the plants had been sprinkled with stardust. He'd heard his mom tell Mia she wanted the garden to be a place to wish upon the stars and believe in the impossible. If he believed in magic, he'd be looking for the person who cast the spell over the house for the evening and ask if he could bottle some of that magic. He stared at his empty hand and decided there must've been something in his drink. It was the only explanation for what had come over him and generated such out-of-character thoughts. As if he ever believed in magic and fairy tales.

He wound around the path and stumbled. Lights inside the fountain cast their own spell over the private hideaway and the scene before him. Mia was settled back behind her camera, drawing laughter from Ava and the adorable Ella. The little girl's innocent laughter a reminder of the joy that had once bounced around the house from him and his brother. For the first time, a memory didn't sour his stomach, but instead comforted. He liked the idea that there could be laughter and lightness and happiness in the house again.

Eddy stepped up beside Wyatt. "Too bad we couldn't grab Mia's camera and capture her in this moment."

Wyatt didn't need a camera. The image of Mia teasing and hugging Ella was already imprinted on his mind in Technicolor. "That's the problem with photographers. They're usually behind the camera, not in front of it."

Eddy captured a photograph with his phone. "Her dad used to have the same look of total absorption when he worked."

Wyatt studied Mia. Her hair absorbed the night, shimmering with the reflection of the tea lights hanging above her head. A softness covered her face, lightness floated in her laughter. Even her movements were graceful, other than favoring her left leg to relieve pressure on her right side. She seemed to embrace every piece of the moment. "I didn't think Mr. Fiore worked stills."

"He didn't," Eddy said. "He looked like Mia does now whenever he filmed. Consumed and enraptured."

"Must be a strong family trait," Wyatt said.

"Except, Mia never looks like that when she's on a film shoot." Eddy nudged a pebble off the paver.

"Maybe she hid it better," Wyatt suggested. He wasn't sure why he felt compelled to protect her, and from Eddy of all people.

"I'd have seen it at least once, right?" Eddy stepped to the side, tipped his head as if he struggled to understand the meaning behind a priceless work of art. "There's something about her tonight that my wife would say is… unforgettable."

Wyatt took another long look at Mia. She'd covered her sky-blue sundress with a floral wrap. The sheer fabric floated around her knees, revealing her bare feet. Forgetting Mia and this evening was going to be a problem. "Maybe it's that you haven't seen her in something other than a hospital gown or scrubs for the past few weeks."

"It's more than her clothes." Eddy tugged on his curly hair as if trying to put the night back in its proper place. "Tell me you don't see it?"

Wyatt saw more than he'd ever admit. He forced his gaze away from Mia's bare feet, dancing around the fountain. "Have you seen the final cut of the documentary?"

"Mia never mentioned that she finished it." Eddy frowned and tucked his phone away in his back pocket.

"I assumed it was done, since it's due Monday," Wyatt said.

"That's earlier than the original contract," Eddy said.

"She mentioned something to do with Howard and the negotiations for the next contracts," Wyatt said.

Eddy nodded. "Howard makes his living on overcommitting. Still I never thought Mia would let us walk away so easily."

Once again Wyatt defended Mia as if she needed his protection. "She's had a lot to deal with between her father's death and her accident."

"That's usually when you rely on your friends the most." Disappointment was evident in Eddy's voice and face.

Wyatt grabbed Eddy's shoulder. "You're here now. Maybe you should make it hard for her to turn her back on you now."

"Is that your plan?" Eddy asked.

He rather enjoyed the idea of imprinting himself on Mia's brain so that she couldn't simply walk away this time. Nothing was the same between them as it had been two years ago. Hearts and careers were never at stake. Not like now. He had no plans when it came to Mia. Except to erase the image of her dancing around the fountain from his mind. But it was like a tattoo, permanent and lasting, etched in colored ink. "I promised my mom I'd help get dessert ready."

"Did you mention dessert?" The thrill in Ella's voice caught everyone's attention.

Wyatt faced the fountain. "I did. It's time to get our brownie tasting under way."

"I cannot wait for this." Ella picked up her walking stick from the bench. "But I'm worried I'll like them all."

Wyatt moved to Ella's side and touched her arm. "You can like all of the brownies, you just need to like mine the best."

Ella giggled and set her hand on Wyatt's arm. "I already promised my dad I'd pick his."

"He doesn't need to know we have an arrangement." Wyatt guided Ella back to the house. "If you pick mine, I'll give you all of the leftovers to take home."

Mia stepped up to Wyatt's other side and

snapped a photograph of Wyatt and Ella together. "No cheating, Dr. Reid."

"This is a private conversation between Ella and me," Wyatt said.

Mia sprinted ahead, her bare feet floating over the pavers, her happiness wrapping around him.

Ella covered her mouth with her free hand, but her smile spread beyond her fingers. "Can I really have the leftovers?"

"Absolutely," Wyatt said.

"Then you need to tell me which one is your dessert," Ella whispered.

Wyatt sighed. "Mia will be mad at me if I cheat."

"You don't want that." Ella straightened, alarm raising her voice. "She might not take your picture anymore."

"I don't like pictures all that much," Wyatt confessed.

"Pictures are the best. They freeze time." Ella tugged on his arm. "And then you get to revisit that time whenever you want. I make pictures in my mind all the time. Then if I'm sad, I just look through my mind and visit my happy pictures."

"What if Mia won't share her pictures with me?" Wyatt whispered back.

Ella tapped her forehead. "Then you just have to make your own like me."

He wanted to share in Ella's innocence. To store every moment in his mind's photo album to revisit again and again. Yet he feared his memories of Mia might be best if they were forgotten, if only for the sake of his sanity and the protection of his heart. A heart he never intended to open.

Chocolate decadence consumed his thoughts for the next hour. The leftovers dwindled as the debates over the best dessert streamed through the house. The salted caramel took the dark chocolate to another level. The hot skillet transformed the brownie. The marshmallow fluff altered the fudge to whatever surpassed decadent. Minds changed as often as samples remained on the serving plates. The only real consensus after the last sample disappeared was that despite their mutual overindulging, they all agreed the only true way to discover the best was to schedule another taste-off. Goodbyes followed after calendars were consulted and a date penciled in.

Wyatt kept to his promise and sent Ella home with a secret take-out package of every dessert. He'd filled it while Mia had explained the rules of the taste-off and his mom had handed out plates and forks. He'd earned himself a new ally for the next taste-off, or so Ella had whispered to him when she'd hugged him goodbye. All in all the evening was a success, but like all good things it had to come to an end.

Wyatt stepped onto the porch, carrying two wineglasses. Mia turned from Daisy's cage and pressed her finger over her lip. A light blanket covered the parrot's cage and only silence surrounded the bird's new cottage, as Evie and his mom called it. Mia opened the door into the garden and stepped into the night, holding two plates with cheese and crackers.

Mia dropped onto the bench beside the fountain. "Sorry, I didn't want to disturb Daisy."

"Because that's now a thing." Wyatt picked up the small wrought iron table and set it in front of the bench for the wineglasses.

"She needs to learn when the house goes to bed, she goes to sleep." Mia balanced her plate on her good leg.

He needed to learn not to get so close to Mia that he could see the copper tint in her amber eyes. Beautiful eyes. "You can't expect me to accommodate a bird's sleeping schedule."

"You just did." She toasted him with her wineglass.

No, he'd accommodated Mia because of the night magic and how she'd looked—sincere and genuinely concerned about a parrot. And because he wanted to know if she'd ever be that concerned about him. He considered dunking his head in the fountain, wondering if the cold bath would clear his thoughts.

Last week he knew exactly what he wanted. Today, everything seemed rearranged like a patient's intestines after abdominal surgery. Now he had to put everything back in its place. End the night and disconnect the magic like turning off the TV. They'd given his mother one lovely evening in her house, a memory to take with her. He'd walked the house without the familiar loneliness beside him for one night. That was enough. "How do you plan to return that cage?"

"Excuse me?"

"Daisy's fifty-two-inch cage won't fit inside my mom's car." Wyatt sat beside her, setting his own plate on the small wrought iron table beside the bench. "I don't think it folds down like a traveling kennel."

"Good thing I'm not putting it in the car." Mia layered a cracker with cheese and added a second tier, lining the cracker edges up.

Wyatt tried to line things up as well to be stored back where they belonged. To set his world back in place. "But you're returning Daisy on Monday."

"That was only if Daisy proved too much for your mom." Mia lowered her cheese and cracker stack to her plate.

"It's too much." Wyatt stared out into the garden. If he looked at Mia, she'd entice him to lower his guard. She'd tempt him to change his mind. To change his world.

"You can't decide that after one day," Mia argued. "Daisy was singing tonight. Your mom was relaxed and happy."

"My mom is exhausted," Wyatt said. "She barely made it down the hall to her room."

"But she hummed the whole way," Mia said. "She deserves to be tired tonight. I'm tired tonight."

He was tired, too. Tired of wanting the impossible. Tired of fighting. "Daisy has to go back to Sophie's."

"Why must you change everything?" she demanded.

The harsh scrape of her voice scratched like claws against his resolve.

She sharpened her attack. "Why must you force your mother out of the home she shared with her husband? The home she raised you in. The home she finds comfort and security in. Why must you ruin her life?"

Wyatt jumped up and paced around the fountain, plugging the holes she'd pierced in his emotional armor. His mom had destroyed everything first: his childhood home, his relationship with her, his memories of Trent. "I have to know if my mom needs help, it's there for her in that instant. Right when she needs it most. Not ten minutes later when it's already too late."

Mia rose from the bench and stood beside him at the fountain. "How long was it before you discovered Trent's body?"

How was it that she read him so well? How was it possible that he let her expose him? Wyatt stared into the water. The image of his face blurred into that of his brother's. "I was a resident, no set schedules. Endless hours. No sleep, except the few hours snatched here and there. I loved it."

Mia grabbed his hand, her shoulder brushing against his. The water rippled, dispersing his image, flooding his present with the past.

He studied their joined hands, his anchor to the present. The perfect fit. But perfect never really existed. "Trent had come over to ask my mom for money. He knew she'd give it to him. She always did after making him promise he'd use it for food. It was past midnight. I'd just crashed in the bedroom, trying to catch a few hours of sleep before my morning shift. I never heard anything."

Mia grasped his upper arm with her free hand, as if he needed more support.

He inhaled and dropped his head back, searched for a star in the night sky. But wishes were useless. "If she'd woke me up, I might've been able to keep Trent at the house until he sobered up. Instead I noticed the leftovers from dinner were gone when I got up. Mom never eats after she goes to bed. I'm the only late-night snack eater in the family. I stopped by Trent's apartment on my way to work. The coroner estimated his time of death to be between five and five thirty in the morning. I arrived at five forty-seven. What if he'd called for help? What if I hadn't hit the snooze button? What if Mom woke me? What if I treated him like a patient and not my brother? What if I hadn't listened to Mom and taken his pain meds away like I threatened to do a month before his death?"

"Stop." Mia faced him and put her hand over his mouth. "You need to stop tormenting yourself like this."

This was what happened when he stopped. All those what-ifs assaulted him and dragged him into an abyss of endless misery. How could he ever stop running? He closed his eyes and let the warmth from her hand chase the chill of the past from his skin.

But the what-ifs hadn't ended with Trent. Another series revolved around Mia.

There was one he could answer right now. He reached up, pulled her hand away from his mouth and brushed a kiss across her palm. Her fingers curled in as if she wanted to capture his touch, hold it there forever. He kissed her wrist, watched her lips part, heard her soft inhale. He ran his hands over her neck, up into her hair, and tugged her forward. This time he held nothing back.

His mouth covered hers, and together they fell into the kiss. He lost himself to everything but the touch of Mia's skin under his palms and the taste of her. The scent of the night-time garden and the sound of the waterfall cocooned them in the moment. He wanted to settle in and never come back out.

Still, he slowed, pulled away to drop a last kiss on her lips, then her forehead before folding her into his embrace. He held her until his heart stopped racing and his breath evened out. Then he held on because he wanted to. Because she felt like she belonged right there, in his arms.

She yawned against his chest yet curled in closer against him.

He tipped her chin toward him, kissed her again. Only this time quietly and easily, as if they had all night, instead of minutes. He stopped before he was ready. Knew he'd never be ready. He cupped her cheek and said, "You need to go to bed. Get some rest."

"What about you?" She leaned against him as they strolled back to the house.

"I'll clean up the last bit from the dessert round and then sleep," he said.

"I can help," she offered.

"I'm not asking." He guided her up the stairs into the house and motioned toward the bedrooms. "Good night, Mia."

She turned around, held the palm he'd kissed up to her lips and smiled. "Sweet dreams, Doc."

And then Wyatt knew. Knew that if he dared believe in the magic between them, his heart would never be the same. His life would never be the same.

CHAPTER FOURTEEN

MIA DROPPED HER camera bag and the half dozen fresh white chocolate blueberry scones from Whisk and Whip on the kitchen counter. Helen declared pastries enhanced the flavor of her green tea in the afternoons. Mia declared it a Sunday to celebrate and filled the teakettle to the rim. Mia had so much news to share with Helen, they'd need at least two cups of tea each. Mia hummed, arranged the scones on Helen's favorite serving plate and wished Helen had been with her at Still Wagging Sanctuary.

The director had cried when she'd opened the envelope with the donation from the Reid Family Foundation. Then Mia showed the director her pictures of the senior dogs, and the woman's kind and encouraging words about Mia's talent made Mia cry. The two women bonded over a box of tissue while hanging out with the dogs in the visiting room and selecting their favorite pictures to showcase on the website. That was only the start of Mia's tears. The Next Stop—Success Village partners wept all over their donation check and Mia's shoulder. Then Mia joined five foster kids for lunch and cried over their stories. To top off the morning's success, Eddy called to tell her one of the boatyards with poor pollution control was performing hull work and their heavy metal-contaminated runoff was heading into the bay waters. She'd taken the ferry and arrived in time to gather more footage. Tonight, she'd finish the documentary.

To think, her run of good fortune had started with the perfect kiss last night. In the perfect setting. Wyatt's embrace last night had made her memories from two years ago seem faulty and lacking. The details of her time with Wyatt weren't for sharing over tea. She tucked the evening inside her heart and hoped the next week would guide her in the right direction. She'd leave soon for Canada and more films, and Wyatt would leave soon for Africa. But their kiss had promised more. Mia dared to believe that more might be possible.

She surveyed the table, adjusted the saucers to match Helen's typical table setting and glanced at the clock. She'd expected Helen to come through the door already. Helen deemed teatime sacred and as such not to be late for. Certain Helen discovered a new hybrid that absorbed her attention, Mia set her dial to a low simmer on a back burner. She slowed to greet Daisy and give the bird a walnut shell. "Treats all around today, Daisy."

Mia pushed through the patio door and called out Helen's name. Outside, gardenias, lush greenery and bees greeted her. And silence. Helen never shuffled around the corner, carrying a water can and new bud clipping. Panic rolled through her like the teakettle about to boil.

She hurried toward the greenhouse. Helen's gray head wasn't bobbing in the window.

As she yanked open the greenhouse door, the teakettle boiled over and seared Mia's insides. Helen lay on the floor, her eyeglasses thrown across the brick floor, one lens broken. Only the fans in the corners of the nursery moved back and forth, agitating the air. Pieces of shattered clay pots surrounded Helen. Soil dusted her face, apron and legs. Mia dropped to her knees beside Helen and checked for her pulse.

That sear from the teakettle dimmed at the slow steady beat of Helen's pulse beneath Mia's fingers. Mia whispered a quick prayer of thanks and cradled Helen's limp hand inside her own. "Helen?"

"Mia?" The squint in Helen's gaze matched

her crumpled voice as if she struggled to clear her cluttered senses.

"What happened?" Mia brushed the dirt from Helen's cheek and noticed the cut just below her eye. "You're bleeding. Let me get something."

Helen squeezed Mia's hand. "Stay. I need a minute to take stock."

Mia lowered to the floor, keeping Helen's hand inside hers. "What can I do?"

"This body doesn't fall like it used to." Helen squinted at the ceiling, but her wince collapsed her voice into a wheeze. "Are my toes moving?"

Mia looked at Helen's feet, her toes wiggled inside a pair of fuzzy flamingo socks. "Where are your shoes?"

"Inside. I wanted a few clippings to color the table for tea." Helen lifted her other arm and touched her forehead. "Things are working. That's progress."

"Was something not working?" Mia pressed.

"My head." Helen patted Mia's arm. "It's nothing."

"You're lying on the floor of your greenhouse after you fell and hit your head." Mia stared at Helen's bright flamingo socks. Usually Helen's crazy socks lightened the mood and encouraged smiles. Not today. Mia searched Helen's legs, questioning whether the pink birds hid swelling or a foot fracture. "This isn't nothing."

"I'm sure my eyeglasses suffered the most damage." Helen dabbed her fingers around her eye and winced. "I dropped them when I fell."

"This was a seizure, wasn't it?" Mia rocked back and forth, willing Helen to deny it. If Helen had a seizure, Mia should've told Wyatt last week about her suspicions. Yet she mentioned nothing as if she'd seen nothing. But she'd witnessed Helen faltering and believed Helen's excuses. And she'd kept it all from Wyatt. The same as Helen kept Trent's condition from Wyatt. That teakettle of panic frothed inside her.

"There's no need to tell Wyatt." Helen closed her eyes. Her pinched tone paired with her thinned mouth. "It's just the new medications."

There'd been every need to tell Wyatt. "Those meds are supposed to prevent seizures." Mia scanned Helen's arms, looking for bruising or swelling. "That's what you told me."

"They do."

"Did you forget to take your medicine?" Mia asked.

"No." The cut on Helen's cheek opened at her prodding. "I chose not to take it. It makes me too tired in the afternoons, and I won't give up my teatime. I've so enjoyed our conversations over honeyed green tea and pastries."

Mia pressed the end of her scrubs shirt against Helen's cut, stopping the blood but not the dread spilling through her. Helen stopped her medication to spend time with Mia. It really was all Mia's fault, but she'd deal with Wyatt later. Helen's blood soaked through Mia's shirt, commanding all of her focus. "We need to get you to the hospital."

"Let's get me sitting up for starters."

Mia braced Helen around her shoulders and helped her sit.

"Nothing to it." The pallor had settled back into Helen's cheeks. "I'm perfectly fine. The hospital can't do anything for me that I can't do here."

Except Helen swayed, covered her eyes with her palm and fell against Mia for support. Even Helen's fragile weight caused stabs of pain through Mia's wounded leg. She clenched her teeth against the throbbing and fumbled to get her phone out of her pocket without bumping her injured arm or jostling Helen too much.

"I won't arrive by ambulance," Helen whispered. "Wyatt will have me admitted to a nursing home before sunrise. I can't abandon my family. You understand."

Mia cringed, accepting the truth in Helen's words. But looking at the older woman splayed out on the brick floor, she considered Wyatt's argument. Perhaps Helen wasn't safe at her home. Yet moving her would cause a wound deeper than any fall. Mia shook herself. All she understood for certain was that she needed help. Fast. "You'll go if there's no ambulance."

Helen nodded against Mia's shoulder.

Ten minutes and several SOS texts and two voice mails later, Ava sprinted into the greenhouse. Five minutes after Ava finished her evaluation, Eddy leaned through the doorway. "Any blood?"

"Only my pride covered in dirt," Helen mumbled.

Eddy stepped inside and rubbed his palms across his thighs. "Dirt I can definitely do."

Ava glanced at Mia. "Open the back-passenger door. Eddy and I will carry Helen out to the car."

"You most certainly will not." Helen's bottom lip stiffened.

"Mrs. Reid, we don't know if you've rein-jured your hip," Ava explained.

"Then we need to test it out," Helen said. "It's the only way we'll know."

Ava said, "This isn't protocol."

"I'm almost seventy years old, my dear." Helen patted Ava's cheek. "I've earned the right to ignore protocol."

"But Wyatt…" Ava said.

Helen cut her off. "My son can walk beside me inside the ER."

Eddy nudged several pieces of the shattered pots under the workbench with his boot. Mia cleared the sharp pieces from around her and Helen.

Ava finally nodded. "We'll help you stand, Mrs. Reid, and take it from there." She mo-tioned to Eddy to move behind Helen. Her orders consisted of a series of silent hand movements and one stern look. Eddy gave a firm thumbs-up and planted himself behind Helen. Satisfied, Ava directed Mia to the front with another series of hand motions.

"Mrs. Reid, I'm on your right." Ava wrapped her arm around Helen's waist. "And Eddy has your left." Eddy curved his arm just beneath Helen's thin shoulders. "On three, we're going up."

Helen unfolded inside Ava's and Eddy's

arms. Dirt floated off her apron and dusted her flamingo socks. Helen's dry lips refused to stretch into a convincing smile. "Nothing to it."

But her body tilted, her head wobbling on her neck like a buoy in the ocean. Mia held up her hands, prepared to catch the frail woman. She needn't have bothered. Ava and Eddy shifted their holds, accepting Helen's weight and steadying her.

Helen blinked at Mia. "Aren't you supposed to be opening the car door?"

Mia scratched her head and glanced at Ava, waiting for her nod. "There's a gate on the side of the house. It's farther away from the driveway, but it's flat."

Eddy adjusted Helen's arm around his waist and edged in closer. "You really do have a secret garden, Mrs. Reid."

"I planted the trumpet vine along the path and gate years ago." Helen's head rolled toward Eddy's shoulder. "It's quite lovely now."

Mia held open the greenhouse door for the threesome. Eddy and Ava supported Helen, lifting her off the ground. Helen's toes barely skimmed the pavers, although she stepped as if walking on her own. Mia sprinted ahead and opened the gate before rushing back inside the house to turn off the stove burner and grab her purse, Helen's go-bag and a bag of frozen peas from the freezer.

The go-bag she stuffed on the floor in the front seat before climbing into the back beside Helen. Eddy handed the keys to Ava and got in on the other side.

Mia wrapped the frozen peas in a hand towel. "This is for your cheek." And maybe the swelling would go down before they went inside the ER and ran into Wyatt.

"I'm not sure what all the fuss is about." Helen brushed her hair into place with her fingers, but a tremor rattled through her body. "I took a bit of a tumble, but I'm upright and talking."

Ava swung into the street, maneuvering through the traffic like a New York taxicab driver without the two-wheeled corners and jarring swerves and horn blasting.

"We should've had tea, Mia." Helen patted Mia's leg as if she was the injured one. "We weren't very welcoming to our guests."

Mia pressed the frozen peas against Helen's cheek. "Next time."

"Tomorrow, Ava and Eddy, we'll have proper tea and act like proper hosts." Helen rested her hands in her lap, limp and fragile and weak. She shifted toward Mia. "Could you cover the two plates of croissants? Otherwise they won't be fresh. There are two."

But Helen held up four fingers, and they'd finished the croissants last week. Ava met Mia's gaze in the rearview mirror.

Mia curled Helen's hand inside her own. "I'll take care of it."

Ava accelerated and sped around a city bus, then cut off a car in the oncoming lane to turn left. The neon blue Bay Water Medical Center sign highlighted the building that stretched across two city blocks. The bright red ER arrow pointed down a one-way street. Ava weaved around several blocks in less than sixty seconds and stopped the car at the main ER entrance.

Eddy leaned over and grabbed Ava's wrist, looking at her watch. "Do you have one of those sensors on your watch that turns stoplights from red to green? Can a normal person get one of those, too?"

Ava laughed. "Sorry to disappoint you."

"We never hit one red light." Eddy climbed out of the car. "Not one."

"I got lucky." Ava shrugged, jogged inside the sliding doors and returned with a wheelchair.

"Impressive." Eddy shook his head. "Really

impressive. Can you teach me your tricks? My wife is due in less than two months."

Ava rolled the wheelchair toward the car. Eddy opened the passenger door. "Or maybe I could just call you to drive us."

Ava laughed. "There won't be blood until the actual delivery."

Helen frowned from inside the car. "Eddy looks like he needs that wheelchair more than me."

Mia patted her friend's shoulder. "You still have lots of time. And I promised I'd be there with the camera to document every precious moment."

Eddy leaned his head inside the car. "Helen, you won't be offended if I kiss you here and wish you well, will you?"

"You're a dear, Eddy." Helen pressed her cheek against his. "We'll be there when that baby decides to make its arrival. Now help me into that chair. I'm not up for battling Ava. She's seems rather determined."

Eddy grinned. "You're going to be fine, Mrs. Reid."

"I know that." Helen accepted his assistance into the wheelchair. "Could you explain it to these young ladies?"

Mia grabbed the frozen peas, wanting to press them against her own head. She'd have to face Wyatt now. How was she going to explain what happened? What was she going to tell him?

The page for Dr. Reid erupted in the waiting area as soon as Helen's wheelchair rolled past the sliding doors as if the chair had triggered a silent alarm. Ava moved to talk to the triage nurse. Mia rolled Helen to the waiting area and dropped into a chair beside Helen.

Helen touched Mia's arm. "He won't blame you, dear. This was my fault."

And Mia's fault for not watching over Helen more closely. Questions skipped through her mind like a movie set on fast-forward. She never should've been gone for so long. She should've called and checked in more often. She'd have gone straight home when Helen didn't answer her last call. But she'd assumed Helen lost track of time in her gardens. Helen had been doing so well. Improving with every day. Helen had encouraged her to concentrate on her film instead of watching over her.

She'd wanted those symptoms to be nothing. Wanted Helen to remain in her home. Wanted Wyatt not to worry. She hadn't wanted to give Wyatt any reason to move Helen into an assisted living center. Now he had all the reasons he needed to check Helen in tomorrow. Mia worried she couldn't protect Helen any longer from the inevitable. She couldn't protect herself either.

Mia pressed the bag of frozen peas against Helen's cheek, below her eye. "He isn't going to be happy when he sees your face."

"Then he'll need to look someplace else." Helen lifted her chin, but her grimace ruined her bravado.

The double doors swung wide and Wyatt emerged. His intense cool gaze pinned Mia in place as if simultaneous high-watt spotlights flooded her. He then found someplace else to look.

Mia's stomach dropped out as if she stood inside an elevator that plunged to the basement.

Wyatt leaned down and kissed his mom. "I'm here to take you back, Mom. The doctors are going to need to run some tests."

Helen patted his cheek. "Whatever makes you feel better."

"I didn't order the tests, Mom." He squatted down in front of her wheelchair. "Right now, I'm just your son. You have a care team ready to treat you, and they're calling the shots."

Wyatt straightened and looked at Mia. Tension angled his jaw and locked his movements. The air stiffened into a brittle silence between them. The condemnation in his flat, cold gaze buckled her knees. He gripped the handles on Helen's wheelchair, turning his knuckles white, then pushed his mom away, taking every unspoken wish in her heart with him.

Mia collapsed into the chair. What was she supposed to do now? She didn't want Helen to be alone in the hospital. Wyatt's shift wouldn't end for several more hours. He'd never let her back there to be with Helen. Mia wasn't family. She wasn't anyone special. She clutched her hands together, seeking something to hold. She didn't want to be alone either.

She cursed Wyatt. Blamed him for making her care. She'd never wanted any of this. Never wanted normal and routine. Her father had told her that she'd have to sacrifice. She'd just never really believed she'd have to sacrifice her own heart.

CHAPTER FIFTEEN

MIA SCRAPED THE last of the broken clay pots onto the dustpan and tossed the pieces into the trash. The evening primrose seeds rested in a row of new pots on the workbench, waiting for Helen's specific instructions for the seedlings' care. The fans no longer tossed the loose dirt from the workbench to the floor in fairy-sized funnels. The solar mosaic glass globes lit the pathways through the gardens and the door-way to the greenhouse. The sleepless only needed to follow the glow from the solar wil-low tree to the bench in the far corner to make a wish in the fountain. Helen's backyard fairy tale was set to rights.

Except Helen wasn't there to point out the night blooms of the moonflower or pluck the ray floret from the chocolate daisy to release its scent into the evening air.

Helen rested in a hospital bed at Bay Water Medical. Mia walked the gardens alone, trapped in Mother Nature's embrace. Yet emptiness entwined her like an invasive weed.

The door on the porch swung open and Wyatt appeared on the top stair. His focus fixed on Mia like a master gardener discovering poison ivy among his prized gardenias. He looked as if he wanted to yank Mia from the garden and toss her in the debris pile.

"I'm almost finished cleaning up." Mia spun around, seeking shelter in the greenhouse.

The greenhouse door never bounced shut behind her. Mia rolled her shoulders, breathed in the lavender to calm herself and stared at the juniper outside the window for strength. She kept her back to the entrance and asked, "How's Helen?"

"Sleeping."

The scratch in Wyatt's voice scraped across her skin like thorns. Mia rubbed her arms. "And the tests?"

"Normal so far."

Mia closed her eyes and gave thanks to whoever might be listening up in the night sky. "She'll be home tomorrow. That's good. She'll like that."

"Did you know?"

Mia pressed her arms into her ribs as those thorns burrowed deep into her bones. "She only told me tonight she'd stopped taking her medicine."

"But did you know?" Wyatt's hand flattened against her arm.

Mia flinched. She turned to face him, stumbling back two steps to put more than a whisper between them. "I didn't check her pill case. Count the pills in every bottle."

Wyatt thrust both hands into his hair as if trying to grab onto one of the chaotic emotions storming through his slate gaze. "You knew her seizures had returned."

Mia jammed her hands into the back pockets of her borrowed scrubs, her gaze avoiding Wyatt, landing on the clean workbench. When had it become so messy between them? "Helen told me the tiredness, the dizziness was nothing to worry about."

"You should've told me." Accusation dripped through his voice.

"Why? So you could worry more?" Mia grimaced. "Or admit her to a nursing home so you could leave sooner."

He shifted his weight from one foot to the other as if preparing to deflect her next attack. "Where were you when she fell?"

"I had a business meeting." Mia held his gaze, searching for something beyond the anger and the blame. "And Helen had checks for the foundation she wanted me to hand-deliver."

"Neither one of you listen. Ever," Wyatt accused. "You both need keepers."

"But it won't be you." Mia backed into the workbench, the hard wood bracing her spine. "After all you have more important obligations in Africa."

"My life is in Africa," he corrected.

"And your mother's life is here. In this house." Mia squeezed the workbench behind her, reinforcing the conviction in her voice. "This is the only place she can find peace from her demons. Don't you recognize what those plants are?"

"Overgrown." Wyatt crossed his arms over his chest.

"That's her grief. That's the pain of a mother losing her son too soon. That's the life she couldn't give to her son." Mia thrust her arm out and pointed toward the gardens, wanting to thrust the understanding into Wyatt. How could he not see the truth? "She was a house mom without a job to return to. Without a husband or kids to nurture. She nurtured those plants. Built a sanctuary to surround her, distract her, love her."

His shoulders rolled forward as if he body-blocked her words. "I love her."

"From a distance," Mia challenged. "On your terms."

"I've made a difference in Africa in numerous lives."

"You've built a distraction. A sanctuary. A place to retreat from your pain." Mia stopped from reaching for him. She wanted to shake him and hold him. To yell at him for abandoning his mom and to soothe his own grief. "The very same as your mom."

"We aren't the same." He shook his head as if preventing the truth from taking root inside him.

"How many plants will your mom need to save and grow to make up for not being able to save her son?" Mia shoved away from the workbench and stepped into his space. Maybe he'd hear her now. "When will you have saved enough patients to make up for not saving your brother and stop running from your family and your own roots?"

"Don't come at me about roots." He stared her down, a sneer curved across his mouth. Disdain coated his voice. "What does the wanderlust soul know about roots?"

"You make it sound like I was born with this insatiable need to travel." She lifted her chin, copied his contempt with her own. "I could settle if I chose to."

"Not according to your father," Wyatt said.

"Claimed it was a disservice to the world to contain a soul like yours."

"This has nothing to do with my dad." Mia crossed her arms over her chest, but refused to step away.

"It's always been about your dad." He pressed his finger into her chest, right over her heart. "It's never been about you. It's never been about what *you* want. Who *you* want to be. What *you* want to do."

She'd always known when her dad had been alive. He'd been her anchor. Now she was all twisted up, questioning everything she'd once known. Everything she'd once wanted. Everything she'd used to want to become. She longed to scream for someone, anyone to tell her who she was. Who she was supposed to be. "You make me forget who I am."

"You only need to be yourself." The edge shifted out of his tone, out of his body. "It's enough."

"No, you don't get it. I'm not enough," Mia said. Her father had doubted her up until his death. He'd have listened to her advice on that final shoot if he'd believed in her. Then he'd made her vow on her life that she'd continue his legacy. And she'd promised. She'd almost died in San Francisco Bay because she'd made him a promise. She'd only wanted her father's love.

"You'll kill yourself trying to get approval from your father's ghost, and still you won't get it," Wyatt said. "You have to love yourself as much as you loved your father. You have to love yourself enough to live your own life, trust in your own art and believe in your own vision."

"I believed just fine before I came to San Francisco." Before the accident. Before Wyatt saved her life. Before she listened to her heart. "This isn't real. Ten days inside four sterile hospital walls and a few weeks here pretending I belonged in your mother's home." Mia pointed toward the door. "But out there is the real world. Out there is my real life. The life I chose."

"That's the life your father chose for you." Wyatt's words landed between them like stones, relentless and hard. "It's your turn now, Mia, to choose the life you want."

Hadn't he been listening? She didn't know what she wanted. Her heart called her a liar. A coward.

What if she reached for Wyatt in this moment? Would he walk away like she'd walked away from him? How could she trust in love? She'd loved her father, and that had never been enough for him to love her in return. She couldn't take the risk with Wyatt, and so she ran. She ran even though she never moved an inch past the evening primrose seedlings. "Are you going to let your mom choose the life she wants, too?"

"It isn't the same thing." He scowled at her. "Stop deflecting."

She pushed back at him again. He'd already pushed her too far into the dirt for her to come out clean. "When has wanting to live out your final days in your home become a bad idea?"

"That home no longer exists," Wyatt said. "The past needs to stay in the past where it belongs."

"Yet you've never dealt with your past. Your guilt won't release you from the past. Until you let it go, you won't ever be truly free."

"You can lecture me when you've stepped up and done the very same thing."

They'd thrown their sticks and stones at each other. Ripped each other bare. There was nothing more for Mia to lose. "And us? Are we better in the past, too?"

"We're leavers, Mia. It's what we do. What we've always done." He flicked his hand between them. "Why pretend this isn't going to end the same?"

"Who says I've been pretending?" But he had. She saw it now. He'd told her to choose the life she wanted. That it was her turn. But he never expected her to choose him. He never expected to have to accept her heart.

"What happens after you finish your film?" he asked.

"With luck, another three-film contract."

"That means more planes and more new countries and no roots." Wyatt circled his arm above their heads, encompassing the house and the gardens with the motion. "And not this. Never this."

"The same goes for you." Mia hooked her fingers around her neck, her palm covering her heart and the ache slicing open inside her. "Or have you decided to choose this over Africa?"

"I've always been headed back to Africa." His face looked more like a wall. "Once my mom is settled into a safer place, it's wheels up."

That ache cracked wide inside her, threatening to yank her into the dark emptiness. There never really was a choice. Not when it came to Wyatt and his heart and his love. "So this is it, then?"

Wyatt nodded.

"You're right. This was all about pretending," Mia said. "Once again, you can convince yourself you tried and move on as the injured party. Except you never intended to try, not now. Not in Africa. Because you never intended to ever give up your heart. You never intended to open yourself up to love."

Mia shoved him in the chest to get around him and to feel if there was even a heart beating inside him. She called herself every kind of fool. She'd considered settling with Wyatt. Putting down roots. She was a fool for believing she could ever be enough. That her love alone could ever be enough.

Mia stopped at the doorway and turned to face Wyatt. "You're excellent at fixing other people, Dr. Reid, but a failure at healing yourself."

THE GREENHOUSE DOOR slammed shut along with everything inside Wyatt. He'd lost his perspective, let his guard down and opened his heart. He'd been too wrapped up in the joy Mia infused into the house. He'd been too occupied believing wishes could come true. He'd been sidelined by the idea of the family he could have. And he'd missed the signs his mother had been hiding from him. Shutting himself away again was the only way to keep those he loved safe.

No matter. Nothing had been permanent. Mia had only ever been a temporary disruption in his world. She'd shown him what they could never have. Neither one was willing to put their heart up for the bargaining. He'd told her in the hospital they made the perfect match.

He shoved open the greenhouse door and strode along the stone path to the gate. He skipped going through the house, knew instinctively Mia was already gone. He headed back to the one place he'd only ever really belonged: the hospital, where his mom was spending the night.

CHAPTER SIXTEEN

WYATT CLOSED THE door to his room and avoided looking down the hall at the other bedroom. He knew the bed was empty. Knew Mia's clothes were gone. He didn't need to step inside her room to confirm anything. He knew because the very air had been stripped of her presence, her joy. A heaviness had settled over the house as if even the walls mourned her departure.

She'd been gone less than a day. No doubt he'd suffocate by the end of the week without her.

He strode through the house, dropped a shelled walnut in Daisy's cage and finally inhaled out on the patio. His mother sat at the wrought iron table, her head tipped toward the sky, a quiet look on her face as if she soaked up the garden's energy to heal her bruised face. She'd passed every test: no internal bleeding, no broken bones, no displacement of her hip, giving her doctors no reason to keep her another day in the hospital. His mother hadn't required twenty-four-hour observation, but clearly, Wyatt had.

For the thousandth time, he told himself it was all for the best.

He placed a pot on the table in front of his mother. The withered and shriveled stem lay limp against the dehydrated dirt. "I warned you not to trust me with one of your grafted plants." Just like he'd warned himself not to let his heart out of lockdown.

His mom picked up the pot and tossed it into the trash can beside her chair. "I've learned after all these years that it can be best to cut your losses sometimes."

What happened to his mother? He searched her face for disappointment or anger. He'd failed her again. Wyatt yanked the pot out of the trash can. "Every single one of your plants is precious and important."

"Yes, they are." She returned her attention to the album and pictures she'd scattered around the table when he'd first brought her home that morning. "But sometimes letting go of the old ones can make room for new growth."

Wyatt hugged the pot.

"Toss it out." She sorted the photographs into piles.

"You can't be serious?" he asked.

She adjusted the brim of her hat to better shade her eyes and studied Wyatt. "That plant is about my twentieth failure at grafting peach and Asian plum. I hadn't really expected it to live."

"That would've been useful information to have weeks ago." Wyatt shot the pot back into the garbage can like a winning basketball shot.

"You'd have ignored it and not bothered to try if I told you." Helen pointed her scissors at him. "There's nothing ever wasted in the effort."

"Except time that might've been spent on something else." Anything else in Wyatt's mind. But he'd never understood his mother's passion for her plants. He'd never understood until Mia made him.

"But now I'm closer to learning the exact combination and method to get it right."

"Will you ever get it right?" Wyatt asked. *Would they ever get it right?*

"Eventually," she said. "It's going to take time and a lot of patience."

"I don't have patience," Wyatt admitted.

"Sit down." Helen motioned to the empty chair across the table from her. "You can't blame Mia for something that was all my fault."

Too late. He already had blamed Mia. But for something that was entirely his fault. Only he had control of his emotions and his heart. "You can't stop your medicine, Mom, without talking to your doctor first."

"You sound just like my doctors at Bay Water." She smiled, small and brief. "I had good reasons."

He had good reasons for chasing Mia out of the house last night, too. Unfortunately, he couldn't think of one this morning. "Your doctors have even better reasons for prescribing the medicine."

She tugged off her hat, set it on top of her work and looked at him. Her serious gaze held his. "I've learned my lesson."

Had he? And what had he learned: that his heart could be broken. That he could be more alone than he ever thought possible. That he'd won, yet celebrating his victory left him hollowed out and empty.

"I can't keep you here any longer. I won't." The seriousness spread from her gaze into her tone, and she set her hand on his arm. "It's not fair to you."

He tensed beneath her touch, fearing he'd won this battle, too. He wanted to stall her words. "What are you telling me?"

"It's time you returned to your work in Africa," she said. "It's time for you to go home."

Strange, he'd started to think he was home. Until Mia walked out and nothing inside him fit right anymore. "Why? Because you learned your lesson and have agreed it's best to take your medicine?"

"Because Trent isn't coming home." Grief hooked on her last word, breaking apart her voice. Her skin paled from her face down across her neck.

Wyatt leaned forward, placed his hand over hers still resting on his arm. "No, he isn't coming home."

"Mothers should never have to bury their sons." Her words lacked texture, as if drawn from the most haunted part of her soul. "I failed him. How could I bury the son I failed to save?"

Wyatt cleared his throat, trying to form words around his collapsed throat. "I failed Trent, too."

She squeezed his arm. Her head shook. The slow motion drew out her anguish. "It wasn't your job to fix him. You shouldn't ever have had that burden."

"I'm his brother."

"And I'm his mother." She wiped her damp cheek with her other hand and never released her hold on Wyatt as if she needed the connection to find her voice. "I want a second chance to make it right."

"We both do." He'd been given a second chance with Mia, and he'd wasted it. Now nothing was right. He wondered if second chances were rare like four-leaf clovers, doled out once each lifetime.

"We're too late for Trent," she whispered.

'Yes." He wiped her cheeks with a dinner napkin from the stack left on the table after their welcome home, Daisy, party Saturday night. "But not for each other."

"I never stopped loving you." She took the napkin from his hand and dried her other cheek. "You'll always be my son. You'll always be that little boy I need to take care of."

"I love you, too, Mom. Now it's my turn to take care of you." He squeezed her hand. "Let me take care of you."

Her first sincere smile since she came home drifted up into her gaze. "Would you mind getting the throw blanket off my bed? The sun warms my face but can't reach my legs out here. I'm a bit chilled."

He stood and looked around the garden. The thick, lush greenery no longer overwhelmed him. If anything, he felt embraced by nature, comforted and protected among the foliage and the flowers grown from his mom's love. He appreciated the sanctuary his mother had built for the first time since he'd come home. Recognized the refuge the garden provided as it offered an escape, a reprieve from the grief and remorse that clung like ice to skin.

He walked into his mother's room and pulled up short. Photographs covered every inch of space on every wall. The same photographs that had once been beside the windows in the family room, once filled the hallways and decorated the shelves around the fireplace. Their artwork from his and Trent's elementary school days littered the entire top of her antique dresser. His father's reading glasses sat folded and waiting in the same spot on the bedside table where he'd left them every night for as long as Wyatt could remember. Everything from his childhood memory book had been crammed into his mother's bedroom as if this was the final resting spot for the past.

Wyatt picked up the blanket, shutting his mother's bedroom door and the past behind him. Downstairs, he draped the blanket over his mom's legs and dropped into the chair across from her. "Why?"

She didn't pretend to misunderstand him.

"Every room, every wall had a memory. A link to my family. Everywhere I looked, I was reminded of how I'd failed my own children. Of how I'd failed as a mother."

Yet she hadn't packed away those memories. Hadn't locked everything inside the attic. She hadn't run away like he had. He'd boarded the plane to another continent and vowed never to look back. Until Mia. Until Mia accused him of abandoning his family, his roots and his own grief. His mother fell asleep each night surrounded by her grief and woke every morning to the reminder of her regrets. No wonder she'd constructed such an intricate and lush garden. She'd needed a place to hide from her bedroom and her guilt. "Why fill up your room?"

"I never believed I deserved peace," she said.

"And now?"

"Now I believe I'll lose the last of what's precious in my life, if I don't let go of my grief and forgive." She clasped his hand. "I can't lose you, too, Wyatt. You're all I have left."

"You haven't lost me." But he'd lost Mia, and he wasn't sure he'd ever forgive himself for that.

"But you're leaving." She lifted her hand to stall his protest. "I won't stop you. But I'm asking that you do something before you go." She paused, but not to draw in one of those deep breaths as if to collect herself. Rather she stilled midbreath as if too scared to proceed.

"What is it?" Wyatt gestured toward the trash can and the dead plant inside, trying to hack through the somber silence. "We've already established I'm probably not the best person to help you with your plants and garden."

His mom blinked, her grin surprised and welcome. "I'd like you to help me pack up the past." She tipped her head toward the house. "Perhaps if we put away the past together, we can move forward with a fresh start."

Wyatt massaged the back of his neck. Was he ready to face the past, let it go and forgive? Would that heal him? Heal him enough for Mia to come back. "A fresh start. We both need that, I think."

"Could you also bring me those brochures you've been collecting?" His mother hung her hat on the chair back and sorted through the photographs. "I think I'm ready to reconsider my living situation."

Wyatt glanced around the patio and searched for the wizard or portal or whatever had altered his world and shoved him into this new dimension. Where he'd talked, really talked with his mom. Where she wanted to discuss moving into an assisted living center. But it wasn't his imagination. This was his reality. How his mom and he had gotten there wasn't important. That they'd mended the fractures between them mattered. That they'd saved what was precious between them mattered. "I'll see if I can find them, and then we can talk."

"I'd like that," she said. "But first you should talk to Mia about moving back here."

Wyatt slumped back in the chair and covered his face with his hands. "We talked last night."

"I doubt that," she said. "If you'd talked, she wouldn't have moved out."

"You spent the night in the hospital. How do you know she moved out?" Wyatt spoke around his hands still covering his face. "Did you check her bedroom?"

"I don't have to," she said. "Aside from your dreary behavior, it's obvious she isn't here."

"It's not like she left her clothes all over the house as markers."

"But she left her mark, in her own way," she said. "If she was still here, there'd be fresh pastries on the counter for our tea this afternoon. There'd be a new tea blend for us to try. There'd be fresh vegetables cut up for Daisy.

And your favorite snacks ready for your midnight food breaks."

"When did you ransack the kitchen?" He lowered his arms and studied his mom.

"I'm well acquainted with the flow in my house," she said.

Whatever that meant. All Wyatt knew was that nothing was the same without Mia. "Okay. That explains everything."

She chuckled. "Mia left her camera on the chair in the kitchen. If you'd talked last night as you claim, she'd have taken it with her now." She sat back and eyed him. "That it's on the chair means she left in a hurry."

Mia had left more than Wyatt behind last night. "You should contact her and give it back."

"There's no need," his mom said. "Mia will be returning for it. It's a part of her now, and things as precious as that we can't ever let go."

"Let's hope you're right. She has talent that she won't admit to."

"Sometimes we're so locked on our paths we can't see the other roads. And it takes someone close to us to show us that we have choices." She trimmed the edges of a picture and smiled at the result. "After all, there's always more than one way to a destination."

Wyatt agreed. He just needed to decide on

where he wanted to go: where his heart led or his mind. He stood, needing to move, to reconsider. "I'm going to check the attic for boxes."

CHAPTER SEVENTEEN

MIA SAT ON the deck of the *Poseidon* and stared out into the bay. She'd been staring at the water since before sunrise, replaying Wyatt's accusations. Replaying every step, every decision that had led her here to this moment. Ironic she'd come to the dock last night to find answers. Find some hidden truth her father had stashed inside the cabin. She'd gone to the boat to be close to her father, and she'd woken up finding herself.

Hard to believe the last time she'd been on the dive boat, she'd almost died. That Sunday seemed like a lifetime ago. Maybe because that was another lifetime when she'd been satisfied following someone else's path. When she'd been certain her father's dream would fulfill her. When all she'd wanted was her dad's approval to complete her. But that part of her had drowned in the bay. She'd just taken a bit longer to realize that if she resuscitated that piece of herself, she wouldn't be living the best life for her.

Eddy's mellow voice carried from the dock before his curly head appeared on the deck. "Couldn't stay away, could you?"

"I slept here last night," she confessed.

Eddy shook his curls and walked toward the cockpit. "Wyatt was right. You really are determined to join your father in the afterlife."

Wyatt was right about any number of things. But not that. Mia spun the captain's chair to look back out at the water. "I don't want to join my father."

"Yet you spent the night here?" Eddy lowered himself into the second captain's chair and spread his long legs out. "The first night the boat was out of dry dock."

"I had no place else to go." She'd have been too close to Wyatt at his mother's house. She hadn't wanted to bother Ava or Sophie. She hadn't wanted to talk. The boat granted her privacy with her thoughts and saved her money. She was going to need every dollar she could find soon.

"What happened at Wyatt's place?" Eddy asked.

"It didn't work out." That was an understatement. It wouldn't ever work out unless they both changed. She was ready to take the first step. She set her hands on the steering wheel and avoided glancing at her friend.

"No, I don't want to talk about it. That's not why I asked you to meet me."

"Okay." Confusion and surrender stretched through the simple word.

She inhaled, watched a brown pelican dive into the bay and plunged into the truth. "It was supposed to be me. I was supposed to be filming in Costa Rica, not my father. I should've been shot, not him. I gave him the location for the cartel's human trafficking exchange, down to the coordinates."

"But you didn't force him to trespass and go deeper into the drug lord's territory."

"I never stopped him." Mia gripped the steering wheel.

"Your father was addicted to the adrenaline rush, to the risk, to the high stakes." Eddy touched her shoulder, pulling her attention to him. "You couldn't have stopped him from getting that footage."

"I should've tried," she said. "I'll live with that regret."

"So that's your plan now. Rush head-on into death." Eddy scoffed before running a hand through his hair and tugging on his curls. "What does that prove? That you're your father's daughter after all."

"I'm not proving anything." She released

the steering wheel and twisted to face her friend. "I'm honoring his memory."

"By dying?"

"By finishing the film the way my father would have."

"He never wanted this." The boat rocked from a swell rolling through as if to bolster Eddy's claim.

"Neither did I." She'd never wanted the dying-for-her-art part. And thanks to Wyatt, she realized she didn't want this life either. "But I never wanted to disappoint him. I wanted his love."

"He used up all of his love on his art." Eddy rested his head on the chair back and frowned at the sky as if he knew her father looked down on them.

"That's become clearer lately," she said. Another insight she owed to Wyatt pushing at her. "If he'd really loved me, he'd have supported whatever dream I had, not just his."

"What are you getting at?" Eddy leaned forward and braced his elbows on his knees.

"I know who I want to be." She lifted her arms. "And it isn't this."

Eddy scratched his chin. "What happens now?"

"We finish the film and secure the new contracts from the network."

"But you don't want this." He circled his hand out in front of him.

"I don't, but you, Eddy Fuller, you do want this life." She grinned at him. "I want you to make your directorial debut on the next contracts. Take over creative direction for Fiore Films. I'll remain a silent partner and, when I have the funds, an investor."

"You're serious." He sat back, ran his palms over his pants and exhaled as if her words slapped against his windpipe.

"Quite serious." Her grin shifted into a wide smile. Excitement pooled inside her. The tension cinching her body loosened. She'd taken the first step and wanted to take another on her path. She was ready and anxious to begin. "We both know that you're the son my father always wanted. You'll carry on his legacy much better than I ever would."

"You were doing a fine job."

She bumped her foot against his leg. "Thanks, but we both know it wasn't my passion. Not like my dad and not like you."

"I'm not sure what to say." Eddy clasped his hands together and chewed on his bottom lip. Still his gaze sparkled like sunlight off the bay as if his mind already sorted through his endless list of ideas.

Mia stood, widened her stance for balance

and set her hands on her hips. "Tell me you'll help me finish this documentary because we don't have those contracts secured yet."

Eddy laughed and pushed out of the chair. "I'll call the guys right now. It looks like it's time for our last working session."

Mia wrapped her arms around Eddy's waist. "I can't believe this is it. You won't have to save me from bad underwater dives or pull me out of muddy rivers or help me hike the rocky cliffs. I'm going to miss you."

"Right back at you. Who's going to take me to tiny villages and threaten the doctor to save my life or suffer your wrath?" Eddy hugged her back. "Who's going to make sure we eat right? Who's going to pack the bug spray, moist wipes and other essentials?"

"Shane can do it. I've trained him well." Mia drew back and laughed. "Besides, there are still cell phones. I can harass you all over text about your poor food choices."

"We'll be counting on it." Eddy released her, then pointed at her. "This doesn't mean you get out of taking the pictures at my son's birth."

"I wouldn't miss it," she said. "Not for anything."

Eddy looked her in the eyes. "What do you do now?"

"I get what I want." At last.

"Does that happen to be a certain doctor at Bay Water Medical?" Eddy wiggled his eyebrows up and down.

"This isn't about Wyatt." Although she wouldn't deny she'd like it to be one day. One day very soon. But right now, she had a path to walk and responsibilities to take care of.

"If we aren't going to dissect your love life, then let's go make a film." Eddy walked to the side and stepped onto the dock. "Let's make Papa Fiore proud."

Mia shook her head. "Let's make ourselves proud. That's what matters."

One documentary complete and two rounds of celebratory margaritas with her crew later, Mia skipped up the stairs to Helen's front door, relieved Helen's car was absent from the driveway. Wyatt wasn't home. She hoped to check on Helen, grab her purse, a.k.a. camera bag, and slip on out before he returned. She pressed the doorbell and checked the driveway again, surprised Wyatt left Helen alone one day after the older woman's fall. She'd have to hurry. He'd most likely return quickly.

"Did Wyatt call and tell you to check up on me?" Helen opened the door and waved Mia inside. "I'm going to need a nap from all the calls and quick stop-ins."

"Wyatt isn't here?" Mia followed Helen out onto the sun porch, noticing the only change in the older woman's gait seemed to be a faster pace.

"He had a meeting and wanted to make a box run." Helen checked the soil of her ponytail palm tree and examined the long thin green leaves. "Wouldn't leave until we agreed on an emergency code I could text him if I got sick or fell."

"That's a good idea." Mia eyed Helen, searching for any wear and tear she might've missed yesterday. But Helen looked content, her hum as she checked her other plants upbeat.

"Apparently not good enough." Helen moved several succulent plants around on the table. "He also called in reinforcements to look in on me. You just missed Ava by less than five minutes. She's off to help a neighbor move out of their building. Evie came over during her lunch break. Eddy, Frank, Sophie and Brad have all called and texted repeatedly." The pleasure in Helen's gaze ruined her attempt to sound disgruntled.

Mia smiled. "We all care about you."

"Don't think I don't appreciate it, but I'd be satisfied with a little bit less attention." Helen held up her arm and drew her index finger and thumb closer together. "Daisy and I missed our afternoon naps with so much company."

Daisy climbed to the top of her cage before sliding down the outside. "When did you let her out of her cage?"

"Evie and I opened the door earlier," Helen said. "We wanted to see what she would do with more space. She seems to like it. Evie read she'll explore more and more each day as she gets more secure."

The cockatoo looked quite at home already. Mia didn't blame the parrot. She'd felt the very same way from the first time she'd walked onto the front porch with Wyatt. And every time she'd stepped inside, she felt like she'd come home. "She'll be perched on your shoulder in no time."

"Not sure we'll take it that far." Helen took Daisy's water dish out of the cage. "But she's good company. Listens to all of my worries and plant problems without complaint."

Wyatt hadn't ever complained about Mia's night terrors. Instead he'd stayed by her side until she'd fallen asleep. They hadn't stayed beside each other last night. They'd both erred last night. Yet Mia needed to focus on her responsibilities before she tackled her relationship with Wyatt. "We all need a friend like that."

"You didn't come here to talk about birds." Helen patted Mia's shoulder on her way into the kitchen. "Your camera is in here on the chair."

Mia followed Helen and spotted the camera bag hanging from the chair back. She hugged the bag and felt a click inside her as if a missing piece dropped back into place. "I also stopped by to give you an invitation to the documentary screening and after-party this Friday night."

"How wonderful. You finished your film." Helen rinsed the bird dish and refilled it.

She'd finished that part of her life, too, and now stepped out on her own without a hand to hold. Now her mom relied on her success. Doubt snuck in. It would've been easier to stick with her father's plan. Live his life. No, she scolded herself. She didn't want easy, she wanted worthwhile. "Where should I put the invitation?"

"Set it on the table." Helen handed the full water dish to Mia. "Would you put this in Daisy's cage while I start the teakettle?"

Mia checked the time on her phone. "It's early."

"Yes, but it's needed, I think."

Mia gathered the teacups and honey from

the cabinet. "I heard you suffered no damage from your fall."

"Only the dent in my pride." Helen pointed to her eye. "And this shiner."

Mia would've preferred a few bruises to her pride over the chunk of nerves banging around inside her chest. She'd broken a promise to her dad and still had to confess to her mom. Mia filled the teacups with hot water and returned the kettle to the stove.

Helen dribbled honey across the top of her tea. "Do you want to talk about it?"

Mia sipped her tea, the hot liquid loosening the scratch from her throat. "I don't know where to begin."

"I usually start at the beginning."

Mia grinned. "But it's true. I don't know where to begin to start my life."

Helen leaned back in her chair and cupped her hands around the teacup. "You start with the first step."

She'd done that with Eddy. Released herself from the film company. Freed herself to follow her own passion. "I managed that this morning."

"You did know where to begin after all." Helen sipped her tea. "What's stopping you now?"

"My mother," Mia said. "I have to talk to my mother."

Helen nodded and reached for her notepad. "We'd planned to video chat this afternoon."

Mia eyed the older woman. "That's convenient."

Helen held up her hands. "And the truth."

Mia finished her tea and ran her hands over her scrubs. Helen slid the notepad toward her. Mia opened the program and dialed her mom.

Her mother answered on the second ring, her face filling the screen. "Mia, it's you. What a pleasant surprise."

"Hi, Mom. Helen is here, too."

Her mom nodded. "Wonderful. Tell Helen I don't mean to be rude, but it's rare that my daughter calls me unannounced, and I'm going to steal this time."

Helen chuckled and walked over to the cookie jar on the counter.

"Mia, I have something to tell you." Her mom's mouth thinned.

She had something to share, as well. "Are you sick? Are you hurt?"

"Nothing like that. I met with a real estate agent last week. I've been considering selling and downsizing to something more manageable."

The breath Mia had been holding escaped.

"Please don't be mad."

That emotion dropped last on the list behind elated and relieved. "Why would you think I'd be upset?"

"I thought you might want to come home," her mother said. "And I was terrified you'd hate me for selling the family house."

"You wanted me to come home?" Mia asked.

"Of course, Mia. A mother always wants her children close so that she can keep them safe." Her mom tipped her head and stared into the camera. "Mia, I hated that I could lose you just like we lost your father. I wanted you both to pursue your passion, but I've lived every day scared to death."

Mia rubbed her forehead. Her mother lived in terror and yet still loved her enough to let her go and follow her dream. Mia's words spilled out like tea running over a full cup. If she said it fast enough, maybe she'd find a quick solution. "Mom, I promised Dad I would make the mortgage payments. I promised him that your life wouldn't change."

Her mom pulled away and covered her mouth with her fingers. "He should never have asked that of you. He had no right to put that burden on you."

Mia touched the screen as if she was really making contact with her mom. "I want to keep my word to him."

"But?" Her mom scooted closer to the screen as if that would give her a better look at Mia.

"This will be my last documentary film. I'm letting Eddy take over the director role going forward." Every time Mia explained the changes, she believed in her decision even more.

Her mom straightened. "What will you be doing, then?"

"I want to stay in San Francisco and see if I can make my photography into a career." Mia glanced at Helen sitting across the table. The older woman nodded, then toasted Mia with her teacup.

"San Francisco," her mom repeated.

"You'd love it here. I do."

The screen shifted as if her mother had picked up her notepad with both hands. "Do you want me to come out there?"

"I don't want you to worry. And there's the stress of flying. And there's the money," Mia rambled.

Her mother cut her off. "Mia! Mia, do you want me there?"

Mia paused and blinked. "More than anything."

"Then it's done." Her mother's smile brightened the screen.

Mia looked at Helen, who nodded again. "Mom, I don't mean for a visit. I want you to come out here and stay."

Her mom dabbed a linen cloth against her eyes. "I'd like that. I'd really like that."

"I know money will be tight. Maybe for a while," Mia said.

Again, her mother stopped her. "Mia, dear, let me book my flight. When I get there, we will figure everything out. And we'll do it together. You really shouldn't worry so much."

Mia covered her laugh with a sip of tea. "If you come by Friday, you'll get to see the screening of the documentary."

Her mother held up her cell phone. "I'm booking now. Love you, dear."

Mia stared at the blank screen, dropped her head on the table and wept. Helen reached over and ran her hand through Mia's hair. For the first time in what seemed like forever, Mia wasn't alone. Helen refreshed her tea, handed her a box of tissue and allowed her to cry until her tears ran out. Mia hugged Helen and disappeared into the bathroom. She needed to clean herself up and leave before Wyatt returned. Her journey had begun. There was more to do before she invited Wyatt to join her.

HELEN WATCHED UNTIL the door to the bathroom clicked shut and then dialed her new friend in New York.

Jin Fiore answered on the first ring. "Helen, my flights are booked."

"Wonderful," Helen said. "I have a guest bedroom ready for you."

"You're certain I'm not imposing?" Jin asked.

"We're going to be family soon, and family is welcome here as long as they want to stay."

"I'm crying all over again."

"As is your daughter." Helen glanced down the hallway, pleased the bathroom door was still shut. "Jin, young people today make love so much more complicated than it needs to be."

"They certainly do." Mia's mom laughed and then sobered. "Do you think they'll finally get it right?"

"Of course." Helen smiled. "After all, they have our help this time."

CHAPTER EIGHTEEN

WYATT SHOOK HANDS with Dr. Samuels, Bay Water's chief of medicine. "Glad you're a part of our full-time staff now, Dr. Reid."

"Me, too." Wyatt walked out of Dr. Samuels' office and checked the time on his watch. He had less than twenty minutes to get home before the first of four general contractors came to his mom's house for estimates on renovations.

Nettie caught him as he stepped onto the elevator. "I've surveyed the staff on every floor for their recommendation and opinions." She shoved a piece of paper at him. "After my own personal interviews, here's my list of the top three home health nurses in the city. I also added my top three home health agencies."

"Nettie, you saved me." Wyatt tucked the paper into his back pocket. "Or rather my mother. You need to come over with your family for dinner and a garden tour."

"You can count on it." Nettie turned at the

call from a nursing aide down the hall. "That's me. You give your mom and Mia a hug for me."

Wyatt nodded and let the elevator doors slide shut. Hugging his mom was simple. He'd see her in less than fifteen minutes. Mia's hug was a little more complicated. He hadn't seen or spoken to Mia since Sunday night. Five days and almost eleven hours, and his breaking point closed in on him.

Fortunately, tonight that changed. And he hoped his first hug with Mia would be one of many to come. He strode off the elevator and crossed the parking lot.

Ava shouted to him from the ER entrance. "Ready for tonight?"

He gave her the thumbs-up sign. That was all he could manage with the nervous excitement twisting through him. He hadn't been this wound up, even as a kid waiting for Christmas morning. Of course back then his entire future didn't rest on whether he got a blue mountain bike or gray one. Tonight, his future waited on one woman and her heart.

He answered several texts about the evening and followed up with several phone calls before he walked into his mother's house. Both Mia's mom and his mom shared tea and scones at the table, their conversation lively and animated as if they'd known each other all their lives instead of less than a month.

Wyatt received welcome hugs from both women. His mother added a pat on his cheek. "There's a gentleman in the backyard talking about an estimate for a ramp."

"He beat me here."

"I don't want my gardens trampled for a ramp," Helen said.

"No trampling will occur, I promise." Wyatt grabbed a scone from the plate. "It's just an estimate." His mother and Jin shared a look that made him pause midbite. Wyatt dug into his pocket for Nettie's paperwork. "I figured we'd talk about this later, so I'll give you the highlights. I'm getting estimates to make a few renovations to make it easier and safer for you to stay in this house."

His mom's mouth opened and closed. Jin grabbed her hand and smiled.

Wyatt tossed the paper on the table. "That's a list from Nettie for the best home health care nurses in the city. I thought we'd interview them together and see if one fits our lifestyle. They can be here while I'm at work."

"You work in Africa," Helen said.

"Not as of today," Wyatt said. "I'm now a full-time employee of Bay Water Medical."

Helen lowered herself into the kitchen

chair. Jin clapped her hands. "That's wonderful news, Wyatt. Your mom thinks it is, too. She's just a little overwhelmed."

Wyatt walked over and kissed his mom's cheek.

She grabbed his arm. "You aren't going back to Africa?"

"Not right now." He looked her in her watery eyes. "And if I return, I'll have your blessing before I board the plane."

His mom wiped at her damp cheeks. "That's good. Very good."

"Besides, my heart belongs in the city." Wyatt bit into his scone and walked out onto the patio to greet the contractor. "Don't linger too long over tea, ladies. We have a party to get ready for tonight."

Helen and Jin's laughter followed him out into the gardens. He'd gained their cooperation from the minute he'd told them about his plan this past Monday. On Tuesday, Ava, Evie and Sophie had joined the crew. And by Wednesday, Eddy and the boys were on board. The only one not in the know was Mia. And she was the only one who mattered. Everything hinged on tonight. He pounded on his chest, trying to force the scone down his suddenly too-dry throat.

Today, he decided, was going to be either the best day of his life or the worst.

A THICK BLACK curtain concealed Wyatt in the back of the private dining room in the Rustic Grill. His position was ideal for the guests' arrival, offering a full view of guests without revealing himself. Laughter blended with varied conversations as the main doors to the dining room slid open. He skipped over Ava's big smile and Eddy's curls and his mother's soft grin, searching the group spilling inside. Finally, his gaze caught the one dark-haired, amber-eyed woman who had stamped herself in permanent ink on his heart. He snapped a picture in his mind of her in that moment: her eyes wide and brilliant, her skin glowing as if she'd been lit from within, her teal dress accentuating everything her favorite scrubs hid. He wanted to wrap her up in his embrace and steal her away right then, but he waited, held still in the shadowed corner.

Mia's gasp caused a shiver to race across his skin. She spun in a slow circle, her gaze jumping from one framed photograph to another. He'd spent the week enlarging and framing his favorite pictures from Mia's expanding portfolio. That morning with the help of Sophie and Ava, they'd transformed the dining room into a private gallery, exhibiting her work.

She stepped closer to the one with the nurse's hand around a patient's hunched shoulder. Rubbed her neck at the one of the burned Labrador puppy wrapped in gauze. Relaxed when she spotted the frame-filling grin of the senior bulldog. And wiped her eyes at the picture of Charlie from the foster home embracing Wyatt. She swayed from one photograph to the next, pausing, sometimes calling out for a guest's attention, sometimes keeping her commentary private. She worked her way around the entire room, stopping and studying every photograph. Her mom joined her, then his mom. Ava shifted beside her before Sophie weaved in. Eddy and Frank bookended her along the length of one wall.

At last she faced the back wall. Wyatt's wall. That's when his breath stopped. His heart rammed into his throat. And time stretched into a deep pause.

Mia's champagne glass smacked against the hardwood floor. She never flinched at the thud, simply stood in the middle of the room and gaped at the eleven-by-fourteen photograph on the easel. The star of the show. The one that Eddy had designed with Mia dancing around the fountain in her bare feet and

Wyatt extending his hand as if to pull her into his embrace. The lights from the fountain cast a shimmering magic over the entire photograph.

Wyatt emerged from the shadows and stood beside the easel.

Mia looked at him and blinked, slowly and deliberately, as if to push the tears out of her eyes. "Did you do this?"

"I had a lot of help." Wyatt lifted his arm to include everyone in the room.

"Why?" Even her voice sounded watery, as if her tears soaked into her.

"Because this is your heart. This is your passion. And you deserve to see the beauty and wonder only you can capture displayed." He stepped closer to her. If he stretched, he could pull her into him. But he stayed where he was, kept his hands at his sides.

"I don't know what to say," she whispered.

"I do." He pointed to the picture on the easel. "I did this because I want that magic in my life, every day, for as long as I can have it."

"What do I say to that?" She shook her head as if confused that she repeated herself, as if all she could do was repeat herself.

"I love you, Mia Fiore." He moved fully into her space, took her hands in his. "I'm saying that I don't want to spend another moment without you beside me. That the best part of my life starts right now. Right here with you."

"I want that, too." She threw herself into his arms, letting her tears pour free. "I love you, Wyatt Reid."

Cheers sounded around them. Shouts of congratulations. Crystal glasses clinked in toasts. Wyatt concentrated on Mia, taking her face in his hands and kissing her until he was sure their knees went weak and their hearts became one. Wyatt indulged in one more kiss before drawing Mia to his side to mingle with their guests.

After the three-course dinner, after the decadent skillet brownies were devoured and the guests tucked into cabs for safe rides home, Mia and Wyatt strolled hand in hand around the dining room. Together they talked about the moments around those single photographs, the people who touched them, the animals who melted their hearts. They agreed to talk about the future tomorrow and let the night be about this moment.

Mia broke away to pull a box from under the table. "It's not as grand as what you did for me, but I have something for you, too."

Wyatt opened the box and pulled out a photo album. The words *To Wyatt, Always re-*

member home is where your heart is were inscribed inside a heart on the cover. He opened to the first page and a series of photographs he'd never seen.

"They're from my private collection. The ones no one has ever seen," she said.

He ran his finger over the picture of the sunrise outside her hospital window. And he understood that these were her heart and soul in photographs. She put them in an album for him.

"I want you to take it with you when you leave for Africa," she said. "To remind you of home. To remind you to come back to me."

He flipped to the end. "There's a problem."

"What?" She reached for the album. "Is it ripped? Torn? Breaking already?"

"It's full." At her blank look, he added, "There are no more pages to add anymore photographs."

"You want to add more?"

"Hundreds and hundreds." He drew her into his arms. "I want one from every day we're together. The good days and the bad. The frustrating and the delightful. The forgettable and the memorable."

She framed his face in her hands. "I'm going to have to be with you every day to take these pictures."

"I'm counting on it."

She raised up to capture his mouth for a kiss with all the magic he'd ever imagined. And right then, their future began.

EPILOGUE

MIA CLOSED THE door at the Pampered Pooch and lengthened her stride to catch up to Wyatt, Ella and Ben. A bulldog tugged on the leash Ben gripped, while Ella held Ben's elbow and her white cane. A beagle mix sniffed the sidewalk, barely pulling on the leash Wyatt held.

"We need to make sure we're home to go over the ribbon-cutting ceremony with the moms." The ribbon ceremony for the opening of the Trent James Rehab Center was the following day. Helen wanted to rehearse to make sure everyone understood the order of events and where they needed to be.

Wyatt grabbed her hand and squeezed. "Our mothers are fine. They're together and most likely didn't stop talking long enough to notice we left the house."

Both Mia's mom and his mom shared tea and scones every afternoon in Helen's kitchen. "I knew they'd get along, but not quite like this."

"They're good for each other," Wyatt said.

Like Wyatt and she were good together. Mia tightened her grip on Wyatt's hand.

Ella and Ben paused in front of the Rose Petal Boutique. The nearest tree was still more than half a block away. Both dogs promptly sat as if on cue. Except the bulldog sprawled on the cement instead. Mia worried something was wrong with Sophie's most recent rescue. They hadn't walked all that far. She could carry him back to Sophie's quickly.

"We're here," Ella announced. Her smile lightened her voice an octave. "I know the exact number of steps from the pet shop to this spot."

Mia glanced along the block, then back at the boutique. Windows anchored the main entrance on each side. Two exquisite bridal gowns with hand-sewn beading hung in the right window display. In the left window, the enlarged photograph of Kellie and Rey—the very one Mia had worked on—stood on an easel. What looked like oversize business cards rested in a holder beneath the ornate wooden frame. Mia leaned down and read: *Mia Fiore Studio.* "That's my name."

"This is your place." Ella jumped up and down.

"Dr. Wyatt says you need your own place.

Now you have it." Ben knelt and scrubbed the bulldog's chin.

"And it's really close to us, too," Ella said. The beagle moved beside Ella, tail wagging and mouth open as if smiling, too.

Mia spotted Sophie, Ava and Evie crossing the street toward them. Helen and her own mother walked between her friends, laughing and chatting like family. "I don't understand."

"It's not as magical at it seems." Wyatt handed the beagle's leash to Ben and stepped in front of Mia "The owner, Josie Beck, is designing Kellie's wedding dress. Josie saw their engagement photo. She needs a tenant to share the expenses and thought you might be a perfect fit."

Ella added, 'You can help each other out."

"Josie contacted Kellie," Wyatt said.

The group of women approached and gathered behind Wyatt. Mia wasn't sure who had the brightest smile.

Sophie raised her hand. "Kellie talked to me when I was there with Pepper, and I called Ava."

Ava waved. "I spoke to Wyatt about it and gave him Josie's contact information."

Wyatt scratched his cheek. "We wanted to surprise you."

"You did this all for me?" She was surprised her voice could be heard above the rapid beat of her heart.

Wyatt nodded, slowly, as if unsure whether to commit fully before holding up his hand. "Nothing has been signed. No contracts entered. This is just an introduction."

"That you put together for me." Mia struggled to form words beyond shouting her love for Wyatt and everyone there. Each one of them was her family. *Her family.*

Again, another slow nod from Wyatt.

"Are you happy, Aunty Mia?" Ella shifted from one booted foot to the other.

Mia touched the sweet girl's arm and took her hand. "I'm thrilled. And speechless you'd all do this for me."

She wrapped Ella in a bear hug and moved on to embrace each of her friends, as well as her mom. Finally, she turned to Wyatt and launched herself into his arms. She brought his face to hers and put all the love streaming from her heart into the kiss. Breathless, she pulled away and framed his face with her hands. "I seem to be setting roots down all over the city."

"Is that a problem?" he asked.

"Not for me. How about you?"

"I'm home wherever you are." Wyatt pulled her to him for another kiss.

Ben groaned, drawing laughter from the adults.

"Come on, kids," Sophie said. "There's still more dark chocolate coconut avocado ice cream in the freezer. Maybe we can convince Ms. Helen and Ms. Jin to taste it."

"Should we wait for Ms. Mia and Dr. Wyatt?" Ben asked.

"The ice cream will be green water if we wait on that pair," Helen said. "I'm too old to wait that long."

Ben laughed.

Ella giggled. "Ben's grandpa says he's well aged, not old."

"I think I like him," Helen said. "Now let's get ice cream and the real stuff, too, not that fancy avocado concoction your mom and Mia like to eat."

Mia set her head on Wyatt's shoulder and watched her family return to Sophie's pet store. She had more in that moment than she'd ever dared hope for.

Wyatt stepped away and opened the door to the Rose Petal Boutique. "Ready to meet Josie?"

"More than ready." Mia walked inside, holding Wyatt's hand.

With Wyatt beside her, she was more than ready to start their new life together.

* * * * *

Don't miss Cari Lynn Webb's

THE CHARM OFFENSIVE

*for another enchanting romance
featuring this neighborhood of caring
friends and family!*

Available now from www.Harlequin.com!

Get 4 FREE REWARDS!

We'll send you 2 FREE Books plus 2 FREE Mystery Gifts.

Love Inspired® books feature contemporary inspirational romances with Christian characters facing the challenges of life and love.

FREE Value Over **$20**

YES! Please send me 2 FREE Love Inspired® Romance novels and my 2 FREE mystery gifts (gifts are worth about $10 retail). After receiving them, if I don't wish to receive any more books, I can return the shipping statement marked "cancel." If I don't cancel, I will receive 6 brand-new novels every month and be billed just $5.24 for the regular-print edition or $5.74 each for the larger-print edition in the U.S., or $5.74 each for the regular-print edition or $6.24 each for the larger-print edition in Canada. That's a savings of at least 13% off the cover price. It's quite a bargain! Shipping and handling is just 50¢ per book in the U.S. and 75¢ per book in Canada*. I understand that accepting the 2 free books and gifts places me under no obligation to buy anything. I can always return a shipment and cancel at any time. The free books and gifts are mine to keep no matter what I decide.

Choose one: ☐ **Love Inspired® Romance Regular-Print** (105/305 IDN GMY4)   ☐ **Love Inspired® Romance Larger-Print** (122/322 IDN GMY4)

Name (please print)

Address   Apt. #

City   State/Province   Zip/Postal Code

Mail to the **Reader Service:**
IN U.S.A.: P.O. Box 1341, Buffalo, NY 14240-8531
IN CANADA: P.O. Box 603, Fort Erie, Ontario L2A 5X3

Want to try two free books from another series! Call 1-800-873-8635 or visit www.ReaderService.com.

Get 4 FREE REWARDS!

We'll send you 2 FREE Books plus 2 FREE Mystery Gifts.

Love Inspired® Suspense books feature Christian characters facing challenges to their faith... and lives.

FREE
Value Over
$20

HOME on the RANCH

YES! Please send me the **Home on the Ranch Collection** in Larger Print. This collection begins with 3 FREE books and 2 FREE gifts in the first shipment. Along with my 3 free books, I'll also get the next 4 books from the Home on the Ranch Collection, in LARGER PRINT, which I may either return and owe nothing, or keep for the low price of $5.24 U.S./ $5.89 CDN each plus $2.99 for shipping and handling per shipment*. If I decide to continue, about once a month for 8 months I will get 6 or 7 more books, but will only need to pay for 4. That means 2 or 3 books in every shipment will be FREE! If I decide to keep the entire collection, I'll have paid for only 32 books because 19 books are FREE! I understand that accepting the 3 free books and gifts places me under no obligation to buy anything. I can always return a shipment and cancel at any time. My free books and gifts are mine to keep no matter what I decide.

268 HCN 3760 468 HCN 3760

Name _____ (PLEASE PRINT) _____

Address _____ Apt. # _____

City _____ State/Prov. _____ Zip/Postal Code _____

Signature (if under 18, a parent or guardian must sign)

Mail to the **Reader Service:**
IN U.S.A.: P.O. Box 1867, Buffalo, NY. 14240-1867
IN CANADA: P.O. Box 609, Fort Erie, Ontario L2A 5X3

Get 4 FREE REWARDS!

We'll send you 2 FREE Books plus 2 FREE Mystery Gifts.

FREE
Value Over
$20

Both the **Romance** and **Suspense** collections feature compelling novels written by many of today's best-selling authors.

Get 4 FREE REWARDS!

We'll send you 2 FREE Books plus 2 FREE Mystery Gifts.

Harlequin® Romance Larger-Print books feature uplifting escapes that will warm your heart with the ultimate feel-good tales.

FREE
Value Over
$20

YES! Please send me 2 FREE Harlequin® Romance Larger-Print novels and my 2 FREE gifts (gifts are worth about $10 retail). After receiving them, if I don't wish to receive any more books, I can return the shipping statement marked "cancel." If I don't cancel, I will receive 4 brand-new novels every month and be billed just $5.34 per book in the U.S. or $5.74 per book in Canada. That's a savings of at least 15% off the cover price! It's quite a bargain! Shipping and handling is just 50¢ per book in the U.S. and 75¢ per book in Canada. I understand that accepting the 2 free books and gifts places me under no obligation to buy anything. I can always return a shipment and cancel at any time. The free books and gifts are mine to keep no matter what I decide.

119/319 HDN GMYY

Name (please print)

Address   Apt. #

City   State/Province   Zip/Postal Code

Mail to the **Reader Service:**
IN U.S.A.: P.O. Box 1341, Buffalo, NY 14240-8531
IN CANADA: P.O. Box 603, Fort Erie, Ontario L2A 5X3

Want to try two free books from another series? Call 1-800-873-8635 or visit www.ReaderService.com.

---

*Terms and prices subject to change without notice. Prices do not include applicable taxes. Sales tax applicable in N.Y. Canadian residents will be charged applicable taxes. Offer not valid in Quebec. This offer is limited to one order per household. Books received may not be as shown. Not valid for current subscribers to Harlequin Romance Larger-Print books. All orders subject to approval. Credit or debit balances in a customer's account(s) may be offset by any other outstanding balance owed by or to the customer. Please allow 4 to 6 weeks for delivery. Offer available while quantities last.

Your Privacy—The Reader Service is committed to protecting your privacy. Our Privacy Policy is available online at www.ReaderService.com or upon request from the Reader Service. We make a portion of our mailing list available to reputable third parties that offer products we believe may interest you. If you prefer that we not exchange your name with third parties, or if you wish to clarify or modify your communication preferences, please visit us at www.ReaderService.com/consumerschoice or write to us at Reader Service Preference Service, P.O. Box 9062, Buffalo, NY 14240-9062. Include your complete name and address.

HRLP18